THE
ROOFER

THE ROOFER

ERICA ORLOFF

MIRA®

MIRA®

ISBN 0-7783-2072-3

THE ROOFER

Copyright © 2004 by Erica Orloff.

www.MIRABooks.com

Printed in U.S.A.

First Printing: May 2004
10 9 8 7 6 5 4 3 2 1

ACKNOWLEDGMENTS

First I'd like to thank Margaret Marbury and
Amy Moore-Benson for believing in the story
of the Roofer and his daughter.

As always, thanks to my agent, Jay Poynor, for his
keen insight, his belief in me and his encouragement.
The first time he read the opening chapters, he was
convinced this book would come to fruition and
sought a deal to bring it to light.

To the members of Writer's Cramp—Pam, Gina and
Jon—for keeping me focused. And for the wine. And
champagne. And occasional delights of Gina's
Minnesota cooking.

To Pam and J.D., for nursing me through the writing
process. To Cleo Coy and Nancy Hines…thank you
for your encouragement and for listening to me tell
you about the book and for knowing intuitively that
this was "it." To Kathy Levinson, for swapping stories,
many laughs, a few tears and years of support and
friendship.

To Mark DiBona. What can I say, "Twin"? Your help
with the scenes set in Las Vegas was invaluable. Your
encouragement meant a great deal to me. Who else
can I call and talk to for two hours about gambling?

To Gloria and Joey, my pal Chris Richardson,
Kathy Johnson…and all the unbelievably supportive
people in my life.

Finally, to my inspirations…Alexa, Nicholas and
Isabella…and my family, especially my father and
mother.

And to that sense of peace when a story is put to rest.

Dedicated with great love and devotion
to the real Roofer—
you know who you are

To take revenge half-heartedly is to court disaster:
either condemn or crown your hatred.
—Pierre Corneille

To take revenge halfheartedly is to court disaster:
either condemn or crown your hatred.

—Pierre Corneille

Part One

Daddy's Wake: Night One

Where does one go from a world of insanity?
Somewhere on the other side of despair.

—T. S. Eliot

1

My first instinct was to look at the corpse. It's what all the Irish do.

We treat our wakes like weddings. There's much drinking and storytelling, a lot of back-clapping and hugs and shouts of hello to long-lost relatives and cousins we only see when we bring out our dead. We dress in black, for mourning, but we go out after the wake and get blind, stumbling drunk. We spend the next day nursing our hangovers, puking our brains out if we were especially close to the deceased and therefore drank exceedingly stupid amounts of alcohol, and trying desperately to sober up and straighten out for night two. We often go for three nights, particularly for popular dead people, as we did with my father. The fourth day is the funeral, and we usually mix our drinking with lunch. By then a hangover pallor has been cast over the lot of us. We intertwine all this drinking and carrying on with equal parts wrenching sobs—an ingredient likely missing from the aforementioned weddings.

But first we look at the corpse.

We lay our dead out in the front of the room in a coffin designed to make it look as if the deceased is merely sleeping. The funeral home even sells you a pillow for the dead person's head precisely for this purpose. It is satin and soft. My father's was ivory-colored, a sign of purity. And it cost a lot of money. More money than you would pay, for example, for a pillow you buy at Macy's that you actually *sleep* on. Real sleeping, not pretend dead sleeping. Funeral homes sell you lots of things, none of which the deceased is actually going to *need* on his or her journey to wherever it is the dead go. In my father's case, people weighed in with their opinions, the general direction of which was down.

Having seen more than my share of dead bodies, and having seen TV shows about forensics and morgues—television for the morbidly curious, those of us who likely look at the corpse first when we walk into an Irish wake—I know a bit about corpses. While the dead body up there in the front of the room may, indeed, look like he or she is sleeping, most definitely, the dead body is not. In fact, the dead body has had its mouth stapled shut so as not to open and allow a swollen, blue-black tongue to protrude. The body has also been drained of all its fluids and filled with preservatives. I think of this as the Big Mac approach to death. Funeral parlors line them up like so many fast-food customers at the drive-through and present to the family a preservative-stuffed *something*. Like fast food, which may be called food but bears little resemblance to *real* food, the body may look like your dear old dad, but trust me, it's the preservatives.

Which leads me to the corpse. Given the fact that my father drank his way through sixty-two years of life, he looked pretty good—and let me do the Irish math on that. He was seventy-two when he died but started drinking daily when he was ten. So he effectively drank his way through sixty-two years of straight vodka and enough beer to satisfy the citizens of Munich during Oktoberfest. We are not talking, by the way, of a glass of beer with dinner, or a nightcap at the hour of the eleven o'clock news before toddling off to bed, we are talking about daily consumption the likes of which an ordinary mortal would end up in a hospital having his or her stomach pumped. My father had the fortunate—or unfortunate—ancestry to be half Irish and half Russian. He liked his vodka, liked to brood, and liked to celebrate St. Patrick's Day. That my brother and I—though not my sister—have inherited this prodigious talent for handling mass quantities of vodka was a great source of pride to Dad. More impressive to him than our grades in school, than the fact that, unlike some of his friends' kids, we managed to keep out of prison.

Another thing about Irish wakes. We say things like, "*They* did such a good job." (*They* being the people who do things like staple mouths shut and put waxy makeup on corpses.) *"He looks good."* And Dad did look surprisingly pink and robust for a dead man.

For years, my brother, Tom, and I, as well as assorted sons and daughters of my father's friends, had been laying bets about when he would have to "pay the piper." Another expression. But in the cosmic scheme of things, it seemed logical to assume a guy who had murdered five people (give or take), been to prison three times, drunk his way through sixty-two years, smoked for forty (gave it up for health reasons...go figure), and had been on the receiving end of a few battles with bats and bricks and other assorted weapons (as well as the giving end), would, someday, have to pay for his sins. Someday he would get cancer, a heart attack or (my money riding on this at two to one odds) cirrhosis of the liver. But he never did.

Tom, who had never figured out a way to stand in the same

room with my father without it leading to a fistfight, looked down at the corpse and said, *"He looks good."*

"Yeah. Pretty amazing." I nodded, perplexed by this seeming defiance of the laws of nature.

"Doesn't seem fair, the son of a bitch."

"No, it doesn't. But then again…"

"Yeah. Then again…"

Tom and I talk to each other in shorthand. When we are together, which is nearly always, there is an instant feeling of being home, like being enveloped in the memory of my mother's rosewater-scented arms. With Tom, I never have to explain. I don't have to try to force my world to make sense. I simply breathe, and Tom breathes, too. Usually a large consumption of alcohol is involved when we are together, as well. But this only makes the shorthand a greater convenience. When drunk, we need barely speak.

We stood over the body of this man, my father, and I thought I would cry. The entire scene was something I had pictured before, and I had imagined how I would act. I thought I would feel something leave me, like my breath or part of my soul. But, strange as it sounds, all I felt was a sense of shock that such a force of rage and power, terror and, believe it or not, humor, was actually just a hull of a body. In the end, we all are, whether we're a killer or a schoolteacher. In the end, they staple your mouth shut and give you a pillow as the consolation prize. End of the game. Thank you for playing.

Tom instinctively reached for my hand. His was clammy. "I hate this, Ava."

I squeezed his hand in return.

Our other sibling, Carol, came through the door in a burst of emotion, immediately falling into the arms of her husband and sobbing her way toward the dead body "sleeping" on the pillow in the Rolls-Royce of caskets. She collapsed onto the kneeler in front of the coffin, not even seeing Tom or me, or seeing us and ignoring us. In general, she put on a performance worthy of an Academy Award nomination.

Carol's little game is she decided a long time ago that she would leave our world to go live in her husband's. And she would never tell her husband—not ever—who we really were, who our father was, and why our lives had made the glossy pages of the *New York Chronicle* three years ago in the longest piece they ever ran—in two parts. Or why we were the subject of a movie with "buzz." Why celebrities courted my father as if he had been somebody famous. Why a certain celebrity and I had slept together, complicating matters entirely. No, Carol liked to pretend that we were normal.

After the *Chronicle* article, I heard she told her husband she had no idea what Dad had done. Apparently her husband, though bright enough to earn an MBA from Columbia and be vice president of something or other, bought the myth that during Dad's stint in Sing Sing Correctional, Carol had assumed he was off working as a traveling salesman. In their polite world, where people really *do* drink just a glass of wine with dinner, this kind of lie passes as truth, just as in our world, saying something "fell off a truck" means you now have twenty identical Rolexes sitting in your underwear drawer.

The O'Neil family most definitely was not normal, no matter what Carol wanted to say to her husband and his family. We were the Roofer's kids. And his long shadow filled that funeral parlor, even as his shell lay in front of me.

His message was quite clear.

I ain't never paid the piper, and I'm still a beautiful corpse. And if you cry over me, I'll break your legs.

Yeah. Dad was sentimental like that.

2

At any wake, the places of honor go to the family of the deceased. This can get complicated when there's divorce and remarriage, but the O'Neils don't divorce. They kill people, and they die. Therefore, with our mother long gone to wherever it is she went after dying—in her case, we assume up—and my father's parents dead and his brother first missing and now presumed dead, that left me, Tom, Carol, and, by proxy, her husband. Four chairs next to the coffin where we were to sit and have people "pay their respects."

However, the crew filing through that door, in packs of wailing and crying women and drunken men, did not pay their respects to Carol. Everyone knew what we thought of her, my father included, and more important, we knew what she thought of my father—and the rest of us. So, though people bent down to kiss her on the cheek and to shake her husband's manicured hand, Tom and I were the ones pulled to the side to hear Uncle Charley or Radar or Sly Eddie tell us a funny story that they thought we should know. Even killings, when told with the right panache, can be funny with this crowd.

Uncle Charley wrapped his burly arm around my waist and said, "You need money for anything, you come see me. You hear?" Charley was my godfather, and I knew he meant it. I kissed him on his beer-scented cheek, a perfume of yeast that seemed to filter through my life like the very air I breathed.

"Thanks. We're fine. He left us pretty well set up."

Charley nodded approvingly. "Good...good. God, Frank was a brother to me. Like we were real brothers."

"I know." I found myself looking down. Paying respects means acknowledging all these wonderful things people say about the deceased. If the dead person happens to be Mother Teresa, I don't believe you'd have much of a problem. People say wonderful things, and the wonderful things are largely true, though perhaps embellished by death. In my father's case, the water was murkier.

When your father is a character more than a man, you don't collect memories of being tucked in or of...I don't know...whatever it is real fathers do. Instead you gather stories, like the ones in the *Chronicle*. Tom has his favorite. I have mine.

One night, long before I was born, my father hijacked a city bus. But as in any story with my father as the protagonist, there was much more to the story than that.

As always, it starts with a humorous setup.

He was in the army, a reluctant and terrible soldier. After a long night of hard drinking with two other privates, my father consuming more beer than his skinny frame could realistically hold, and yet not seeming to get drunker, though always getting funnier, this led to a little brawling. Then after some pool-playing and events involving a hooker or two—including one with a glass eye (and he could act out this element of the story with great abandon)—he and the two other soldiers needed to get back to their base. Trouble was, they missed the last military bus heading to Fort Dix, New Jersey. What was a stranded soldier to do? The answer, at least where my father was concerned, was to commandeer a *civilian* bus. In their army greens, he and his pals physically threw off the driver. Then the three soldiers none too gently removed the civilians who had paid their fares, thinking they would be going home after a long second shift or a night waiting tables, when in fact they would soon be abandoned roadside, after midnight, on a cold, wet November evening.

Next, the three soldiers installed my father at the wheel (because as in all stories with my father as protagonist, he was in the center of the action), and off he drove toward their base. What my father and his two cohorts hadn't counted on, of course, was the military police, with their white armbands proclaiming "M.P." and their ill humor registering on their faces. They also hadn't anticipated their drill sergeant, fed up with their barely veiled disdain for Uncle Sam.

Unfortunately for the burly and gravel-voiced drill sergeant, he elected to stand in the middle of the road, blocking the bus, in the glare of its brilliant headlights. He waved his arms wildly in the air, in the internationally recognized sign language of "Stop, you motherfucking idiots!"

However, my father was at the wheel. My father. And he did what came naturally to him. What all of us who knew him understand was the only acceptable course of action.

He ran *over* his sergeant, breaking both of his legs. He crippled him.

Growing up, I found ways to think my father was brilliantly funny.

Give me a vodka on ice and get me rolling on a tangent, and

I can regale you with story after story. The drill sergeant tale is actually one of the best, the most classic. And until very recently, I thought it was the funniest. The razor's edge is always precarious black comedy.

I have danced, my whole life, on that edge. My father took his family with him to the precipice. Seething over authority, disdaining it. Hating cops and sergeants. Despising priests. And teachers. Even kindergarten teachers with their ebullient smiles and rosy cheeks. And anyone who worked an honest job for a day's wage, like bankers, accountants, and pretty much most of America. We learned to love bookies and hit men, and ex-cons. Occasionally a union boss. We broke bread with men who murdered and men who gambled. I never knew any differently. Never believed rules were made for our family, too. In fact, I never stopped to think, as I danced this daughter's dance with him, that the drill sergeant might have had a family, even a daughter. Or he might not have deserved to have had his kneecaps snapped in two by the very large wheels of a very large bus. I never thought about it.

My father's life was, quite simply, folklore and legend. He was grander and larger than any other father I knew, and it wasn't until much later, meeting people away from the cocoon of my family, that I ever thought there was something vaguely antisocial, strangely hostile, about his behavior. About his life. Something that was darker and more dangerous, like the shadow of a stranger coming into your room.

My family even had sayings to reflect all we believed. "If you aren't cheating, you aren't trying hard enough." "A day without larceny is like a day without sunshine."

There were the parties. Three-day benders marked by godlike displays of drinking. The strangers using the bathtub as a urinal. The men coming into my bedroom and sitting on my bed at

2:00 a.m. to tell me Polish jokes and how tired I was the next day in school, but it all seemed like fun at the time.

The bare-knuckle fights. Being hidden inside an end table when my junkie uncle went crazy and started hurling lamps around as if they were children's toys. Enjoying ice cream with the same uncle when he came down off his high. Wasn't that how it was done? How you forgave?

Learning to play poker before I learned my multiplication tables. Learning how to shoot craps, and pitch pennies, and learning every barroom trick there is to earn a fast buck in a grungy bar. Figuring out the ten-point-must system as I watched boxers beat each other's brains out.

Drinking Cokes, age nine, in a bar in Hell's Kitchen, and learning to pee quickly in the barroom bathroom with the bare bulb shining pale light on dirty tiles, before someone came in or pounded on the door, drunk and needing to puke.

Perhaps all this story needs is context. That is what I tell myself. For isn't it all funny? If I tell the stories just right—with the right inflections, the wittiest dialogue—they are. It wasn't until I met people whose fathers obeyed the law that I understood what I thought was funny was really something else.

I thought all I needed was to place this within a history. To help people understand that what seems like anarchy was really survival. My father was a boy bitten by rats. A young man who grew up with the aura of the Westies—New York's Irish gang—and gangland murders drifting over his life like a heavy smog hovering over the city. A man who felt it was all right to push someone in front of a bus or run over a sergeant. With my father cast in the leading role, what's not to understand?

But three years ago, it all unraveled.

Three years ago, a journalist named Jack Casey hunted for, then found, me. And he had a story to tell. About my father.

About events that happened a long time ago. And the dance I had been performing on the edge of an alcoholic abyss stopped, and I realized I was simply on the edge, with only one place to go.

3

Tom and I walked into John's Bar after the first night of the wake and found a booth in the back. When I was a little girl, I thought this was the most spectacular place in the universe. Other children dreamed of Disney World. Tom and I prayed fervently, even as we learned catechism, that Dad would come into our bedroom and say, "You wanna go out, kids? Let's go down to John's for a few."

I'd sit on a bar stool like a canary on a perch and dangle my legs, drinking Cokes out of highball glasses, fishing out maraschino cherries with my fingers and lining up peanuts like little soldiers on the bar. I noticed the men with no teeth, the drunks nodding off on their stools, their greasy-haired heads striking the bar, waking them up again. But I never thought this was strange. In my little-girl world, this just added to the magic of the place.

Sitting in a hard wooden booth now, I looked around. Tom had gotten us two vodkas as a salute to the old man, and sat down across from me.

"To Dad." He raised his glass.

"To the Roofer," I replied.

We nursed our vodkas, pacing ourselves for a long night, though neither of us is much of a pacer. Dad's friends would be wandering in soon, and then the real drinking would begin. For now, it was Tom and me.

"You smell the puke?" I asked him, looking toward the bathroom door across the aisle and down the wall apiece.

He lifted his nose. "Yeah. Smells like someone lost it in the bathroom."

"I haven't been here in years. Did it always smell like puke?"

He nodded.

"How could I not *notice* it smelled like this?"

Tom shrugged.

I reached over to the wall and dug into the nicotine residue with my fingernail. At some point, the wood paneling may have been a light oak. But now it was burnt-brown from decades of cigarette smoke clinging to it. A cloud of smoke hung over the bar like a fog on the Hudson River.

"Were the walls always this disgusting? Look at this...I can write my name in the nicotine."

Tom suddenly downed his vodka like a shot. "Yeah."

"So how did you remember and I didn't?"

"I come in for a drink now and again. I...whatever. I just like how it feels when I come in. I went through what you're going through years ago. The place is gross. But it feels like home."

"Normal families...they go back to the first house they lived in and say 'I don't remember my bedroom being so small.' They bring their first bicycle down from the attic to give to their own kid and can't believe they used to have to stretch to reach the pedals."

Tom stared at me with those fathomless blue eyes of his. No

one can read him. It's like he's empty, disturbed, though I some-times know what's behind those eyes.

"Well, don't you think it's pretty fucking *odd* that we're sit-ting here discussing puke, Tom?"

"It seemed cool at the time. I don't know what you want me to say, Ava."

"I don't know, either. It just reminds me what freaks we are."

"Yeah."

"And that moose head over the bar."

"What about it?"

"It used to be brown. Its fur is pitch-black now. Do you know how disgusting that is?"

"So it ain't the Plaza, Ava."

"Please. It's only a step up from the sewer." I swirled the ice around in my glass, then asked, "What's your best mem-ory of him?"

Tom shrugged. "I don't know."

"Come on. You have to have *one*, for Christ's sake."

He thought for a minute, then spoke quietly. "Okay," he sighed. "It was when I graduated from the academy, and he showed up—even though he broke my nose the first time I said I was going to be a cop."

"You were so handsome in your dress uniform. Dad was pret-ty proud. And annoyed. Typical. Can't have just one emotion go-ing on at a time in our family."

Tom snorted a laugh. "Your favorite?"

"I don't know. Maybe when he came home from prison—the first time—and the first Saturday morning he was home, we watched all the cartoons together. Him smoking cigarettes and laughing at Bugs Bunny. Drinking a beer. And then we watched the Creature Feature show. Godzilla or something. And I remem-ber hiding my eyes and curling up into his chest. And it was like the first time I'd had someone to protect me from the Creature Feature in so long. It made me almost cry."

"I used to protect you from Godzilla, Ava. I used to check under your bed every goddamn night."

"I know. But face it...Godzilla could have eaten you as a snack before he came after me. I don't know...I just liked having a daddy. I thought we were like other families. You know...a dad. A mom."

Tom stared off at the black-haired moose. "I'm going for two more vodkas." He slid out from the booth and made his way through the smoke to the bar. Someone patted his back, undoubtedly an old friend of Dad's. Tom was a blend of both of my parents. He had my mother's thick, blue-black hair and blue eyes, and my dad's lanky but muscular build and a dimple in the center of his chin. Women turned to stare at him whenever we were out, but he was oblivious. He was oblivious to almost everything but this constant raging battle in his head to keep from swallowing the barrel of his gun. He'd been out on psychiatric leave once. I guessed that at the rate he was drinking lately, another one wouldn't be far off. Or a wake. And I couldn't bear the thought of laying him out in his dress blues, which was why I stuck to him constantly, covered him with a blanket when he passed out on the couch, made him breakfast, fed him dinner. I tried to get him to forgive himself. We *both* had blood on our hands, but he couldn't see that. I played tricks on him, and he saw right through them—I watered down his vodka, or hid his bottles. Which just meant he went out to drink.

I'm hardly a poster child for Al-Anon, which advocates right there in the book they give you to let the alcoholic hit bottom. Let the alcoholic slide into that abyss. Let him stew in his own alcoholic nightmare like the worm at the bottom of the tequila bottle. Sure. Bottom in my family means a suicide or a prison stint or someone gets murdered. I don't see anything in their little Al-Anon rule book about that. Their stupid twelve steps mean nothing in the face of someone getting stabbed to death in your living room or hanging himself from the shower curtain rod in the bathroom. Let go and let God they say. One day at a time. Like a fucking cliché is the answer to my prayers.

I went to Al-Anon meetings at the urging of Vince Quinn, who plays my father in the movie. A room full of mostly women talked about their husbands getting a little sloshed and threatening their precious middle-class existence. I wanted to kill all those women myself. They had no fucking idea about my life, my problems. Fuck the twelve steps. Fuck Al-Anon.

And while I'm at it, my own vodka consumption isn't exactly in the "social drinking" category, either. So fuck AA.

Tom came back with two more vodkas. With one under our belts, we both immediately drank the second faster. I don't think anyone in my family knows how to drink slowly. Especially once one drink is in our system.

"Okay, Tom, so if your best memory revolves, remotely, around Dad breaking your nose, what's your worst?"

"Why dredge this shit up, Ava?"

"I don't know. Maybe it proves I'm not crazy." I knew what I wanted him to say, what he never would say.

"What the fuck good does it do to talk about this?" His voice trembled.

My poor Tom. I reached out to hold one of his hands. "You know, Tom, in the *real* world, people go to therapists to talk about this stuff. The force made you see one."

"Yeah, and the guy declared, Ava, that in the history of him being a therapist, he never heard a worse story."

"Are therapists supposed to tell you things like that?"

"No. Which is why I think there's no point in talking about it."

"I know, but if we can't talk to strangers, we can talk to each other. Daddy's dead, Tom."

"No kidding. I saw him in his fucking casket."

"Well, don't you feel anything? It's all so surreal. You know, when you were looking at him in the casket, didn't you think he was going to open his eyes any second and tell us it was all a joke?"

Suddenly, Tom smiled. He has a brilliant smile that literally changes his entire face. When he smiles, he doesn't look crazy. For a moment there, he didn't look like a cop a vodka bottle away from swallowing a bullet. "Honest to fuckin' God, Ava, I did think that."

We both laughed and downed our vodkas.

"Okay, Ava. My worst is…you know…Mom…and seeing him go crazy." He looked away.

"Yeah. That was bad. Mine is the time he made me go live with Uncle George. I remember crying until I threw up, but he still made me go."

Tom slammed the table with his free hand. "Fuck this, Ava. Fuck this! Let's talk about something else. Please, baby. *Anything*."

"Okay," I looked around. "So, you know, with industrial solvents and everything, you think they could ever get these walls clean?"

"Not a chance, baby. Not a chance." He smiled again.

"If it ain't the darlin' O'Neil children." Tony Two-Times came over to our booth. Two-Times earned his name from two murders he committed, both of which he managed to be acquitted of, though all of Hell's Kitchen knew he was guilty. I always found this an impressive display of the justice system, which weaved its way through my life like a thread in a piece of cloth. It was always about putting one over on the D.A., on the lawyers, on the prison system, on the cops. Tom was the exception, but he'd never make detective because he consorted with "known felons," though I know he was approached about going under deep cover one time precisely because of his connections. But his drinking always held him back. Anyway, Two-Times was in the piece in the *Chronicle*, too. How he made a mockery of the system.

"Hey, Uncle Two," I smiled.

"I'm real sorry about the old man. But he lived right. Played the game his way."

Tom stood to go get more vodka.

"Sit down, you little asshole," Two told him. "Like I'm letting you fuckin' guys pay for a drink with your father laid out in a goddamn casket. No motherfuckin' way. I'll be right back."

Two made his way to the bar, not an easy feat, given his emphysema and considerable poundage, which made him walk in a manner that looked like he was going to fall over at any moment. Behind his back, we used to call him the Weeble. I looked up at the front door and saw a steady stream of ex-cons and bookies making their way into John's.

"You ready for this?" I eyed Tom.

"What?"

"The heavy drinking?"

"Yeah. I'm ready."

"The deal is, Tom, when I feel like I have to puke, take me home. I don't want to add to the…general scent around here. I prefer to puke in the comfort of my own bathroom."

"Deal."

"Swear it?"

"Yeah."

"And make me drink two glasses of water."

"Now *that* will make you puke, darlin'."

"No. It wards off a hangover. You get a hangover because the alcohol dehydrates you. And make me take a Percocet and one vitamin B-12."

"Anything else?"

"No. Just that if Vince shows up, don't let me go home with him."

"Got it."

Two came back with vodka, this time in larger glasses. I took a deep breath and tried to pace myself, but before too long the nicotine-stained walls of John's were swimming. Tomorrow was going to be very ugly.

4

They say there are no atheists in foxholes. There are rarely any atheists hanging over a toilet bowl after a night of drinking, either. My father used to say that people who beg God to make them feel better from all the alcohol they drank were pussies. They bargain with the man upstairs, "I swear to God, I'll never drink again, just make this stop." As if God is going to feel sorry that you decided to do your twelfth tequila shot. Famine and war, murder and child rape…and yeah, He's going to stop the revolutions of the earth and take the bed-spins and hangover-shakes away. Sure. If you're going to drink that much, Daddy said, you should take the consequences like a man—even if you're a woman.

In the middle of the night, I woke up, my head throbbing. The room was spinning like an amusement park ride. I tried to steady my gaze, but I grew sicker just opening my eyes, so I felt across the bed with my arm. No one was there. Vince hadn't come home with me. Better yet, I hadn't fucked someone else to prove I was over Vince.

I wondered when I would get over him. I rolled onto my side and curled into a ball, clutching my stomach. There were days when thoughts of him felt like knives in my gut. When I picked up a magazine with his perfect face staring out from the cover—publicity for the movie—all I could remember was the last time I was with him, in this apartment. The last look he gave me, the last time we laid eyes on each other, I saw only pity. And to an O'Neil, nothing was worse than pity. Not even murder.

I slid one leg out from under the blankets and planted my foot on the floor to try to make the spinning stop. Vince hadn't come to the bar. I remembered that now. He hadn't been at the wake. I could remember back that far. But I couldn't recall how I'd gotten home.

The first time I experienced a blackout, I was frightened. I was also, probably, fourteen. Then, after a while, blackouts became a curiosity. I liked to see how far back I could go to the point of blackness. It's like a heavy velvet curtain in an old theater closes over your mind at one particular moment in time.

After many years of practice, most of the nights I blacked out did come back to me in fits and starts—though after a while I realized I probably didn't *want* to remember whatever it was I forgot. But I had slowed my drinking considerably in the last two years, so as not to encourage Tom and because I had fallen in love. Now I was out of practice, and so I squinted and struggled to remember at what point the night disappeared. The line of demarcation was a shot bought for me by an ex-con named Sal the Chin, who'd done time with my father—though Sal's stint was much longer. Twenty years. He went in a young man of twenty-six and came out looking like a very old man. The Chin liked to drink shots of whiskey—with a proof so high if you rubbed two sticks in the vicinity, they would probably catch on fire—

washed down with a beer. I did the shot, and then I looked across at Tom and said, "I'm going to be sick. I'm invoking our deal."

I could remember nothing after that. Now I struggled to my feet and stumbled to my bathroom. Shielding my eyes even from the glow of the night-light, I saw I had thrown up, as evidenced by a towel and washcloth with telltale signs on the floor next to my toilet and a fierce heartburn in my chest and aftertaste in my mouth. That was good news. Throwing up meant I would sober up sooner and maybe have a chance at being halfway normal by morning.

I opened the medicine cabinet and saw row upon row of bottles of pills. Tom would swallow a bullet. If I did it, I would take a lot of pills, just like my mother. I hoarded them, though I didn't really want to die. At least I didn't think so. Or not right now. I couldn't leave Tom. I hoarded them because she hoarded them, and maybe in some way, I wanted to be like her.

I grabbed two Percocets for my headache and washed them down with water that I scooped into my hands at the sink. I stared into the mirror. Talk about Creature Feature. Mascara had run down my face, and I had classic raccoon eyes. My black hair contained dried bits of what I assume was a colossal vomit session. You'd never know that when I am showered and in clean clothes, with a little lipstick and maybe some powder on my pale white skin, that I am pretty. I wear my hair past my shoulders, and in the genetic lottery, I got my father's hair, which means it has a lot of curl to it. When I was small, the kids in school used to call me Snow White for my alabaster skin against my dark hair. If they only knew how far from a fairy tale things were.

Turning off the light, I realized I was still in my clothes. I didn't even want to think of what had managed to get on my black "mourning dress." I slipped out of it and put on my bathrobe. I padded out to the living room where Tom slept on a pullout bed that we never bothered to fold back into the couch. No one ever visited us. Anyway, Tom and I liked to watch scary movies together, lying in that bed with takeout. He had trouble sleeping through the night and always liked noise, so the television was a constant backdrop to our lives.

I walked over to him, his face illuminated by the flickering television. I leaned in close to make sure he was breathing. I learned to do this after the first time my mother overdosed. It seems I have spent my entire life leaning over people I love to make sure they're still breathing.

Making my way to the kitchen, I pulled out an ice pack from the freezer and poured myself a glass of grape juice. A guy in a bar once told me there was something in grape juice that helps cure a hangover, and I have been keeping the Welch's grape juice company in business ever since.

I went back into my bedroom. Tom's and my apartment is actually a two-bedroom co-op, and I have owned it since I was five and my father stumbled on a deal. He paid cash and put it in my name to cheat the IRS, though I didn't move in until I was out of high school. Hell's Kitchen has changed. Yuppies moved in on the fringes of our neighborhood, and suddenly my apartment is worth a ridiculous amount of money.

The second bedroom is full of junk. Not junk, really, but our mother's things, including her clothes, which neither Tom nor I can bring ourselves to give to the Salvation Army. Tom would rather sleep on a pullout couch with zero privacy and keep his clothes in an armoire in the corner of our living room than get rid of a single thing that belonged to our mother. Sometimes, in the night, when I would go to check if he was breathing, he wouldn't be in his bed. I would immediately panic, assuming he'd killed himself, but then I'd hear someone in the second bedroom and I would find him there, among her things, just sitting and maybe looking at old photos of her. Sometimes he'd be crying. I usually just sat next to him without saying a word and kept him company until he simply got up and went back to bed.

Ice pack on my head, in my bedroom, I thought about her. Most people have the sense of serenity or acceptance that when both their parents die, they each go to the same place and are together again. Considering I, and everyone else who knew my father, assumed they headed in opposite directions, I didn't have that calm, that feeling somehow all was going to be okay and they were both at peace. I guess peace has eluded all of the O'Neils all our lives, so I don't suppose death should be any different.

When I first found my mother, she looked like she was sleeping, except for the vomit trickling out of the corner of her mouth. She didn't leave a note, but we had always known she was crazy. Even at six, I knew she was crazy. But what a delicious crazy it was. My father's crazy was about murder. My mother's crazy was about bringing you into her world and loving you so intensely you spent the rest of your life comparing love to hers.

5

My mother, Mary Callahan, wasn't from Hell's Kitchen. She was from Queens, an entire train ride away from the world in which my father grew up. In New York City, a train ride can make all the difference. So she knew nothing about my father and his crew when she met him at a dance hall. All she knew was he walked as if he ruled the world, and he had a chivalrous air about him, because if anyone so much as looked at her while they were out on a date, he would walk over to the guy and bust him in the face. For some reason, she found this charming, just as I am sure pit bull owners think their dogs' jaws of death are enchanting. They grow on you.

Somehow, Mary Callahan, with her working-class parents and her Catholic-schoolgirl sensibilities, fell in love with Frank O'Neil. No one understood it until later. No one could believe her parents didn't object to the marriage. Why they seemed only too glad to hand her over to a man whose very muscles, very hair-trigger nerves reeked of violence. Grandma and Poppy Callahan were quick to pack her bags and give her a big wedding with a full Catholic mass before my father figured it all out.

On the other side of the train ride, everyone understood that my father took one look at the stunning Mary Callahan and decided he had to have her. He bought her a delicate wristwatch with diamonds on the face on their third date. Scratch that. She *thought* he bought her the wristwatch. It fell off a truck—like ninety percent of everything we owned.

Their wedding pictures are like any wedding pictures of that era, except for the extracurricular activities of the wedding party. For me, looking at the photos, I cannot help but see blood splattered. If you count my father, the best man and the groomsmen, between the five of them, by the time the black-and-white wedding photos were being snapped at a wedding hall in Bellerose, Queens, they had killed nine people—including one by dismemberment. The *Chronicle* explored that in enough detail to make me sick, and to fascinate Hollywood.

In their pictures, my mother looks radiant, my father beside her with his lopsided, half-drunk grin. He looks a little tired, courtesy of an all-night bender the evening before with his closest pals and a half-dozen hookers. My mother's dress was ivory with a long train and pearls hand-sewn on the bodice. He wore a black tux. She carried a small nosegay that she told me was filled with her favorite flower—lilies of the valley.

But sometimes I stare at the pictures. I even pull the wedding album up three inches from my face. Was it there? In those blue eyes of hers, the color of Tom's, gray in the photos, was it already obvious she was insane?

Three babies came in quick succession, along with the first jail stint my father did after marriage, for breaking and entering. He copped a plea and only had to serve six months. He left my mother with enough money to cover expenses in his absence.

He wrote to her from prison, those letters now in a box somewhere in my spare bedroom. They urge her to hold on, because
by then he knew. I think she scared the shit out of him. This tiny little woman, ninety-five pounds sopping wet, scared him
more than facing down a guy with a buzz saw who wanted to do
his own dismemberment job on my dad's legs.

The other part of it, of course, is that he may have loved her.
This is debatable. I think that in my father's world, whatever
passes as love was the feeling he had toward her. I think when
she walked into the room, his stomach tightened. I think when
he heard "Fly Me to the Moon" by Frank Sinatra, he thought of
her in a way that resembled love. I think he would have killed
anyone who tried to harm her. But I've spent a lifetime wondering what love is and wondering, most especially, what love
was to Frank O'Neil. Whatever it was, by the time his prison
stint came along, my father understood very clearly that he was
sold a bill of goods by my maternal grandparents.

I don't remember much about those days he was gone—that
time to Rahway because he committed the crime in Hoboken,
New Jersey. Carol is the oldest, Tom the middle child, and I was
the baby. But I do remember that Tom cooked for me. He made
me cereal in the mornings and hot dogs for dinner, and he taught
me how to dress myself. I don't remember Carol. I don't know,
quite honestly, if this is because I hate her, and my mind, under
the burden of all this blood and violence, has excised her from
every scene, like someone cutting a face out of a photo. Or is it
because she was already distancing herself from Tom and me? All
I know is I seem to have spent my entire life with my hand in
Tom's, and her hand was nowhere to be found.

I also remember, vividly, the door to my mother's bedroom—
my parents' bedroom—because it was always shut during
Mom's bad days. We approached that door as a penitent Catho-

lic might approach the cavern of Lourdes on a pilgrimage. It was sacred, almost frightening. We didn't know what was behind it. Of course, we knew the room contained a bed, a dresser, two nightstands, two lamps. But Mom was our fallen saint. We prayed for her; we sat outside the door for days hoping she might come out. I trotted out every prayer I'd been taught at St. Agatha's and improvised a few. I even said rosaries. Much later, I gave up on God, but I might as well have back then for all the good it did.

We could hear her crying, though now that I am officially a grown-up, I recognize it, in my memory at least, as more like keening. The sound from behind that door settled into a rhythmic pattern that rose and fell. At its height, it gave me goose bumps, and my teeth chattered involuntarily. I recognized it for the sound of a ghost woman. She wasn't human. She was my mother, but she was behind that door possessed by something neither Tom nor I could understand.

And then the door would open a crack. It might be weeks later. We would peek our heads curiously around the corner, and there she would be, lying on her side, dark circles that belong only to the insane beneath her eyes. They weren't circles like I get after a few nights of restless or no sleep. They were nearly ebony, like black eyes or bruises. Her skin against them was a pale white. She was wraithlike. A wisp of a woman in a bed, a woman we hoped would come back to us. We never knew what, if anything, she ate while she was behind the door. We never knew if she slept, if she took pills, if she ever called anyone on the telephone.

I remember whispering "Mommy?" the first time the door cracked open. She smiled weakly, always a half smile, and she squinted, as if trying to recall who she was and who these little Irish-Russian urchins were who looked at her with hope mingled with terror.

"Come, my babies," she would say, and gather us into her bed. She was bony and frail, but Tom and I nestled against her. Carol, already, was carving her life of resentment. She would kiss my mother but then retreat. So it was Tom and me always. We would lie snuggled to her, one against each tiny breast we could feel beneath her dirty bedclothes. We would lie on her like children do seeking their mother's warmth, clinging to her for our very lives. For her life.

Then came the breathless delirium. Within days, when we came home from school, she would be rearranging the furniture and painting the bathroom, racing from project to project, chattering a mile a minute until we could scarcely understand what she was saying. Through it all, she kept laughing, delightedly, and talking of our father as if he would be home any day, though we knew he was gone for six long months. We were rapt with adoration. She was out of that room, she was alive, she was full of life. We laughed with her…at first. Dancing in the living room to the albums she and my father loved—Louie Prima, Frank Sinatra, Benny Goodman, Bobby Darrin.

Then the energetic delirium would go on for a time we innately understood was not human. Days and days she wouldn't sleep. She spent the food money on presents for us, useless junk and baby dolls, and she tried to get Tom and me to stay up with her all night long. We would try. God knows, I tried, so thankful to be near her. We watched the late show and the late-late show on the color television my father stole. Tom and I both would nod off, but always I remember her poking me in the ribs, saying, "Don't fall asleep. Be with me, darlings. Be with me. Let's *do* something. Come on now, darlings, darlings, I love you." She talked incessantly to keep us awake, her face inches from ours, her pupils dilated with madness. We were her "darlings," repeated until I heard that word in my head like a chant—I still do some nights when Tom and I are in that room with her things. She haunts us.

Let's do something. This meant, usually, baking twelve dozen cookies at three o'clock in the morning. We would feast on chocolate chip cookies for breakfast, lunch and dinner, loving them at first, then tiring of the monotony. Or we would perform for her, scenes from her favorite television programs. We would sing and dance until we literally dropped. And then she would let us stay home from school for days, still trying to keep us from falling asleep, desperate for our company. We would stay awake until we literally threw up from exhaustion, and then she might relent and let us nap.

Once a week, whether she was behind the door or pacing the living room calling us "darlings"—up or down, we'd be visited by one of my father's friends. Two-Times and Uncle Charley visited most often. Charley would poke around in the refrigerator to see if there was any food. He considered twelve dozen home-made cookies food, so the fact that milk and juice and eggs, and anything that resembled dinner, were missing was ignored until Two-Times came. Two was a man who believed in "three squares," and if the refrigerator and cabinets did not contain some semblance of real food, he either went shopping himself or took Tom, Carol and me out for dinner, which we would wolf down as if it was our last meal on death row—an analogy that seemed especially appropriate for my family.

Two had his own way of checking on our health. Each weekly visit he wrapped one thick, beefy hand around my upper arm—I being the baby and needing the most watching—and measured just how skinny I was getting. Sometimes Two followed me and Tom home from school and made us stop for ice cream to fatten us up. He handed us money...not much, because we were kids and would have blown it on candy probably, but enough to let us stop at a grocery store if we needed. But what kid thinks she needs milk? We lived on crap and looked like orphans.

My father's brother, George, visited us. But I remember little of him. To me, he is the evil puppet master behind that theater curtain. He is shrouded in red velvet and muffled, as if I can't quite make out what he is saying, let alone who he was. What he was.

We never visited the dentist or the doctor while my father was in prison. We were truant from school. We lived our whole lives in that apartment. We lived and breathed the life of my mother.

I remember moments when she would stroke my hair, and she was neither up nor down. Maybe she was so exhausted from staying up for a week that she finally just settled into her brain…but I remember her stroking my hair. She looked at me with eyes I could not see reason in and told me she loved me, that she would rather die than harm me. And I believed her.

Tom and I lived our lives nestled in the arms of our mother, with only each other to keep the darkness at bay. We learned to soak up her love when she was out of bed and to fear each day she stayed behind the door. We learned to check to see if she was breathing as she slept—hot breath on our faces, chest rising and falling. We were children who later counted the pills in the medicine cabinet and stood guard over the very air entering her lungs. We never rested, not really. We've been tired all our lives.

6

Terror and laughter are an intoxicating cocktail. When my father came home from prison, the first thing he did after walking through the door was pick me up and toss me high in the air. This was his standard greeting for me. Once, on my third birthday, he dropped me, leaving the right side of my face bruised and blackened in all the pictures. But even after that, I never asked him not to, or even screamed when he did it. I laughed and squealed with terrified delight. To have asked him to stop would have meant I wasn't special because throwing me up toward the ceiling was for me alone.

After he put me down on the day he returned from Rahway, he kissed Carol on the top of her head, tilting her chin so he could see her freckles, then he hugged Tom. He never kissed Tom or told him he loved him. That was for the girls only. Two-Times stood in the doorway, rocking back on his heels in his Weeble-like way, smiling at our reunion. He'd gone to pick Dad up in his shiny Pontiac, which I later found out was pieced together in a chop shop in New Jersey.

"Look at this." Dad knelt and flexed the bicep of his right arm, showing off a brand-new prison tattoo—my name with a lop-sided heart beneath it. Only he wasn't just referring to the new tattoo, but to the size of his biceps. "Daddy did a whole lot of push-ups while he was away," he boasted, as if push-ups and a new physique were the sole purpose of his extended "vacation." "Look at these muscles, Tom," he said, flexing both arms like a bodybuilder.

"You're like Superman," Tom whispered with awe, touching Dad's arm. I felt it, too, as if a rock had been implanted where his old muscles used to be. His biceps seemed twice the size than how we remembered. He went away with lanky, snakelike arms and came back with pythons. He was beefier all over. Only now do I realize that in prison, rather than growing thinner, the in-mates beef up because they feed them starches morning, noon and night. It fills the prison population up cheaply. Instant pota-toes at lunch. More potatoes for dinner. Oatmeal for breakfast. All lumpy and unappetizing. But the prisoners eat it, anyway. Mealtime breaks up the monotony of the day out in the yard, the nights in the cell. That and the fights. My Dad shanked a guy who'd cheated him out of a pack of cigarettes. Dad wasn't caught. It was the highlight of his stint, he told me years later. He'd got-ten his enemy deep in the kidney, which was later removed.

"Yeah, Tommy, little buddy, Superman. That's your old man. So…where's Mommy, kids?" my father asked, standing up and stretching. My eyes darted down the hallway toward the door. Two-Times jerked his head in that direction, too. I guess he hadn't the heart to tell my father what he'd find when he got home.

"I was fuckin' afraid of that." Dad sighed and went into our tiny kitchen for a beer. We all stood in the hallway, watching him with curiosity, and because with Two there we'd never all fit in the kitchen. Dad sat in a kitchen chair, shoulders slumped, and stared at the wall, covered in a black-and-white wallpaper, courtesy of the tenants before us. His beer, which Two had put in the refrigerator to chill the night before as a homecoming gesture, was downed in two swift chugs. Dad put the empty Schlitz can on the table and buried his face in his hands. He leaned over and opened the refrigerator again, not for another beer but to survey its contents. He looked at me, out in the hallway, and commented on how thin I'd become. How I was wearing dirty pajamas though it was three o'clock in the afternoon, and how Tom and I had not had haircuts in six months.

"You look like a fucking hippie, Tom."

Tom, eight years old, nodded and looked down.

"I'll take all you kids for haircuts tomorrow."

Finally, after what seemed like a long time, with us and Two afraid to even breathe, my dad stood and said, "Well...lemme go give your mother a kiss."

He walked slowly down the hall and stood in front of the door. He put his hand on the doorknob and waited again before finally turning it and going inside. We still didn't move. None of us. Two was as rooted to his spot as a tree. It was as if he had sprouted roots in our apartment, the way oaks grow into concrete and blacktop in the city over time.

Eventually, Carol retreated into her bedroom and slammed the door shut. My legs got tired. The backs of my knees ached from standing so straight, so worried, so tense. I sat down cross-legged on the floor. I stared at the door, willing my father to get my mother out of that bed, where she had gone three weeks before, never to be seen by us in daylight since.

Occasionally, I would wake up at night and hear her shuffling in the kitchen, rooting around for a box of crackers or something. I would stare at her from Tom's and my bedroom, craning my neck from my twin bed so I could see what she looked like. She wasn't my mother. She was a ghost of my mother.

But with Daddy home, as long minutes ticked by, we waited for my father to emerge with her. I imagined her restored to the pretty woman in the wedding pictures with the strangely vacant stare, but beautiful nonetheless. Tom sat down next to me in the hallway. I slipped my hand in his. Daddy would fix this. This was what we had waited for. Those six months we had counted the days. We had fed ourselves and dressed ourselves. We had done everything right with the hope that when he returned he would fix what was broken.

But when he came out hours later, he was alone. His already pale prison skin, almost translucent from lack of sun and—I found out later—a stay in solitary, was even whiter. His eyes were moist, and he shared a look with Two-Times that spoke of what was behind that door.

I remember feeling as though my stomach had dropped through me to the itchy brown carpeting beneath me. We had waited for our savior, so certainly wrongfully convicted as we'd been told, to return and resurrect the body of Mary Callahan O'Neil. But our savior might as well have been the plastic glow-in-the-dark statue of Jesus we kept on a bookshelf. Our mother wasn't healed. It was that room. That room held her hostage. Behind that door was something, some beast holding her there. And Frank O'Neil was as powerless as two children.

"Hey, kids, let's get you guys some pizza and then off to bed," he whispered, and I remember his voice sounded strange, as if spoken through a tunnel, far off and distant.

"Is Mommy coming out for pizza?" I asked. Tom's nails dug into the flesh of my palm, warning me to shut up.

"No. Mommy's resting, baby doll. Mommy's resting."

I looked down so my father wouldn't see my tears. The

O'Neils don't cry. It's an unspoken rule. Tom's nails dug still harder into my hand to keep me from crying—or himself. We willed each other to be strong.

Dad lifted me up, and I nestled my head against his neck. He smelled of prison. He smelled of men who kill. He smelled like my beloved daddy.

Later that night, when he tucked me in, he kissed my forehead, and I heard him choke back something that sounded like a cutoff sob. An anguished half moan from somewhere inside him I didn't know. He was frightened by what he had seen behind that door. He had gone to Rahway, but what he found at home was more torturous than solitary. He was more afraid of what Tom and I had faced, alone, every day for the last six months. Our cage had no bars, but it was darker and filled with the cold snakes of insanity.

7

My mother emerged from behind the door about a week later, in time for Thanksgiving the following Thursday. She cleaned and scrubbed and stayed up all night, every night, preparing for the Thanksgiving feast, which could only mean one thing—the invasion of the grandparents.

Both my grandmothers shared one common characteristic: neither could cook. Vegetables were boiled to a putrid pale mass of congealed slop, and meat was overcooked until turkey was actually more like Shredded Wheat, stringy and tasteless. The gravies the two grandmas concocted differed only in their color. Both sides made it lumpy with thickened bits of flour that stuck to the roof of your mouth and made swallowing decidedly difficult without a chaser. My mother rounded out this triumvirate of abysmal cooks, and consequently Thanksgiving day usually meant eating a lot of canned cranberry sauce and trying to avoid anything that had been on or near a stove or oven and, even accidentally, touched by these three women. For the adults, a veritable lake of alcohol was consumed to make the day more bearable.

As soon as Grandma and Poppy Callahan walked through the door, they handed Tom, Carol and me a silver dollar each. This was their one indulgence for us, and they doled these out like Kruger-rands. They dressed in their Sunday-best clothes, his a dark blue suit, white shirt and striped tie. She wore a pale blue dress with a high, librarian-like collar. Her hair was stiffened by a can of Aqua Net hairspray. The previous year her hair had caught on fire after Uncle Charley dropped a match in it while standing behind her chair and trying to light a cigar. Uncle Charley had thought quickly and patted it out with his bare hands and a dish towel, though she had to cut her hair frighteningly short to fix it. In the year since last Thanksgiving, her Brillo-pad-like hair had finally grown back to its full bouffant potential, though she glared at Uncle Charley all day.

My mother's parents were only vaguely interested in what we did. As they pressed a silver dollar into our palms, they asked about our grades and our friends, but they always ate and left as soon as possible. I don't think they wanted to know about that door their daughter hid behind, most certainly didn't want to know about their son-in-law's nefarious activities, and even more certainly didn't want to break bread with Two-Times, Uncle Charley and Benny C-note, our neighborhood bookie and a steady employer of my father as "leg-breaker of the year."

I think they actually hurt Two's feelings. He was always so polite to them. "Yes, sir, Mr. Callahan. No, ma'am, Mrs. Callahan." We ate on bridge tables set up in our living room, and he passed the potatoes and tried not to curse, but the sheer number of tattoos on his arms and even knuckles (not to mention my father's tattoos) caused Grandma Callahan to sit even more erect and stiff than usual.

In the end, too, I think they wanted to go back to Queens,

keep our pictures on their out-of-tune piano, but never actually deal with their daughter—or us. The entire time Dad was in prison, they never even called our apartment.

The O'Neil grandparents, on the other hand, never gave us silver dollars. Grandfather O'Neil usually arrived with a bottle of Jameson's and didn't stop drinking until it was all gone. Like my father, he had an uncanny ability to hold his alcohol. Grandmother O'Neil, who had arrived from Russia when she was twelve, scowled her way through the evening. She never spoke English in my presence, though I was quite certain she understood it and could speak it. Instead, she spoke Russian, and when we children didn't understand what she was saying, which was one hundred percent of the time, she slapped our hands and called us *СЛАБОУМНЫЙ*, the Russian word for idiot.

The O'Neils and the Callahans had been enemies ever since the wedding. The cause of the rift was never fully explained, though rumors have circulated through the neighborhood for years that it involved a craps game in a back corner of the wedding hall, as well as a toast by the best man, Uncle Charley, that referred to sex in ways generally not used in pool halls, let alone at weddings of virginal Irish brides. The Callahans were not amused, but the O'Neil side soon figured out my mother was mentally unbalanced and therefore their son had gotten a raw deal. Dad's father, consequently, delighted in tormenting Grandmother Callahan, usually by telling jokes containing any of the following words: *douche bag, pussy, cunt* or *motherfucker.* He collected these jokes all year long to delight the Thanksgiving table.

That the grandchildren were innocent of the roots of the feud did not matter to either side. In my entire life, I saw the inside of the Callahans' two-bedroom, one-bath home, which backed up to train tracks, a total of three times, all involving funerals and wakes. I saw the inside of the O'Neil apartment, a fourth-floor walk-up in a decaying building, twice a year when my father used to drop off money or some of his stolen property to them for safekeeping. Because all visits with my Russian grandmother involved having my hands slapped until they were red and raw, I often hid at my Uncle Two's apartment down the street when I knew Dad was heading over to his parents, until he couldn't wait any longer and would leave without me.

This Thanksgiving, Grandfather O'Neil was midway through a joke whose main punchline was clearly leading toward a colossal case of mistaken identity involving an old woman misidentified as a young prostitute, a dog, a blind sea captain, and the use of an actual douche bag. Finally, Grandmother Callahan had quite enough.

"Mr. O'Neil, there are ladies and children present and—"

"Come on there, Rita. It's nothin' these kids haven't overheard down at John's."

"John's? You don't mean that filthy bar, do you?"

"Yup. Show 'em the Amazing Coaster Trick, Ava.... You gotta see this trick she learned on Sunday."

"Sunday?" I watched my grandmother carefully. Her very pointy nose actually twitched with rage. I opted not to break out my cardboard beer coasters and demonstrate the trick I had mastered, courtesy of the sleight of hand of the three-card monte king, Joey Quick. Sunday was supposed to be church day. We seemed to worship at the Church of the Divine Keg.

Two-Times, anxious to play peacemaker, tried to change the subject.

"So...did everybody watch the Macy's parade this morning?"

No one spoke. My father had frozen, fork poised in midair, and Benny C. was eyeballing the carving knife, should the meal turn to bloodshed.

Grandfather O'Neil could not leave well enough alone. He couldn't leave *disaster* enough alone.

"So you gotta listen to the end of this joke."

Grandmother Callahan rose, very dignified, and said, "Ed, we're going home."

With that, my father threw his fork against the wall, slammed his fist down on the card table and picked up the carving knife. A gravy boat fell onto its side, and several drinks spilled. "Park it, Rita."

"I beg your pardon?"

"You heard me. I'm home from the joint, and I'm *going* to have a turkey dinner. And though I'd like to belt the two of you for not even checking on your own fucking grandchildren while I was away, we all know what the fuck is going on here. So sit the fuck down and eat your turkey before I put a baster up your fuckin' ass."

My grandmother's eyes widened, and her nose twitched even more, like a rabbit's, but she reseated herself.

Grandfather O'Neil made a move to open his mouth and finish the joke, looked at the carving knife, which was held tight in my father's left hand, and shut his mouth. My mother was by now crying, tears rolling down her face and dropping onto her turkey. My father leaned over and kissed her cheek, gently pushing her hair back behind her ear. He took her hand in his free one. She visibly calmed down at his touch.

"All right. It's over. Everybody eat your turkey. And save room for dessert. Mary made an apple pie. You'll eat it and like it."

Two-Times looked quite pleased by that prospect. We ate in silence, finished our tiny bits of shredded turkey and plates full of cranberry sauce, and cleared the table for dessert and coffee.

When my mother's parents left, they didn't kiss her goodbye, nor did they acknowledge my father. The men settled in to a high-stakes poker game. My mom retreated to her bedroom, where she quickly downed an entire bottle of Seconal. My father, needing more money by the tenth hand, went into the bedroom to get some out of his underwear drawer, found her and managed to get her to the hospital in a cab, he and Two first carrying her down the stairs of our apartment building like a sack of potatoes. Dad was hyperventilating and saying "Please, God, let her fucking make it" all the way down to the lobby of our building until I could no longer hear him and they were out the door. Benny C-note baby-sat us, teaching Tom, Carol and me how to shoot craps, playing with us for Cheerios. He even cheated. For cereal.

Tom, Carol and I never cried, even as they carried our mother down the stairs. Two told us to "keep our chins up." And like good little O'Neil children, we did what we were told.

My mother lived. That time. And both sets of grandparents never came to Thanksgiving together again.

8

My mother's suicide attempts came closer and closer together. With more and more pills. The obvious solution was to take her pills away. Dad did. And then one night she swallowed a bottle of baby aspirin and half a bottle of rubbing alcohol. She survived, but it had been very close, and my father, Two-Times, Uncle Charley, Tom and me, even Carol, began watching her in shifts.

I tried to be inconspicuous, even as I invented stomachaches and headaches to stay home from second grade. A doctor at Bellevue had placed her on lithium, which she spat out and refused to take. He also gave her other drugs with fancy names I couldn't pronounce that my father said didn't seem to be doing what they were supposed to do. All I knew was her wild mood swings had settled into a daze. She sat on our couch, her hair unwashed and uncombed, and watched soap operas and game shows. She didn't even bother to switch the channel. It stayed on channel two if that was what the television was tuned to, and channel five if that was what we happened to have watched last.

Mom sat on the middle cushion on the couch, precisely in the center, her hands in her lap. I sat beside her, my hand touching hers. She never held my hand, never clasped it, but she didn't withdraw from me, either. Sometimes I would pet her leg like a child might pet a cat. I instinctively wanted to soothe her, wanted to make her better.

At night, when he was home, my father would carry her into their bedroom. Sometimes he bathed her, placing her in the tub like a little girl. He didn't know how to do her hair. So he washed it and let it dry, unstyled. Sometimes he would cut out pieces of hair that had gotten too matted. After a while, her hair was jagged and messy-looking. She began looking more and more like a crazy woman, like the women we saw on the streets sometimes.

Two-Times came by, along with Uncle Charley. We also had a new addition to our household. Pinky was my father's latest sidekick, so named because he was missing the pinky of his right hand, lost, he said, "in a disagreement" with his bookie when he was a teenager. Pinky did the grocery shopping, and he cooked for us sometimes, too. He was a great cook, better than our mother. He made chicken cacciatore and spaghetti in meat sauce—from scratch, not even from a jar.

Pinky, with his Brillcream-slick hair and "Guinea-Ts"—muscle shirts that showed off the tattoo of Jesus Christ on his arm, seemed to like being around Tom and me. We were a fresh audience for his wild tales, and I never knew whether to believe him or not. Would a man set on fire really be able to throw himself down a flight of stairs and run out into the street and have to be shot to finish off the job? Tom and I discovered that having Pinky in the house was better than watching *Starsky and Hutch*. Tom wanted to take him to school for show-and-tell.

One night in February, my father said he wouldn't be com-

ing home because a particular truck driven by a particular Team-
ster was due to be "delayed" on Route 17 in New Jersey, whereby
my mother and all the wives and girlfriends of my father's crew
would be getting new rabbit-fur jackets.

Tom and I were in our room. Tom was feeding our goldfish,
Sam, a bloated, overfed, lazy fish that mostly hung around the
bottom of his bowl. I was playing with my Barbie dolls. Their
pink clothes and little pink shoes were so far from my reality. I
meticulously lined up their accessories, marveling at them. Mom
came into our room and sat down on my bed.

"Do you two know Mama loves you?"

We were both too shocked to see her in a clean nightgown
speaking to us to even answer, so we nodded.

"Come here, Tom." She held open her arms. He ran to her and
hugged her fiercely, pushing her backward on my bed. She laughed and kissed his forehead. "Now, listen to me, Tom——" she
raised herself up on an elbow, and he moved over and sat beside
her "——I think you are a very smart boy. Too smart to end up losing your finger, like Pinky, or going to jail, like Uncle Charley.
So I want you to promise me you won't become a gambler or a
wise guy. You will become a good man and do good things."

Tom nodded.

"Promise me."

"I promise."

"Good. Now, get on your pajamas and brush your teeth."

"I love you, Mommy," he said, calling her Mommy and not
Mom. He hadn't called her Mommy since he was my age—a
baby.

"I love you, too. Very much."

Tom went to the bathroom to change and brush his teeth,
leaving my mother and me alone. I was still marveling at her.
She had done her hair. She looked like she was supposed to look.
Like our mother. Like the pictures we had of her.

"My baby. My baby, Ava." She held out her arms to me. I climbed up on her lap, and she put her face to my cheek, then kissed my head, my hair. She smelled me, inhaling my Johnson's Baby Shampoo scent. My babyness. Though I wasn't really a baby anymore, just small for my age.

"I love you," she whispered. "I love you. And I love your daddy. I'm just tired."

She held me until Tom came back. She helped me change into my pajamas. She tucked us both in. She kissed us. She kissed us like she used to kiss us. She kissed our forehead, then each eyelid, then our nose, and each cheek, and then our lips.

"Can we have pancakes in the morning?" I asked, my throat tightening with happiness, blinking hard.

She paused, smiling a faraway smile, as if pancakes and warm maple syrup were a dream she once had a long time ago, like a fairy tale of a family. "Hmm…pancakes. Sure. You can have them." She stared at me. "Remember, I love you both."

She turned out the light, looking at us from the doorway, framed like a halo by light from the kitchen. Then she went to Carol's bedroom and tucked her in. We could hear their sweet murmuring, and we fell asleep blissfully.

The next morning was Saturday. I ran out in my pajamas to the living room where Tom was already ensconced with *Bugs Bunny.* "Is Mommy up yet?"

He shook his head. It was the Bugs episode where he traveled to Mars. Tom was laughing and wearing his pajama top and his underwear—Superman underwear with a big *S* in the crotch. Believing Mom was now well, for I had seen her the night before, vibrant, sane, alive, I didn't even knock on her bedroom door. I ran to it, unafraid. She was cured. I rushed in to ask her to make me pancakes.

She was facing the door.

Her eyes were wide open and frozen in their blueness. I stood by her, touching her skin, now cold. Vomit had trickled out of her mouth. She was sick. She was sick again. I took her tightly balled hand in mine and knelt at her bedside, as a child says prayers.

I knelt there, unable to move, cold myself, then hot as if a fever had taken over me. I moved my lips. I moved them more frantically, but no sound came out, not even a rush of breath. I started trembling, shaking, my teeth chattering loudly.

Tom came into the room. We lived our lives in some state of hyperalertness. We watched people at dinner tables and waited for them to make a move for the carving knife. We listened for noises in the night. We listened for gunshots and the sirens of police. I had gone to ask for pancakes, and now I was silent. That was enough to bring him to my side. He took my free hand, and with his other hand he stroked her bare arm. We didn't cry. We didn't move, except for the involuntary shaking that had taken over both of us.

Some time later, Two-Times let himself in with a key. What must he have seen as he opened the door? Two children, hand in hand, frozen, a body on a bed. I remember him screaming "No!" and I remember he raced to us, and he cried as he lifted each of us up and sat us on the couch with the TV on.

"Stay here, kids. Stay here." He went into the room with her body, shutting the door behind him. Mom had gone into her room the night before, the coroner later told my father, and took a combination of aspirin, Valium she had been secretly hoarding for a long time, and a pint of gin.

Two-Times shut her eyelids and wiped the vomit from the bed and the corner of her mouth. He put a blanket over her as if she had fallen asleep. He knelt by her bed and said the Hail Mary. I know all this because he told me one night when he was very drunk. He did all these things so my father would see her, the love of his life, as he would want to remember her.

Then he left the room and went into Carol's bedroom. She was watching her own TV set, not interested in our cartoons. We heard her crying. Then Two-Times shut her door and stood in front of my parents' bedroom, like a sentry.

My father came home a little before noon with two fur jackets on hangers. Two-Times's sizable body blocked the master bedroom. He nodded to my father, almost imperceptibly. My father rushed at Two. He punched him in the jaw, leaving a red welt, and later a bruise, as Two wrestled him to the floor. All the while, my father was screaming and cursing. The word "fuck" reverberated through our apartment again and again. The lady who lived below us even pounded on her ceiling with a broomstick, which she sometimes did when my parents' parties got too raucous.

Finally, when it seemed as if my father had calmed somewhat, Two allowed him into the room. We heard our father wailing and cursing God and Grandmother and Poppy Callahan. He broke a lamp, the mirror over her dresser, picture frames, and punched his fist through their medicine cabinet mirror, requiring stitches in our kitchen later, administered by Pinky, who was apparently quite talented at removing bullets and stitching people back together again.

Eventually, an ambulance arrived. They took our mother away with a sheet over her face. Only after she was gone did Dad seem to remember we were there, on the couch, watching television, too numb to cry. He sat down next to us. We were watching the Creature Feature, as mesmerized as our mother had been by what was flickering back at us.

"I thought you were afraid of Godzilla, Ava?" he whispered, patting my knee.

I shook my head.

After that day, I was never afraid of the monsters on TV again.

9

We didn't go to our mother's wake. Instead, we watched as a steady stream of half-familiar strangers brought us food until the pans of ziti and lasagna and trays of cookies and desserts literally couldn't fit in our kitchen anymore. Our refrigerator was so full, frost was accumulating on the sides when we opened it to peek inside. We piled trays on the bookshelves in the living room, and trays on my bed. Tom, Carol and I nibbled at sweet sugar cookies dipped in dark chocolate. And Two-Times nibbled at everything, having a taste from nearly every tray that came through the door, then replacing the aluminum foil with an expression of guilty pleasure.

Tom and I hid under the long table set up in the living room, our own personal fort, as people poured into our apartment the two nights of the wake to stay up drinking with my father until dawn after viewing our mother's dead body in the funeral parlor several blocks away. The party was loud, not somber, and no one seemed terribly sad.

Two-Times knew we were under the table. Drunk, cheeks

flushed red, sweating profusely in the crowded heat of the apartment, he kept lifting up one side of the tablecloth and peeking at us, winking and patting us on our heads. We listened to the men, their talk littered with their usual words of *fuck*, and *cunt*, and *a-hole*. We tried to place snippets of conversation with the owners of the voices.

"The fuckin' Mick didn't know what hit 'im."

"Sad fuckin' end to Mary. Sad fuckin' end."

"Can't say as I'm surprised."

"Those poor babies."

"Yes…those poor babies."

The women gathered in little clusters, clucking about Tom, Carol and me. But not one of them had been my mother's friend. All the times my mother had been too sick to cook for us, none of these women brought ziti or trays of antipasto, or chocolate cakes made extra moist with homemade recipes. Now that she was gone, suddenly we had more food than we could eat. I would be sleeping with four casseroles…yet where had they been, these women?

Staring out from beneath our mother's best white linen tablecloth—not stolen, but given to her by her grandmother, whom we'd never met—at the shiny Sunday-best funeral shoes of the people in our lives and our father's life, I don't remember thinking about my mother very much. Instead, my grief was quiet. It whispered to me in the night when I woke up and couldn't fall back to sleep after they had gone. My grief came to me in tiny shards of glass that pierced me when I walked by their bedroom door, when I knew that she wouldn't be on the couch to touch, to stroke. What I felt in place of grief was fear. Shivers passed over me, and both Tom and I would find our teeth chattering at odd moments. All children have mothers. That was the truth, I knew. Without one, we were utterly alone.

Though she had never been well, not that we could remember, she had been there, in our house. She had been ours, our mother, imperfect and crazy, but she belonged to us. Now she belonged to the angels, and we wanted her back.

The women who came to our apartment were cheap-looking and ugly. I hated them all, even though they brought cookies. I hated them for being alive when she wasn't. Some of them weren't mothers. I remember feeling an anger curling up in my stomach and nesting there for a long winter. Why couldn't God have taken a woman without children? Why couldn't he have taken one of these hideous women with too-dark lipstick and bright blue eyeshadow? My mother's beauty had been undiminished even when she sat dazed and unresponsive.

During the two days leading up to the funeral, my father slept in. Pinky came over each morning and cooked us eggs and made us toast with thick slabs of butter. We weren't very hungry, but we listened to his stories, thankful, I think, for something other than the silence and the stale smell of old cigarette smoke from the night before. Tom and Carol and I would try to clean up from the party, gagging at the sights and smells of cigarettes stubbed out in glasses of Scotch and gin.

In the afternoon, alone with Tom in our bedroom, he and I didn't speak. I remember lying in bed for hours, trying to comprehend what life would be like with just our father. With just men around us. I couldn't count all the dollar bills that had been thrust into my palm all the years of my life by them. All the times I had been patted on the head, taken to bars and taught tricks with coasters and napkins. But now who would touch my cheek with featherlight fingers? Who would comb my hair? I needed a mother, we all did.

After two nights of the wake, the next day was the funeral, which we children were to attend. I wore my best dress, with

full crinoline that itched my legs. I put on black patent-leather
Mary Janes and white stockings, and Tom wore the suit from his
first communion, which was too short in the sleeves, but no one
would notice, or so Two-Times told us.

"You'll take off the jacket when we get to the luncheon, Tom,"
Two said, his meaty fingers struggling with the tiny knot of a little boy's tie as he helped us dress.

"I'm scared, Uncle Two," Tom whispered.

"Eh…nothin' to be scared of, kids. Your mom looks like she's
sleeping. 'Cause she is. She's sleeping in heaven now, but…" He
sighed, struggling with the words. "You just hold on to my hand
or your dad's hand. You go up to the kneeler, and you say a
prayer and you say goodbye. And then you visit with all the people and then the priest is going to say some prayers. And then
after the cemetery we go to a nice lunch." Two seemed very
happy about the lunch.

Walking into the funeral parlor, I was terrified. My heart raced
like a baby rabbit's, and I remember breathing so fast I thought
my lungs would explode. The place was packed full of the people from the apartment, packed so tight it was standing room only. The entire room, echoing with gossip and flashes of laughter
a moment before, fell silent as we children walked in, Carol first,
then Tom, then me. Women looked away and dabbed at their
eyes. I saw pity, though I didn't yet know that's what it was.

The air was stifling. I was overwhelmed by the scent of gar-
denias. Thick and cloying, the flowers suffocated me. All those
flowers, huge arrangements towering over me, taking over the
room. I started crying, and my knees buckled. In an instant, I
was picked up by Two. He took me toward the coffin, weaving
through the people, though they parted as much as they could
in that crowded parlor for us, the motherless children.

My mother did look like she was sleeping. In fact, she looked better than she had in a very long time, though her skin was plastic-looking and unnaturally pink-cheeked. Yet her hair was "done" the way she would have done it, the way she looked in the picture framed on the coffin. I buried my head in Two's shoulder, and he brought me to a chair, where I sat next to Tom and tried to avoid looking at her.

Grandma and Poppy Callahan were there, their faces pinched. They never cried. Nor did they kiss me when I was sent over to say hello to them. My grandmother made a kissing sound, but her cool, dry lips never touched my cheek. Grandma clutched a pressed handkerchief, but she never used it. Even Two used a hankie at one point, blowing his nose so loudly that he startled the priest and made him have to start the Our Father all over again.

And that's all I remember. Before I knew it, we were at a luncheon. People were drinking and laughing and gossiping. My father was smoking and drinking and hugging people. I remember standing in a corner of the hall my father had rented. Carol, uncharacteristically, chose to stand with Tom and me. Our backs were to the wall, and I surveyed all the life going on around us. It was as if my mother had never existed at all.

Part Two

Daddy's Wake: Night Two

I am sworn brother, sweet,
To grim Necessity, and he and I
Will keep a league till death.
                    —*William Shakespeare*

10

The morning of the second day, I heard Tom violently vomiting into the kitchen sink. Yet another reason we rarely cook at home.

I struggled out of bed myself, with only a slight pounding in my temples, thanks to the pharmacological miracle of Percocet. I brushed my teeth, collected my vomited-on towels from the night before and deposited them in my laundry basket, then put on my blue terry-cloth robe. Making my way out into the living room, I didn't have to squint in the sunlight. Tom always kept the shades drawn so it seemed like a cave.

"Hey, Tom," I called out, my voice a leftover rasp from shouting over the noise in John's Bar the previous night.

"Hey," his gravel-voice replied from the kitchen. He coughed several times, then I heard him gargle with water. The coffeemaker was brewing. I sat down on the pullout couch and stared at the television, tuned to one of the morning shows that deliver your news with lots of perkiness. Tom emerged from the kitchen with two cups of coffee—his black, mine pale cream-colored with two and a half teaspoons of sugar.

"Thanks, Tom."

"Tonight's funeral-hump night. I wonder who'll show."

Funeral-hump night is sort of like Wednesday. Hump day. The first night of the wake is packed. The second night the parlor is usually full of only the most faithful friends, or people who can't make first or third night. The last night is the heavy party night, the prefuneral send-off, standing room only.

I shrugged. "De Silva's assistant left a message on the machine yesterday morning saying most of the film crew and actors are coming tomorrow. As well as the publicity people. Tonight, I assume it'll be the usual. Uncle Two said he would pick up Pinky."

Pinky had married into money. None of us knew how he did it, but fifteen years ago he married a divorcée on the rebound, a Park Avenue beauty sixteen years his junior who delighted in antagonizing her entire old-monied family by marrying a guy with a missing finger and a rap sheet a mile long. They said it wouldn't last through their honeymoon in Tuscany and Lake Como. But Pinky had surprised all of us. Not only did he seem to genuinely care about Patricia, he had managed to keep her very happy. Five years ago, they bought a six-bedroom house in Sands Point, Long Island. We hear he plays golf every Wednesday with a bunch of doctors.

Tom shook his head. "Pinky...was the surprise of the bunch."

I laughed, taking a sip of my coffee. "And once the *Chronicle* article came out, it just made them the darlings of the country club. People fight to have them at their parties."

"Do people even get it?"

"Hmm?" I sipped my coffee.

"These guys aren't conflicted pussycats. The TV shows, the movies...do the people who love mob movies understand Dad and his friends play with real bullets?"

"Who knows, Tom? Blame directors like Michael De Silva. The movies glamorize them all. No one's ever gotten it just right."

We drank the rest of our coffee in silence, watching the morning host flip her blond hair around and smile at the actor she was interviewing about his latest Hollywood blockbuster.

"Ava?"

"Hmm?"

"Promise you won't go crazy?"

"No." My stomach tightened. "I don't make promises I can't keep. Not in this family."

He sighed and looked down into his coffee mug. "I threw up blood again this morning."

"Christ, Tom! You've got to get that checked out."

"I know. Wouldn't that be ironic?"

"What?"

"The old man dodges bullets and buzz saws his whole life, and I end up with cancer or something?"

"Fuck, Tom, you're burning a hole in your gut with vodka. You have an ulcer. You're not dying of cancer. You're killing yourself. Like Mom."

"Fuck you!"

"Fuck yourself!"

I stood up from the rumpled unmade couch and stormed into the kitchen and looked in the sink. He had scrubbed the porcelain with Comet so that it gleamed in the otherwise untidy kitchen. Tom was a clever and sneaky son of a bitch. I dumped out the rest of my coffee and put the mug in the dishwasher, a tiny narrow model made for small kitchens. We were lucky we could fit a meal's worth of dishes in it. My mug was a dorky World's Greatest Sister one with a red heart on one side. He had put it in my Christmas stocking.

My hands trembled as I closed the dishwasher. I hated fighting with Tom.

Fighting with him was like losing my life preserver and bob-
bing along in the ocean alone, swallowing huge gulps of brine until I was dead. So I tolerated everything. The drinking, the rages,
the bickering, the tears. I needed him. He told me things, like he
was bleeding, to keep me tied to him. I had to take care of him.
I owed him. We both knew it. And so I did what I always did.

"I'm sorry, Tom," I whispered, walking to the doorway and
looking at him lying back on the opened couch, a lit cigarette in
his mouth.

"I love you, baby." He glanced at me.

"I love you, too." I walked back toward my bedroom. "I'm going to shower and then take a walk."

"Okay," he said, blowing a smoke ring, his eyes utterly vacant.

That night at the wake, Jack Casey came through the door
with two other reporters, one from the *New York Times*, and Uncle Charley. Jack's intense black eyes darted to me immediately, and he didn't stop to kneel at my father's body. In fact, he
didn't even look, which made me wonder if he was really Irish.

"Ava." He seemed to be at my side in four strides of his long
legs. "I'm so sorry."

What was there to say? I just nodded.

"Can I take you out for dinner after this?" He looked around
at the gathering wise guys. "You could use a break from all this."

"I don't know, Jack."

"Come on...not for an interview. Not for anything but an old
friend making sure another old friend gets a meal in her. You look
tired. And too thin."

I glanced over at Tom, who was laughing with Charley and
Black Tom, who wasn't really black but was instead dark Irish,
with the thickest ebony beard and hair any of us had ever seen.
He also wasn't really named Tom, but that was another long

story involving a case of mistaken identity during an armed robbery.

I said softly, "I should stay with my brother Tom."

"You can meet up with him later. With this crew, they'll be going until two o'clock in the morning."

"That would be early for them. Give the gang a little more credit."

Jack laughed. "Please, Ava?"

I nodded. "Okay. But no deep, probing questions."

"Deal." He kissed me on the cheek, then took a seat, observing all the people coming in. I knew how his journalistic mind worked. I could almost see him, as his eyes darted back and forth, mentally separating the real-deal gangsters from the wannabes, the cops from the bad guys. In this neighborhood, that line was often blurred.

In a moment or two, I forgot about Jack Casey as Pinky came in with Patricia and Two-Times. Patricia wore an elegant black dress, her highlighted blond hair in a classic bob, and Jimmy Choo shoes. Pinky was dressed in one of his trademark Italian custom-made suits. Jack Casey's *Chronicle* article and then book had been so detailed, he had even found out the name of the tailor where Pinky had them made. Pinky looked handsome, tanned, relaxed. On his remaining pinky was a diamond ring.

"Thanks for coming, Pinky, Patricia." I kissed them each on the cheek.

"Your father was a true gentleman," Patricia offered. In all my life, I don't believe I had ever heard Frank O'Neil called a gentleman, but Patricia meant it as a compliment, so I didn't point out to her that gentlemen don't carry switchblades. They don't piss in the kitchen sink. They don't do many things, but why bring it up? After all, the purpose of an Irish wake is to celebrate and lie about the dead.

Pinky held his hand out waist-high. "I remember when you were this big, Ava. I still can't believe it every time I see you, sweetheart." I was everyone's sweetheart.

"I remember the time you and Dad took me to the Ringling Brothers circus at Madison Square Garden. We ate peanuts until we were all sick, and I got to pet an elephant before the show. Hard to believe how long I've known you. Tom and Carol had the chicken pox that night, so I was the only one who could go. Remember?"

"Remember?" he said. "Don't you remember I *got* the chicken pox from those two little brats? I was sick for a week after that fuckin' night. Who knew that I never caught 'em as a kid? I'm lucky I don't have scars on this beautiful mug o' mine."

We all laughed, but I laughed at the irony of a man missing a finger worried about chicken pox scars. Then he and Patricia excused themselves to go kneel at the body. Seeing them at the red-velvet-cushioned kneeler, amid rows of flowers, reminded me of church. It was as if they were worshipping at the Church of Frank O'Neil. God of all things unholy.

When viewing hours were over, Father McCann closed with a prayer. Squint Coonan, from one of the longshoreman locals, began singing "Danny Boy." Suddenly, everyone was singing. Men were swaying, arms slung around shoulders; women were wailing. It was time to get out of there.

I approached my brother and whispered in his ear. "I'm going to get something to eat with Jack Casey. I'll see you where? John's again?"

Tom nodded, his eyes steely. "Be careful." He didn't trust Jack Casey.

One piece to Jack's puzzle was missing, and Tom and I held the key to it. But I knew Tom and I would both die with the secret. When people came to our wakes, they could guess and wonder all they wanted. But no one would ever know.

Jack walked over to me and helped me drape my black shawl around my shoulders. We made our way through the crowd, on their last chorus, and out into the street where we hailed a yellow cab. We climbed in, and he told the driver to head over to a little Italian place called Café Rosa's. He knew the maître d', who sat us in a corner table, very private, toward the back of the restaurant.

"How are you holding up?" he asked me in the candlelight as our waiter poured us Pellegrino and I ordered a vodka and Jack a draft beer.

"As well as someone whose father just died can hold up, I guess. Some moments I feel totally fine. The next it seems surreal. It hasn't hit me yet, in some ways. And I haven't really even cried yet. Not really."

"How's Tom?"

I sighed. "Tom is...Tom."

"'Nough said."

I looked at my watch. About now, Tom would likely already be three shots into the night. Without me there, what little conscience he had was free to slide down into the bottle. I tried not to think about it and instead looked at the menu. I wasn't hungry, but when the waiter returned with breadsticks, I ordered manicotti and Jack ordered shrimp scampi.

Taking a breadstick, Jack took a bite, then asked me, "Has the cast of the movie come by yet? De Silva and them?"

"No. Tomorrow. And I guess it's likely they'll show for the funeral. De Silva sent an enormous floral arrangement."

"The big one with the red roses?"

"No. That one's from Pinky and Patricia. De Silva sent the huge standing white wreath."

"Oh...that one. Couldn't miss it." His eyes twinkled a little. In fact, for all the flowers, you would have thought a head of state had died. Or the pope or something. There were floral arrangements in the shape of dice and horseshoes from Benny C-note and the guys Dad went to the Belmont racetrack with.

I spread my napkin on my lap. "De Silva seems really broken up about losing his new 'best friend.'"

"I know they ate together at De Silva's restaurant in Tribeca a lot. Who would have ever thought your father would make Page Six of the *Post*?"

I shook my head. "One of the many strange twists in a twisted life."

"Hear from Vince?"

I shook my head. I know it hurt Jack that I fell in love with Vince. But I think Jack cared about me enough to be grateful I fell in love with someone, anyone. Even Vince Quinn.

"Nothing?"

I shook my head again.

"Don't worry. He'll show tomorrow. If he cares about you at all. And you know he does. He has to."

"I doubt it, Jack. You don't know what went down. Not all of it."

"I'm a good listener."

"Yeah, well, I'm not a good talker."

"Now, that's a news flash." He winked at me.

I smiled at him. Then tiredness consumed me. I stifled a yawn. The previous night, coupled with the day before that I spent picking out a coffin and satin lining, had exhausted me. I felt numb. Jack and I didn't speak much. When dinner came, I ate a few bites, then pushed the food around on my plate.

"Can I tell you something, Ava?"

"Sure."

"I wanted to hate your old man. I really did. And part of me hated him like a son of a bitch, but part of me loved the way he told the whole wide world to fuck off. He never backed down. Never repented."

"Now, there's an operative word. Tell me…all your years of catechism…do you think he's in hell?"

"You don't believe in heaven and hell. You told me that."

"I said I didn't *think* I believed. But I believe in ghosts. Sort of. So maybe I believe in hell. It doesn't matter, anyway…what I believe. I asked you what *you* believe."

He shrugged.

"You do think he's in hell. You just don't want to say it."

"Maybe. I don't know if there's an absolute. Maybe he gets to the pearly gates and God says, 'Hell's Kitchen is a rough neighborhood. You have to survive on its streets, so you get a little extra dispensation for your sins.' What do I really know about theology, Ava?"

"Just wondered…. Do you think I'll go to hell?"

"No. That's crazy talk, Ava."

"What about Tom?"

"Ava…stop thinking like this. You look tired. How about I get the check and take you home?"

"I should go to John's…keep an eye on Tom."

"He's a big boy."

"I know. But this is Tom we're talking about. I should check on him, anyway."

"Ava…your dad's gone. You don't have to be Tom's baby-sitter. Maybe it's time you lived your own life."

My own life. He might as well have said move to Mars. Fly. Make time stand still. I had never had my own life. The one time I tried, I failed.

"Thanks, Jack. But you just don't understand."

He shook his head, looking sad, the way he might look at my wake someday. "I wish I did, Ava. But you won't let me."

Jack pulled a hundred out of his wallet and paid the bill. He held out his hand and helped me from my chair. He hailed a cab. He wrapped my shawl around me tighter so I didn't catch a chill. He did all of those things because he was my friend. Maybe my only friend.

Tiredness overwhelmed me in the cab. "You know…maybe I will let you drop me off at home instead of John's. I have another whole night of this and then the funeral. And right now, I feel like I could just collapse I'm so tired."

He gave the driver my address, then turned to me. "You don't let yourself get sick. Keep your strength up."

"Thanks. And thank you for dinner. Coming tomorrow?"

"Probably. And the funeral. I have to write about the funeral." He looked intently at me. "I'm sorry. That sounded really bad."

"It's what you do. Just like I do what I do."

The cabbie stopped at my address. Sliding out of the cab, I didn't turn back as I climbed the steps to my apartment building. I unlocked the outer door where the mailboxes were, then the inner lobby door. Next I trudged up the stairs to my and Tom's apartment. Unlocking the door, I turned on the lights and walked into my bedroom and changed into my pajamas. Flopping on my bed, I stared at the ceiling, then rolled onto my side. A picture of Tom and me and our father sat on my nightstand.

I felt grief climb up in my throat like acid. I didn't want to cry. I always felt if I started crying I might never stop. So I tried to think about other things and found my mind drifting to Jack Casey. Back to before we were ever friends.

11

Three years ago, I walked into Kelly's Tavern to have a quick drink before going to see my father and Tom, and whatever assorted pals were around, for our weekly family dinner. In fact, I thought I would have two quick drinks, because dinners with my father were occasions to dread.

As Tom and I grew older, we fought with our father more and more. Everything from Tom's decision to become a cop to my inability to "settle down" and find a good husband were fair game for explosions, from fistfights to thrown plates of food. Somewhere along the way, perhaps in his anguish over my mother's death, or his melancholy as more and more of his friends died when lifetimes of street justice and hard drinking and drugging caught up with them, he'd gotten angrier. He started to smell of violence before I even got close to him. The apartment smelled of it. Or maybe he had always been that angry, but getting older took away any inhibitions that might once have made him just a tiny bit more soft or human.

Joey Quick had died of a stroke the previous year. Two-Times's only son, Rocky, had been gunned down in a drug deal gone horribly wrong four years before. Sonny got colon cancer and withered away to bones six months ago. Heroin had claimed Bobby Snow. Dutch Sullivan had been shot outside a bar. No one saw the shooter. Death was closing in on my father. Sometimes I thought of my father sitting in his armchair in that apartment, hearing the scratching sounds of the Grim Reaper tapping on his door.

When I arrived at Kelly's, Todd Kelly, the owner's son, was tending bar and jerked his head toward a man in the back booth.

"That guy's been askin' after ya, Ava."

I squinted in the dimness. "Give me a vodka on the rocks," I said, craning my neck. "He look like a cop?"

"Nah. Not a cop. At least he says he's not. That was the first thing I asked him. Doesn't look like one. He seems to know you come in every Sunday, though. You want me to bounce him outta here?"

"No. I don't think so. Not yet."

"'Cause if you want me to, just say the word." Todd looked at me adoringly, courtesy of an ill-advised one-night stand two years before.

"I'll let you know. Thanks, Todd." I reached for the vodka he poured me and walked to the back booth.

"Who are you...and what do you want?" I stared at the man sitting there, sizing him up. He had brown hair, the color of toasted almonds, and almost black eyes. A smattering of Irish freckles scattered across his nose. His jaw was square and clenched, and he wore his hair long, over the collar of his shirt. He had a single scar on his cheek, a small, jagged line. He kept on his black leather jacket, I assumed because every time the door to Kelly's opened, a blast of January chill flew in and caused a draft.

He stood to shake my hand. "Jack Casey."

I didn't take the offered hand, so he sat down, acting neither surprised nor annoyed. "I was wondering if I could have five minutes of your time."

"Depends. You a cop?"

"Nope."

"Lawyer?"

"Nope."

"Have we met?"

"Not until today. Why don't you take off your scarf and sit down. I promise you, I'm not a cop. I just want to talk to you."

Warily, I sat on the red leather-covered bench opposite him. But I kept my scarf on, I guess because he asked me to take it off.

Jack Casey gripped his mug of dark beer in both hands, took a deep breath, and said quietly, "Does the name John Corrigan mean anything to you?"

"No. Though I have to tell you, most people in this neighborhood go by nicknames, so that doesn't mean anything. Why are you asking?"

"Well...he was my uncle. My favorite uncle. He was also not—" he rolled his eyes upward, searching for the words "—what would I call it? An upstanding citizen. He was a bookie. For one of the longshoremen locals. A drunk. And he was murdered. A long time ago. You couldn't have been more than four."

"Okay...well, I never heard of him, so I don't know that I can help you. Or would want to."

"Just hear me out. I asked for five minutes. That's all." He looked at the watch on his wrist and started speaking more quickly. "I'm a journalist. I work for the *New York Chronicle*. Freelance. And I have literally spent the last ten years of my life researching *one* story."

"Well, you must not make a lot of money, then," I quipped, taking a drink of my vodka.

"I write a lot of stories, but this one…this one is my life's work. I don't care if it takes me ten years or twenty years. I'm writing the story of this neighborhood. Of the men in it. The men who created it before all the yuppies started moving in and turning it into another excuse for The Gap and yoga studios. You think this neighborhood would have needed a yoga studio ten years ago?"

I laughed, despite myself.

"So what do you want, Mr. Casey?"

"I'd like to interview you. About your family."

I stared at him and shivered, more from the thought than the chill, but I didn't respond.

"Did you hear me?"

I nodded. "I heard you. Not a chance."

"What if I told you Tony Two-Times has already agreed to speak with me?"

"Wouldn't matter. Uncle Two can do what he wants."

"What if I told you that I know where you come from? That I know about your mother, that I know about your life, because bits and pieces of it trickled into my life. In some ways, our lives intersected. And what if I told you that if you ever got tired of it all, of the violence and the ugliness of it…tired of watching your brother come in here and kill himself drinking every night until you drag him home—and I know about that, too—that I can offer you, in exchange for the interview, everything you ever wanted to know about your family."

"I already know everything I need to know about them. If you think that by telling me they take book, or loan-shark, or they might have broken a few legs in their lifetime, that you're surprising me, you're wrong. And if you think I need someone else to tell me what I've been through, or what my brother does to himself every chance he gets, or what, precisely, I'm tired of, you're even more wrong."

"No. I offer more than that. I offer a look at it all. Everything. The truth. The good, the bad and the ugly."

"I've seen more ugly than you can possibly imagine." I stared at this stranger, liking his face, but not liking what he was saying. I wasn't sure why I sat there listening to him. I was weary. I had dragged Tom home the previous night after Todd called me and said Tom had puked in the bathroom of Kelly's, slipped in it and cracked his head on the sink. Two-Times helped me lug him up the stairs to my apartment, swearing he would never tell my father. If my father knew, it would just mean a fistfight at the dinner I was delaying going to by drinking a vodka and listening to this stranger.

"But there have to be pieces missing."

"Sure. Don't you have pieces missing? Doesn't everybody have them? But when you fill in my blanks, it's going to be more of a horror show than *The Brady Bunch*. Thanks——" I stood up "——but I think I'll leave well enough alone."

"Wait." He lightly touched my hand. "Let me buy you a drink at least. You gave me your five minutes. At least let me do that."

The O'Neils aren't known for passing up free drinks. So I sat back down and ordered a vodka from our waitress. He ordered a second Guinness.

"So you've really worked on this story for ten years?"

He nodded. "I used to come here and visit my grandmother. She lives maybe eight blocks over. And my family was...pretty colorful. And I always just knew I wanted to be a writer, and that one day *this* was the story I wanted to write."

My vodka came. "You like writing real *happy* stories, I take it."

He laughed and took a sip from his mug.

"To me...it's not happy or sad. It just is. It's the truth."

I tossed back my drink in a swift single motion. Standing again, I offered him my hand. He seemed like a decent enough guy. Let him write his story. Without me.

"Nice to meet you, Jack. Good luck with your story."

"Nice to meet you, too." He stood up. "Ava?"

"Hmm?"

"One more thing."

"Yeah?" I wrapped my scarf around my neck.

"What if I told you I had a pretty good guess about what happened to George O'Neil? Your uncle George."

I tried not to let my face reveal anything. I thanked God I had drank two vodkas. My voice steady, I stared down at him and said, "I'd still say I wasn't interested."

I turned and walked out of Kelly's, quickly, not even looking back. I half jogged a block, my eyes stinging from the cold. I arrived at a quiet street corner two blocks from my father's apartment, the apartment I'd grown up in. Just the mention of Uncle George panicked me, and I leaned over into the gutter and threw up.

Jack Casey had no idea just how weary I really was.

12

I have agonized for most of my life, deciding who was on a "need to know" basis. My father needed to know virtually nothing. Tom needed to know only slightly more than my father.

The first man who broke my heart, really tore it apart and then minced the pieces in a Cuisinart, was David Grecco. He didn't even *really* break my heart, but he was the first guy to dump me and make me feel like my heart was in physical pain. And Tom made sure he never forgot that you don't do that to Ava O'Neil. And you especially—most especially—do not cheat on her with your ex-girlfriend. Because if you do, well...suffice it to say, that handsome jaw of David Grecco's was wired shut so he couldn't perform oral sex on said ex-girlfriend, which was precisely what I'd caught him doing.

While I may have briefly thought David Grecco deserved what he got, as time passed I realized that I hadn't loved him after all, that I probably wasn't capable of loving anyone. And from that point on, in fact always, I understood that I had to protect people from the two pit bulls in my life. Even if that meant lying.

I wasn't sure where that left Jack Casey.

After throwing up in the gutter, I wiped my mouth and gulped cold New York air. The sky was already like a winter's midnight, the streetlights casting a glow on the street corners. I fumbled in my purse and popped a wintergreen Life Saver, then walked to my father's apartment, a burning, gnawing nervousness in my chest. Climbing the narrow staircase, I opened the apartment door. Dad was in the tiny kitchen cooking what smelled like sausages and peppers.

"Hey, baby girl," he said when I walked in. The apartment was easily a hundred and fifty degrees, thanks to an overactive radiator that didn't know how to shut itself off in winter. We'd stopped complaining to the super fifteen years ago. Underneath my coat and sweater, I had on a black tank top, which I stripped down to, already sweating. The oven wasn't helping matters in the kitchen, either.

"Hey, Daddy." I kissed him on the cheek. He was freshly shaven. Sunday dinner meant a clean shave, cheap cologne, a fresh shirt. I leaned over the oven, opening the door and catching sight of the onions and peppers and spicy sausages sizzling in an aluminum pan. "Want me to slice the bread?"

"Sure...where's Tommy?"

"Coming, I guess." I glanced at my watch, then pulled a bread knife out of the drawer. "Is Uncle Two coming?"

"Yeah. Charley, too. And that dingbat Charley's seeing. What the fuck is her name?"

"Charlotte."

"Yeah. Fuckin' Charlotte. She's got a big ass and an even bigger mouth. I don't know what the hell he's thinking. Remind me to put some fuckin' rat poison on her sausage. She's such a goddamn cow she'd chow it down without stoppin'. Hey…check under the sink. Don't I have some roach spray or something I can feed her?"

"Another pleasant Sunday, Dad," I mumbled as I sliced into the bread, still warm from the bakery.

"Don't fuckin' give me that, Ava." He paused, wiping at the sweat dripping down the side of his face. "You know, every fucking time you come over here, you put one foot in that door and you already got some wiseass comment to make. You and your brother. A pair of fuckin' brats you turned out to be."

I sighed and threw the cut bread into the wicker basket my father had on the Formica counter. I mopped at sweat forming on my own brow. "And every time *I* come here, you've got some fucking comment to make about me and my life."

"What life? All I ever say is maybe it's time you think of settling down. It's not right that you and Tommy are holed up over in that apartment. Him fuckin' drunk all the time. He's a fuckin' lowlife."

"Pot calling the kettle black."

He slammed down the fork he had for stirring at the peppers. "You wanna fuckin' fight? Is that what you come over on Sundays for?" I saw the little vein on his temple pulsing a deep blue.

"Yeah. I *really* love this. Look, Dad, when I date a halfway decent guy you call him a *worm*. When I date a neighborhood guy who's goin' nowhere you tell me he's a creep or a *thug*. I can't win." I stopped slicing bread and stormed into the living room. I could hear him, banging pots and slamming the refrigerator door, the oven door. We replayed this scenario every weekend. Different meals, same bullshit.

Walking into the living room was like walking back into my childhood. Not much had changed since the day my mother died. He had gotten a new couch a few years ago, but it was beige just like the old one, minus cigarette burns and stains, but pretty much identical with three square cushions to sit on and roll-top arms. The furniture was arranged the way my mother had left it. Her photos were everywhere, in black and white, a few in color. Each one stared at me, making me feel guilty that I could remember so little of her. I had a movie in my head of the memories, specific frames I played over and over in my mind, like the Zapruder film of Kennedy getting shot, but it was like chasing a ghost and putting my hand through the air and grasping at nothingness. I couldn't really feel her anymore.

I walked over to the bar my father kept on a set of shelves. The O'Neils had no books. Only booze. Bottles of vodka, gin, Canadian Club, and V.O. whiskey lined the shelves, like the spines of books would have in someone else's apartment, neat and all in a row. I poured myself a tall vodka and tonic. Warm. I was damned if I was going to go back into the kitchen with him for something as stupid as ice.

Drinking down the warm cocktail, I tried to calm myself. But I couldn't. Calm was a state of equilibrium I could only achieve chemically. I sat down on the couch and tried to breathe. A few minutes later, I heard Two-Times walk through the front door, recognizable by his heavy, out-of-shape breathing, more like a wheeze. They spoke quietly in the kitchen, and after handing my father a box of éclairs from the overpriced bakery down the street, Two grabbed a beer from the fridge and came into the living room, still wheezing. He took off his coat, revealing a short-sleeved Hawaiian shirt underneath it.

He kissed my cheek. "How ya doing, sweetheart?"

"Good." I patted the sofa, and he sat on the cushion next to me. "Two?" I lowered my voice. "Can I ask you something?"

"Shoot."

"I met a reporter today. He said you were going to talk to him for a *Chronicle* article on the neighborhood. Is that true?"

He nodded. "Sure. Your father might, too."

I gulped more of my drink, then whispered, "Are you two out of your fuckin' minds?"

"You gotta watch that fuckin' mouth, Ava."

"Sorry. I forgot about your delicate sensibilities. Now answer me. Are you crazy?"

"Nah. You know, we watch *The Godfather* and...what was that movie with...you know, they shoot the guy in the foot?"

"Goodfellas?"

"Yeah. And it's always about the Italians, though I'm half Italian, and...they don't ever do something about the Irish. About this neighborhood. We don't get our due. And...what the hell? It's not like we're gonna tell this jerk-off anything that could get us fuckin' arrested. I don't know. I kind of like the idea of telling about this place. Before the fuckin' yuppies arrived with their strollers and their Starbucks. Now, that's not right. That is most definitely not right. Not this neighborhood. Four dollars for a cup of coffee. We don't need that here. It was better the way it used to be. I want *that* in that magazine."

"Sure. And so you're not going to get arrested...because why? You think you're smarter than this guy?"

"Oh, Ava. Most definitely."

Most definitely. Of course, I was talking to the man who beat two murder raps, but I was very uneasy. He may have been smart, but something about Jack Casey told me he might be smarter. And I knew if Tom found out they were talking to him, he'd go ballistic. The mystery of George O'Neil was to remain just that.

And then, as if perfectly timed with my thoughts, Tom came blowing through the door. "Hey, Ava," he sniffed, wiping the palm of his hand across his nose. I looked at Two; Two looked at me. Tom was coked up, and this "most definitely" did not bode well for a peaceful Sunday dinner. Not that we had a lot of experience with peaceful dinners. I imagined that other families in other apartments and homes passed bread and butter and smiled and made *polite* conversation. I imagined Carol was discussing the weather at that precise moment. Rat poison would never be mentioned. I never envied Carol, but that Sunday, hearing my father already slamming drawers and cabinets and plates, my sense of dread was so thick it choked me. I longed to be at another dinner table. Even Carol's.

Tom made himself a drink. A vodka, warm. He would avoid the kitchen, too. He hadn't been wearing a jacket outside, and his arms and face were flushed and ruddy.

Next we heard Charley and Charlotte make their way into the apartment, greeting my father and putting their coats on my father's bed. Uncle Charley came over to the couch, leaned down and gave me a kiss. Charlotte greeted Two and me. Charley took one look at Tom, saw the jitters in Tom's hands, and rolled his eyes and made the sign of the cross.

"Dinner!" my father shouted, coming in with heaping plates and bowls of food. I went into the kitchen to help him cart all of it to the two card tables set up in the living room, the only place with room enough for us all to sit.

We sat down warily, like prize fighters sizing each other up in the ring. Conversation was cautious, with all eyes on my father, his vodka bottle and Tom. Dad stuffed his face, too preoccupied with his sausage and peppers at first to notice his son's sniffling nose and the persistent tic Tom got whenever he did cocaine. But after Dad satisfied his growling belly, it was time to pick on us.

"Charlotte, you eat like a fuckin' bird. What? You don't like my cookin'?"

Then to Uncle Two, "Two-Times, you big fuckin' bastard, you eat like a pig. Save some for the rest of us."

That was life with my father. No middle ground. Just quicksand wherever you stepped. No place was safe, nothing you did was beyond his rage, nowhere to run, nowhere to hide.

"Tom?"

Charley glanced at Two-Times. We all inhaled a collective breath.

"Yeah?"

"Look at me."

Tom did.

"Fuckin' little bastard!" My father rose in one swift motion and backhanded Tom so hard his head literally bounced back on his neck. I heard a sickening sound, a gurgle, as blood spewed from Tom's nose and half choked him. His nose bled into his sausage and peppers, onto the table, down his shirt.

Tom wasn't a little boy anymore. He was six feet tall, and he did one hundred push-ups each morning. I knew. Sometimes he made me count. As Tom looked down into his own lap at the blood, I watched him clench his jaw. He raised his pale eyes to mine. I saw it. Like a glacier moving down a mountain, a blanket of coldness settled into his eyes. My teeth chattered even in the heat of the apartment. Charlotte's little hamster eyes, beady and brown, moved in shock around the table, not knowing whether to pretend she hadn't seen all this, to continue eating or to run to the other room for her coat. Two-Times pushed his chair back, ready to pull my father and Tom apart if he had to. Charley also pushed his chair back and took his hands from the table.

In an instant, pouncing like a tiger on a lame zebra, Tom had toppled my father over in his chair, his hands around my father's throat.

"Not in my fuckin' house!" My father's hoarse voice rose, his face growing redder. Charlotte screamed and Charley and Two-Times rose up out of their seats in near unison, literally prying Tom's hands off my father's throat, finger by clenched finger, the blood from Tom's nose spraying my father's face, and my arms and chest, as I stood and tugged on his arm. Both Charley and Uncle Two were needed to pull Tom up, and then Charley held him back as Two placed his considerable body between them, one arm outstretched to my father as he got up from the floor.

"Tom, we're leaving," I screamed, watching my father and him square off. "We're leaving!" When Tom wouldn't even turn to look at me, I climbed over my father's toppled chair and got in Tom's face, my eyes and nose inches from his, blood still pulsating out of his nose with each heartbeat throbbing in his jugular vein. "Let's go."

The coldness was still there, the icy, dead eyes I knew too well from my mother, but he heard me, somehow, took my hand and nodded. My father tried to come at us, Two-Times blocking him like an NFL linebacker.

"You fuck!" Daddy taunted. "You fuckin' drug addict piece of shit and that whore sister of yours!"

Charley called out, "Just get out of here, Ava. Take him home and straighten him out."

We left, me without my coat or sweater, speckles of blood smeared in sweat on my arms. We took the stairs two at a time, me pulling Tom, racing to get him out of the apartment building before my father decided to chase him and finish the fight. My father was screaming down the stairs that we were not to leave Sunday supper.

"Get up here and finish your dinner!" he boomed at the top of his lungs, as if anyone wanted blood-covered sausage.

"I'll come by later, Dad," I called up to him, hearing the apartment door slam.

Out on the street, Tom and I said nothing. We walked back to our apartment, Tom keeping one hand to his nose, occasionally stopping to spit into the gutter or down a sewer grating. We reached our apartment building, climbed the stairs and silently opened the door to our place. I went to the freezer and got an ice pack, then went into the bathroom to find an old towel. I wet it under the sink, feeling like some sort of fucked-up Florence Nightingale, administering to the family war-wounded. Tom sat on the pullout couch, leaning his head back, pinching the bridge of his nose. I walked over to him and mopped at the blood with a damp corner of the towel. I handed him the ice pack, gritting my teeth and shaking my head.

"You shouldn't go there when you're fucked up, Tom."

"I'm not fucked up."

I sighed in the silence. "Yeah…sure you're not. You need to stop this. What's wrong with you? Huh? Are you crazy? You have a death wish?" The questions spilled out in the semidarkness. I was cold from the walk, tired. I wanted a hot shower. I wanted to wash Tom's blood off of me. "You're crazy—and you're killing me, Tom."

He bolted upright, spilling the ice pack to the hardwood floor, and grabbed my hair, pulling me very close to him. "Don't say it," he said through his teeth.

"You're hurting me." I spoke evenly, hating him in that moment. Hating him for what we were. And then I felt instant regret, like grief, from someplace dark and damp inside me. To hate Tom? *My Tom?* I let him hold my hair in his death grip. *Let him kill me if he wants.* Sometimes I welcomed the pain because it let me know I was alive. His other hand came up to my throat, his thumb caressing the hollow and then tracing up to where he could feel my heartbeat in my neck. I stared at him; the drugs stared back. And then as quickly as he had tightened his hand into my hair, he let me go, my scalp throbbing. He started crying, putting his face in my lap, blood still seeping from his nose and onto my jeans, warm and sticky.

I stroked his hair, thick and blue-black, letting it twine around my fingers. Tom, *my Tom*. And then I knew.

I'd have to meet Jack Casey again.

I'd have to do the thinking for Tom and me and Two-Times and my father. I would have to protect us all.

13

Two Sundays later, I had tracked down Jack Casey through the *Chronicle*, and we met for dinner in a small Italian restaurant on the Upper East Side. I wore a simple black velvet dress, a garter belt and stockings, and no underwear, determined to give him a blow job, sleep with him, do anything to keep him from completing the story of my life, of my father's life, of the neighborhood where I had lived forever, and where I was certain I would die, alone with my brother, in our apartment.

"You look great, Ava." Jack smiled as I took my seat in a corner back booth.

"Thank you." I smiled. I wore full makeup, my hair loose and curly. The small diamond-faced watch that had been my mother's adorned my wrist. I fingered the band as if it was a talisman, praying her ghost would help me.

He ordered us a bottle of red wine and made small talk. Where had I gone to school? Did I ever think of leaving the neighborhood? What did I think of all the yuppies who had moved in? Yankees or Mets? Rangers or Islanders? Knicks or Nets? Giants or Jets? Like he had to ask. True New Yorkers—in my neighborhood—go down the line: Yankees, Rangers, Knicks, Giants.

"Do you work?" he asked. I finished my glass of wine, and he poured me a second.

I shook my head. "I live with my brother. I don't really have to work. I tried temping once." I playfully shuddered. "Office job." I shook my head. "Not exactly my strong suit....I was fired on my second day. But I occasionally bartend for my uncle Larry. I pick up shifts here and there. Ask me to type, no thanks. Ask me to pour liquor...that's more like an O'Neil."

"What place?"

"The Shamrock."

"I know it. I've never seen you there, though."

"Like I said, it's here and there. I cover shifts for people on vacation or if someone has an emergency. All cash. It's really not bad."

"So what do you do with your time?"

"Let's not bullshit each other. You seem to know a lot about us. My brother is a full-time job...so is my father." I stared into his eyes and tried to convey to him how much I loved them both. I willed him to realize that he didn't really want to do this story after all. Backed up with a blow job in a cab ride home, I was certain he would forget it all. Ten years of a story. A lifetime of research. Forgotten as I went down on him. I had a lot of faith in my blow jobs.

We ordered dinner. Manicotti for me, and a veal chop for him. He signaled for a second bottle of wine. A merlot with an eighty-five dollar price tag. After the waiter brought it and uncorked it, Jack looked across the table and then reached over for my hand. I let him. His own hand was large, the fingers strong, and he absentmindedly rubbed his forefinger up and down on my wrist. He withdrew his hand, maybe in a chivalrous gesture. Little did he know I wasn't wearing underwear.

He stared at me, looked away, then held my gaze. "I didn't mean to corner you two weeks ago about this story, Ava. I didn't mean to blindside you."

I shook my head. "You didn't. Not really. I was more afraid you were a cop."

"Your brother's a cop."

"He doesn't count."

He gave me a half smile. "Guess not. I've heard stories of you dragging your brother home. You're tough."

"That's what they tell me."

His smile evaporated. "Can I ask you something, though? In all seriousness?"

"Maybe."

"No bullshit then, between us. Your brother's a wreck... your old man is the neighborhood wise guy, so where does that leave Ava? Aren't you entitled to a life?"

I shrugged. "I have a life. Maybe you wouldn't pick it, but it's mine."

"Can I ask you something else? Kind of important."

"You can ask. Doesn't mean I'll answer."

"Do you know who your father and Two-Times and Charley were in their youth?"

"The Father, Son and Holy Ghost?"

He laughed, his eyes a little glassy from the wine. I reached over to the bottle and poured him some more. *Drink up, Jack Casey.*

"No. Not *that* trinity. Actually... a trio of murderers."

I hesitated, then finished pouring. "Jack, the first time I saw you, I told you that you weren't going to shock me. I know they're not choirboys. Two-Times isn't called Two-Times for nothing. We all know he did it. Twice. More than twice. We just can't call him Five-Times."

"Ava...the three of them are the *Roofers*. That's what the article is really about."

The waiter brought us salads, and I tried to steady my mind and not let the wine overtake me. I had no idea what the hell he was talking about, but he said the Roofers in the way someone says "Jack the Ripper" or "Ted Bundy."

"You honestly don't know who the Roofers are?"

I shook my head and picked at a piece of romaine lettuce with my fork. "Apparently, they're my two uncles and my dad. After my mother killed herself, they were all I had. Them and Tom."

"And George O'Neil. Until he disappeared. See—" he looked at me "—I do my homework."

"Fine. So...the Roofers, if they're all I have, do I want to know more, Jack?"

"Probably not. But you can only ignore the truth for so long."

"What is with you and the truth? There is no truth. Not in my neighborhood. Whatever you say, I know that life is not black and white. Truth isn't black or white. My world is gray. So is yours. Let's just leave it at that."

He stared at me until I had to look away. "You're so beautiful, Ava. You deserve better, you know. As fucking clichéd as that sounds. I didn't start this story interested in you, Ava. You were a tiny little piece in this. But as I went on, as I saw you around, in bars, as I followed up on leads and interviewed people...you became a big part of it."

"What are you saying?" I asked, but grabbed my wine as I waited for him to tell me. I felt cornered, like when my father got in one of his moods and berated me, endlessly.

"We're bound together, you and I. By a murder that took place at five o'clock in the morning thirty years ago. My uncle, John

Corrigan, was murdered, I think, by your father, Tony Two-Times and Charley Rafferty. The Roofers. My aunt Teresa, his widow, went crazy and came to live with us…. She sat in a room in the back of our apartment, and then our house on Long Island, and never budged until she died of cancer five years later. And my whole life I swore I was going to find out what really happened."

"Why? Will that bring her back? Or him, for that matter?"

"No. That's what's got me so torn up inside. Damn…I listen to stories about them, and they're—you've got to hand it to them."

"The Roofers?"

"The Roofers, Roofer Boys. They used to drag people up to the rooftops and throw them off. Or they'd go up there and wait, like they did with my uncle John. He liked to smoke in the early morning, when he was just getting home from the bars, before climbing into bed. So he went up to the roof one morning, drunk out of his mind, lit a cigarette, and they just grabbed him and threw him off. A witness on the street says he screamed until he hit the pavement. It's not like jumping from the Empire State Building. You're not dead before you splatter. They grabbed his legs and under his arms, and they heaved him over the edge."

"I'm sorry, Jack." I spoke the words, but I didn't really mean them. If I started feeling sorry for every crime my family was involved with, I'd be sorry forever. I wanted more wine. I wanted to breathe, to escape from this conversation. But I thought of Two-Times and my father agreeing to talk to Jack Casey. Too dangerous. So I stayed put.

"They ruled the neighborhood. Your father, Tony Two-Times and Charley. Tony wasn't even called Two-Times then. Just called him Big Tony. They didn't like my uncle. He took book, was a rival, though not nearly as powerful. This all got down to territory when King Conway went to prison and your father and Two-Times took over his collections. Charley helped them. And my uncle was just a fly in the ointment. Got in the way. So they took care of things their own way until no one in the neighborhood would face them down. They literally ran the place. No one would mess with them once they'd roofed a few guys. Legend mixed with reality until they became something bigger than life."

I looked off at the bar. Couples laughing, people drinking. Other tables with lovers, married people, old friends. It was as if the real world had a party, and I was never invited. Instead, I was invited to the back room. To the ugly world, to the alley-way. I was out *there* with the garbage and the drunken puke, the stale piss. That was where I belonged.

"Why dredge this up, Jack? This is all stuff so many years old that I'm not even sure you'd get at the truth you say you want. You know these guys like to bullshit people. They tell stories to make themselves tougher, smarter, bigger than who they really are or were."

"At first, it was to get even. Can you imagine my uncle fight-ing for his life? It's a personal crime. Not like shooting someone from far away. My uncle John had to have clawed at these guys, wetting himself, pleading with them not to throw him off. Cry-ing, spitting, weeping, shrieking, praying for someone to hear him. Because he pissed someone off, he just got pitched down into an alleyway like a trash can? Like a sack of shit?"

I remembered Uncle Two coming into my room sometime after my mother died. He sat on my bed and told me the story of Little Red Riding Hood, complete with mimicked voices and sound effects. "Why, Grandmother, what big teeth you have!" Then he made me say the Hail Mary and the Our Father, and when I told him I was afraid of the dark, he told me that my mother and his mother were both in heaven together playing canasta.

"But Mommy doesn't know how to play canasta," I told him.

"That's okay, kid," he'd said, "'cause my mother is the canasta queen. She even cheats. Trust me, they're winning. And now they're both your guardian angels. You don't have to be scared of the dark."

I tried to reconcile that Uncle Two with the big man throwing Jack's uncle off a roof, watching a man piss all over himself. Killing someone because he'd angered one of them. Because they didn't want to pay a gambling debt. Or they didn't want the competition. Because they were hardwired for violence. An unholy triumvirate. I wasn't stupid. I knew in my heart they were dangerous men, but for the first time, I was sitting across a table from someone who had suffered because of my family. Jack Casey was a product of the life these men lived, just as surely as I was.

"I'm sorry, Ava. Sorry to stir this all up. I wish, more than anything, that the path to my uncle's murderers didn't also lead to your door."

"I can't make them saints, Jack. I can't even tell you what I think of all this. You see my brother as a wreck, I see him as my savior. You see my father as a thug, a mobster, I see him as the man who loved my mother even though some days she didn't even know his name and couldn't remember how to brush her teeth. I see a man who not a few days ago sat down with his family for a Sunday dinner." And actually, after Tom's cocaine-and-blood-drenched sausage Sunday, we'd had a lovely roast chicken the following week, last week, and no blood had been shed. For that I was told I could thank the Hail Marys Uncle Two said he recited in church.

"Ava...this is beyond gangster and mobster stuff. The Roofers were known to do it for kicks. Not all of it was over bad debts or revenge. Sometimes they just did it because they had nothing to do and it was a slow Saturday night. I mean it. The guys they tossed weren't saints, either, but that doesn't mean they deserved to fly off a tenement roof. The Roofers ruled the neighborhood because, even as far as the Westies go, they were sociopathic. They killed when they were bored."

"And you think if you write about them.... What? It's your revenge?"

He looked down at his plate. "I'm not even sure what I want to accomplish. Do you want to hear what I think happened to George O'Neil?"

"You know, Jack—" I felt a too-familiar gnawing in the middle of my chest "—what I really want is to eat dinner, drink this bottle of wine, have an anisette, and go home and fuck you."

The candle on the table flickered, and in the soft light, I saw Jack Casey's eyes blink quickly. We ate our dinner, we ordered anisette. We took a cab to his apartment, a loft down in Chelsea. And we were fucking before we even made it three steps into the apartment.

Sliding down to the floor, he pulled my dress up, then kissed me harder. "Would you let me save you?" he whispered.

I nodded. He pulled his shirt over his head as I unbuckled his belt. As soon as he entered me, I knew I had him. Jack Casey thought he was saving me. But he had no idea I'd drowned long ago.

14

I needed to breathe.

That night I fell asleep in Jack's bed, a king-size mattress and box spring on the worn parquet floor of his loft. I lay on my side, my ass pressed against his hips, and stared out the floor-to-ceiling windows at the glimpse of sky above the city buildings, the blessed sky filled with all that *air*. He stroked my hair, my shoulders, tracing my body with his fingertips. I never fell asleep with anyone before. The idea filled me with strange thoughts that I might die there in his bed.

My whole life, whatever men I've known, I've bolted before dawn, though occasionally I've passed out, which is different. Every nerve in my body wanted to get up and run away. He had fucked me once and made love to me once. He fucked me once in a fury of need, and a second time in a way that told me he really had come to care about the little girl, now a woman, whose father had killed his uncle, whose mother had killed herself. I couldn't imagine someone knowing about me and not running the other way, but the second time he entered me, he put his hands on either side of my face and made me stare up at him. Made me look and see it was *him* and not anyone else, least of all the demons in my head.

As I lay there afterward in the dark, he whispered, "I won't let anything bad happen to you anymore, Ava." I felt the blackness of sleep come find me, much as I fought against it. I didn't want his hot breath on my neck. I worried I would suffocate in my sleep.

The next morning, sun drifted through a filter of clouds, playing tag between the apartment buildings before finally warming my face until I awoke. Sunlight was foreign; my apartment was usually pitch-black, the better to face a throbbing hangover. I was afraid to roll over and look at Jack. I just wanted to be home. Eventually, he stirred.

"Hey…" he whispered, "I'm going to go get us bagels and coffee." He kissed my shoulder. I rolled over and watched as he got up and dressed in sweatpants. Once he was out of bed, I felt safe enough to look him in the eyes and smile. He was boyish in his pale gray NYU sweatshirt, looking like he could still be in college.

"I like mine with two and a half sugars and milk," I said.

"Sure thing, beautiful," he grinned.

As soon as I heard the elevator clang shut, its metal sounds echoing in the loft like a lion's cage being swung closed in an old zoo, I got up and padded over to his desk. He had a laptop and a four-drawer green metal file cabinet, and a pile of papers. I didn't know the first thing about computers. Not even how to start a laptop. Tom and I were lucky we could manage our VCR. So I looked, carefully, through the papers, trying to sift through them without displacing anything. I saw my name and Tom's name and our phone number scribbled on a piece of paper. I saw a photo of me, a copy of one from a softball game. Tom and a bunch of cops had played a pickup game. My head was tossed to one side, and I was smiling. I could barely remember the day. Cops' wives had come and talked to me with their bouncing babies, and I had felt so uncomfortable that I'd downed a lot of beer. Babies. Every time I saw a mother with a baby, I wanted to cry. I remember spending the day near the keg, afraid to go near babies. I missed my mother, and the idea that I would ever be one was beyond my imagination. Raise a baby in that apartment with Tom? I knew I had no chance for a life beyond that apartment.

Chilled, I understood that if Jack Casey had that softball picture, then Jack Casey was talking to cops. Every guy in the photo was a uniform. They were in sweatpants and T-shirts, but they all had badges. I recognized three guys Tom drank with. Together, they formed a dangerous quartet, each one as on the edge as the next. I recognized a cop I once dated, and a few who frequented the same bars Tom and I did. If Jack was talking to cops, I was even more frightened. People in my neighborhood didn't talk to cops. Tom didn't count. Tom was one of us; besides, he was a crazy cop. I stared at the faces in the picture. What had these men told Jack Casey?

I moved still more papers. I found obituaries, including a photocopy of my mother's obituary, in which it said she died of "natural causes." Back then, they said things like that. We grew up embraced by lies in all we did, even in how we died. There was an obituary for Two-Times's son. One for Jackie K., an old-timer who I thought had jumped to his death, but now I wondered. And beneath that, five obituaries for either "jumpers" or suspected homicides. Old clips, yellowed.

More clips about the Westies and their RICO trials in the 1980s. The government had gotten some of them for racketeering. Clips about murders. Old police photos in black and white, the blood looking like so much chocolate syrup in puddles on the floor.

Seeing all those newspaper stories, photos and notes, I felt like my life wasn't my own. It was something you could read about. It wasn't a life, but a strange story enmeshed within a neighborhood. It was as if the blood of my family had been added to the very concrete that was poured as they built the apartment houses and sidewalks. We lived in it. We died in it. My life has never been my own. First it belonged to my mother, then it belonged to Uncle George. Now it belonged to Tom. He possessed me. I tried to decide what I would say to him when I returned home.

I walked over to the filing cabinet, opened a heavy drawer, and felt my breath kicked out of me. File after file of the names of people I knew. Two-Times, Pinky…their neighborhood names and their given names. "O'Connor, Timothy F., aka Pinky"; "O'Rourke, Louis, aka Black Tom." I opened another file drawer. We were all there. "O'Neil, Ava."

I wedged my fingers in my own file and pulled it out. I could barely read his handwritten scrawl. Besides the softball picture, he had one from a Christmas party held at John's. I stood between my father and Tom, in a line-up of the neighborhood. Some of the guys had on Santa hats, and I was wearing two Christmas-ball earrings and laughing. Tom had his head on my shoulder, a big grin on his face. My father's face was turned to kiss my cheek. We looked, for the photo, like an ordinary family. But on the scribbled pages, facts spilled out. I lived with my brother, who was a known alcoholic who'd already been put on leave from the NYPD for psychiatric problems. My mother had killed herself after six attempts. I didn't remember six attempts. He knew more about me than I did. Six times. Six times she had decided Tom and Carol and I were not enough of a reason to live.

"O'Neil, Frank." My father's file was thick. His prison stints, his mug shots. Then there was a diagram. It looked like a family tree. Only in this web of circles and straight lines, the lines represented, not children, but connections to deaths. Many lines led to my father, and the names were unfamiliar to me, except John Corrigan, who I now knew was Jack Casey's uncle. I stared at the line and the little circle, in Jack Casey's handwriting. He wrote himself notes and half thoughts. *Why? Motive? Opportunity?*

That line, that single line, now placed my whole family in danger. If he published the article, in a magazine revered for its glossy journalism, we would never again live anonymously. Jack Casey had researched us into family trees of sins. Shaking, I stopped reading and sat down on the bed, pulling on my dress, shoving my bra and stockings in my purse, feeling waves of panic crashing against me until I was certain I wouldn't be able to stand.

I had to do something. The O'Neils were known for doing things. I had to stop this.

Taking a deep breath, I went to the filing cabinets and pulled out files. The file on Rocky, Uncle Two, Pinky and me. On Tom. Even on Uncle George. I pulled them all out and shoved them into the wastepaper basket. Then I rummaged through my purse for a book of matches.

"Damn!" I couldn't find matches or a lighter. I raced over to the kitchen and opened all of Jack Casey's drawers. Silverware. Measuring spoons. A drawer full of chopsticks and little packets of take-out ketchup and soy sauce and mustard. My heart raced. Finally the last drawer I pulled open was what I wanted. The junk drawer. A ball of twine, assorted batteries and loose change. And a book of matches. Grabbing them, I went back to the wastebasket. I pulled up a file and set it on fire. I lit another file, then another one, feeling the heat on my face as they took flame. I dumped more files into the wastepaper basket and watched as the orange-and-red flames and smoke grew higher, eating away our lives, licking them with destruction. The paper shriveled. I put another file on the flames. The heat radiated off my cheeks. Jack wouldn't have his notes. He'd have to stop caring about this story. He had me now. It was an even trade.

The elevator clanged again. I looked away from my fire as Jack let himself into his apartment.

"Holy fuck! What are you doing?" he shouted, and raced over to the wastepaper basket. He looked over at the file cabinet drawers, each one pulled out and nearly empty, with papers scattered on the floor.

"Jesus Christ!" He grabbed the comforter from his bed and stifled the flames. Smoke billowed. He ran to his kitchen and opened a bottom cabinet, throwing out pans until finding a fire extinguisher. He raced back and aimed at the wastebasket and put it out, smoke choking us, filling the room, along with water and foam. I coughed, my eyes tearing and blinking rapidly from the acrid air, my hopes doused.

When all that was left of the fire was a thick smoke and horrid smell, he grabbed me by my shoulders, coughing himself. "Are you all right?"

I didn't answer him.

He shook me gently. "Ava! What were you thinking? What? Did you think if you set the files on fire it would stop me? Don't you realize I have it all on disk? I have it all on computer disks and backed up. I have a backup of my backup. Ava...Jesus Christ..." His breath came in quick gasps, and he let go of me and sank into a chair, putting his head in his hands.

Jack looked up at me, his eyes red and filled with tears. "Ava...they're gonna kill you. This whole life. It'll kill you in the end. Those files are full of death, Ava, honey."

I didn't move, still absorbing the fact that I had lost. The recognition of it traveled through me.

Jack's hands visibly shook. "This whole place could have gone up. Would you have left? Would you have burned down the whole building and just walked out the door?"

"If it would have stopped you. Or I would have just stayed and burned with it."

"So you slept with me to stop me."

"It didn't work."

A tear slipped out of the corner of his eye and traveled down his cheek. "Ava...let me care about you. Let someone get you out of there."

"Don't bother.... Will you put this in your story?"

"No. I'll leave this out of it."

"Jack?"

"Hmm?"

"I want to know... What do you think happened to my uncle?"

"George? I think he may have been murdered by King Conway."

"King? If you say that in an article, you could find your fingers lopped off for the fuck of it."

"Is that what bothers you? Nah. Don't worry about me, Ava. To a man, these guys are getting off on having their stories told. They like to brag, and half of them tell me exaggerated lies, anyway. I have to weed through to the...truth. Or what I think is the truth."

"If I asked you...if I begged you...would you drop it? Would you not do it?"

"Why?" He reached a hand up and stroked my cheek with his thumb.

"I don't want my family in it. I don't want my brother in it. I think you're crazy for doing it. Crazy. But if you have to do it, leave Tom and me out."

"There's nothing in it that's going to harm Tom…or you."

"Would you not do it?" I stared at him, willing him to say he would stop.

"I can't." His face was smudged with smoke.

"Why not?"

"Because there's no justice. Not for people like my uncle. Nothing's going to happen to these guys. No one is going to go to jail. There's no case, no witnesses. No DNA that's going to reach back through the years and send anyone back to Sing Sing. But maybe I was dumb enough to believe my professors at NYU. Maybe there really is truth."

"Truth is for suckers and assholes."

I picked up my purse.

"Stay for breakfast."

"I can't."

I put on my shoes and reached for my shawl, which was draped over a chair.

"Ava, don't leave mad."

"I'm not mad."

"Look…for me…last night wasn't about the story." His face was still shrouded in the now-dissipating smoke. "I decided a long time ago I wanted to meet you. I'm going to keep in touch, okay?"

I fought tears and nodded, then rushed out the door. I entered the cage of an elevator and took it to the ground floor. Even in the cage, I felt freer than in Jack's apartment.

Hitting the sidewalk, I gulped in cold air. I fell into a rhythmic walking, not wanting a cab yet, just calming myself. I had been penned up all night, and now I was free.

Eventually, I hailed a cab and took it back to my apartment. Tom wasn't home. He was on day shift. Entering the apartment, I felt my entire body relax with a relief I couldn't explain. I may have just as easily been caged at home, but it was a prison that felt entirely familiar. Like a lifer walking his cell, twenty steps to one corner, turn left, ten steps, turn, twenty steps…my cell was my own.

I stripped out of the previous night's dress and put on my bathrobe. Then, for the first time in a while, I went into the second bedroom. My mother's dresser stood against one wall. The mirror had a crack in it from the morning she died when my father hurled a lamp. I ran my finger along the dresser and then sat down in a rocking chair. Next to me was a trunk full of her old clothes. I pulled out a soft blue sweater I tried to tell myself still smelled like her. I picked up a picture of her and rocked and held it. I convinced myself that in that room full of her things, the scent of mothballs and dust, dark and cold, that I could breathe more freely than out there, outside this place, with a man like Jack.

15

I lived in a world without witnesses.

No one saw my father hurl men off of roofs. No one saw who killed King Conway's son in a hail of gunfire. No one saw Pinky kill the rat who Tom said was going to cooperate with the cops. No one saw anything. It was how we lived, blind to everything but one another.

True to his word, the fire I set didn't deter Jack Casey from pursuing his story. If anything, I fanned the flames of truth for him. He searched for witnesses, as if he had something to prove to me. As if by finding still more victims, it would convince me to leave my world for one that wasn't blind to truth and justice.

He called me one night, after he'd had a few beers by the sound of his voice. "Ava...come with me. Leave the neighborhood. Get away from your family."

I lay back on my bed and stared at the ceiling. I didn't hate him for pursuing the story, just felt an overwhelming dread. I would fall asleep at night and wake with a start, convinced someone was in my room, watching me. Everywhere I went, I felt eyes on me.

"No. This is where I'm safest."

"Safest?"

"I wish I could explain it, but I can't. It's what I have. It's what I know."

If I couldn't stop Jack from writing his story, I'd set about convincing my father and his friends not to talk to him.

"What if they trace old crimes to you?" I confronted my father in his apartment. I found him sitting in the dark, drinking his vodka straight.

"What fuckin' old crimes? Ava, you worry too much. I tell you what they got. Nothin'. They got nothin'. No witnesses, no fucking DNA. No fuckin' nothin'."

"What if he found a witness, or a witness came forward after reading the story?"

"Ava, listen to me." He leaned toward me, his face still in shadows. "If someone came forward, they'd be a dead man. There is nothin' that happened in this neighborhood that has any witnesses. It ain't the way we do things. He wants a story, I'm gonna give him one that'll make me famous. Maybe I'll go on *Larry King*."

Larry King. My father needed to be on fucking *Larry King* like he needed a bullet to each kneecap. Daddy continued to drink in the dark, ignoring me, his way of making me leave, so I did. Two-Times had already made it clear that the Starbucks and strollers had pissed him off enough that he was determined to "set the record straight" about the neighborhood. That left Pinky for my quest.

But Pinky's coiffure had gotten decidedly fancier since he married Patricia. He got manicures, leaving his nail beds pale and shiny, and he wore suits that the Teflon Don, John Gotti, would have killed for in his heyday. Pinky had already agreed to talk on the record to Jack Casey, as did Black Tom, Joe "Brickhouse" Cleary, Uncle Charley, and Jimmy "the Grease" Sullivan.

All I could do, I decided, was convince Jack Casey that he was right, that King Conway *had* killed my uncle George. That, and keep Tom far away from Jack.

The *New York Chronicle* magazine article expanded like a living thing. It grew so large that it required almost two full issues. Jack Casey appeared on every major news network. He was suddenly a "mob expert." He garnered a book contract in the mid six figures. Fame, respect, money, he had it all now because of my father's story.

I bought the first issue as it went on the stands. In black and white, it broke down murders into stats.

Two-Times had committed, likely, seven gangland murders. He'd been tried for two, and acquitted. He liked Cuban cigars, espresso after a heavy meal, three squares a day and mass quantities of beer. He mourned his son's death from a drug overdose and hated that bookies were arrested more than dealers.

Pinky was allegedly responsible for six murders. He favored a bat and, once someone was dead, an electric saw. Though he had once used a serrated knife and done the cutting up by hand. Later, he liked less bloody methods. He had his suits custom-made by a Mr. Chang who was from Hong Kong. He liked his initials sewn on the cuffs. He never had children "that he knew of," but he liked to donate money every year to Little League because he thought baseball was as close to heaven as it gets, and he worshipped the Yankees, once keeping a body in a restaurant walk-in freezer for two days because of back-to-back home games.

My father, who loved my mother enough to bathe her by hand, who walked me to school almost every day, had roofed a handful of people, including Jack's uncle. He was a legend for the way he enjoyed making people suffer. "Suffering leads to truth," he told Jack.

Jack's words made my father and his friends—and all their victims—come alive.

In the summer of 1975, three young men, two of them by this time fathers, waited with the pigeons on the roof of a cold-water tenement on Fifty-first Street on NewYork's West Side. The pigeons slept, their heads tucked into their wings, one or two cooed, starting to rise with the sun as it began its ascent near dawn.

Frank O'Neil smoked an unfiltered cigarette, holding it between his thumb and forefinger and taking deep drags in the way of tough guys who smoke almost angrily, inhaling deeply. He and his best friends, Charles Rafferty and Tony "Two-Times" Reardon, waited for John "Shorty" Corrigan. They were waiting to do a "heave-off" job, to throw Corrigan off the roof.

To understand this story, the writer must first confess that John Corrigan was his uncle. Not just any uncle, but his favorite uncle, half wise guy, half clown. And to understand the story still further, we must understand the neighborhood. For Frank O'Neil and his friends, raised with a toughness that would make the fictional Corleones think twice about messing with them, it was nothing to walk into the Sunshine Bar and see, floating in jars of preservative liquid, the testicles of men who'd wronged the owner of the Sunshine, a neighborhood book and shylock king. In general, in Hell's Kitchen, in the Yorkville of their youth, in Alphabet City, in any of a dozen of NewYork's rough neighborhoods, you don't travel without a pack, and you don't enter bars that keep testicles in jars without being able to hold your own. You have to belong there. And these men did. For Frank O'Neil, the right-hand man of the loan shark king, named, literally, King Conway, to all who know him, the streets were mean, but they were home.

Frank O'Neil, the Roofer Boy as a young man, lived in a neighborhood known for nicknames, where tracing a person involves knowing not just his

baptismal name but his street name. He was, even for this place, a hard case.
He was married to the most beautiful woman for twenty square city blocks.
She also had bipolar disorder and a cabinet full of antipsychotics and lith-
ium, which did nothing for her, leaving Frank and his murderous sidekicks
to tend to his three children. It was Frank's idea to roof Shorty Corrigan.
Shorty was honing in on the territory of King Conway, and besides, it was
always a good idea to shore up your reputation with a few well-placed roof
jobs. Which was how he came to be smoking on the roof of a tenement, wait-
ing for the predictable loudmouth, Corrigan, who always had a smoke and
visited his pigeons in the dawn hours after a night in the bars. He'd be drunk,
his reflexes off, and he was a mere five foot five, anyway. For Frank, Char-
ley and Two-Times, it would be like tossing over a sack of sugar....

When the article came out, Jack wanted to have dinner with
me. We met at a dark-wood-and-brass steakhouse near Ninety-
third Street.

"Jack...what's wrong?" I asked as the maître d' pulled out my
chair and I slid into its soft forest-green-leather plumpness.

Jack clearly had a few cocktails head start on me. "I thought
doing this article, getting a book contract would make me feel
a certain way. This is all I've wanted for as long as I can remember. But it hasn't made me feel better. I feel worse."

"Why?"

"Did you watch Charlie Rose two nights ago?"

"No. Creature Features and old movies...no talk shows...sor-
ry."

"Don't apologize. It's just that...every show, every fucking interview...they all think these wise guys are gods. They make
them sound like a cross between teddy bears and iconic murderers. Legends. I—" He held his head in his hands, then
punched at his forehead with his fists. "I must not be a very good
writer if I couldn't make people hate them."

I exhaled and signaled the waiter, who looked at us awkwardly with Jack clearly distraught. I ordered a vodka. "I don't know what to say, Jack. I don't hate them. I don't think they're heroes, either. But you have to admit, they do..."

"Don't say it. Don't say they 'have a code.'"

"But they do."

He stared at me now, his face glowing orange by the light of the small hurricane lamp on our table.

"Is it wrong to kill, Ava? Unequivocally?"

"I don't know. Do you think so? You were raised here just a neighborhood or two over. You tell me."

"I don't know. You hear me? Do you hear what's coming out of my mouth? I spend all these years doing this fucking article, and I ended up just as conflicted. Maybe I need a shrink."

"What would a shrink know about this shit?"

"Then I guess you're stuck listening to me."

I reached across the table and took his hand. "I can listen. Better than I can talk. You know that as well as anyone."

"I wanted, all along, to do it for me. For my family. And then when I found out about you, when I met you, I wanted to do it for you. I wanted to show you...what, I don't know. I wanted to show you how bad it was so you would leave them. But they're heroes now. They're fucking heroes."

I felt a little bit sorry for Jack Casey. There was no journalistic justice, just a country full of movie buffs who thought that Don Corleone and Scarface were criminal cool.

After dinner with Jack I stopped by the Shamrock to find Tom. Usually, I would see Two-Times there, and we would cart my brother home. We believed we were hiding this from my father. I did it so they wouldn't kill each other. Two-Times did it because he'd lost a son to drugs, and all he had left were Tom and me. But Tom wasn't at the Shamrock. My father was, however. Along with every familiar face from the neighborhood. They were making noise like tonight was a wedding, a celebration.

"Ava!" my father called to me, both arms raised in the air in greeting. I hadn't seen him this happy since the Giants won the Superbowl. That was occasioned by a two-day drinking binge of gallons of vodka. Tom's binge extended three days. Come to think of it, I nursed a nasty hangover that seemed to last until Wednesday.

I sauntered over to the table. "Did someone win the lottery?"

"Come on and sit down with your old man here. Pull her over a chair." He gestured to a young tough guy I barely knew. The kid got me a chair, and I joined the table. Someone poured me a beer.

"Raise your glass now," my father said. "Wait until you hear this."

I raised my glass. Everyone else looked at me, and I was uncomfortable. They all knew the inside joke, whatever it was. The million-dollar secret, and now Dad would tantalize me until he spilled it. He was happy. How utterly foreign to his face, that grin. Except when with Two and Charley and Pinky. They could make him smile. Tom and I made him angry.

"Want to know what we're celebratin', baby girl?"

"I don't know. Do I?" I asked cautiously.

"Of course you do. Guess."

"Dad...I can't. Just tell me."

"All right then." He looked so pleased with himself. "I had dinner tonight with Michael De Silva. The director. They're makin' a movie about me. And payin' me to be a fuckin' consultant. Baby...I'm a Hollywood star."

With that, the table erupted into hoots and hollers and loud whistles. I smiled, then downed my beer in one shot. If I thought *Larry King* was a bullet in both kneecaps, this was a shot to the temple.

16

I thought my family lived in a murky world with topsy-turvy values. Soon I learned Hollywood was even murkier.

The director Michael De Silva, whose movies had glamorized "the mafia" for all eternity, including one that won the Oscar, found a new pal in my father. Suddenly, they were the best of friends. The funny thing is my father always thought De Silva's movies were about "pussies." The men in them cursed, and they killed, but they were also stupid, and at some point their lack of intelligence, and their addictions to cheap women and violence, brought them down. My father, in his own mind, of course, was brilliant. Far more brilliant than any of the heroes in De Silva's films—at least that's what he told us all.

"See, baby," he said to me over Sunday dinner with Two-Times and a young sidekick named Mickey. "De Silva likes that when we were young, we ruled the streets here. And we never got caught. But also, he likes our values. That we're loyal."

"Values?" I raised an eyebrow. They had a code of loyalty, I'd give them that. But values?

"Don't fuckin' look at me like that." My father slammed his hand down on the table. I began to wonder how it was our card tables had held up over the years, though one had a depression in the center. "See?" He swept a hand back and looked at Two-Times. "See how she looks at me? What did I fuckin' do that was so bad that my two smart kids hate me so much? The other one, I understand," he said, spitting about Carol, "but these two. Can you tell me that, Two?"

Two avoided looking at me and shrugged. Then my father turned his attention to his new ally, Mickey.

"I hope you fuckin' respect your parents, Mick. Don't take lessons from this one."

Mick nodded. He looked about eighteen, and what I noticed about him was his perpetual hard-on. The front of his faded Levi's always looked as if he had stuck a medium-sized rock there. Hence Mick's nickname in the bars with the ladies. According to Tom, they called him Mick the Prick. They said it was as big as a porno star's.

Returning his glare to me, my father sneered, "What...you don't think we have fuckin' values?"

"Dad...did you even *read* Jack's article? Let me see if I get this straight—you roofed his uncle because he had a 'big mouth.' You didn't like him, Charley owed him a grand and didn't want to pay, and he insulted you, so you roofed him. That's family fuckin' values, all right. So glad De Silva respects the way you do things."

My father's hand shot out to my face so quickly, I didn't see it coming. It was a slap, not a punch, but it felt like someone had physically burned my cheek, as if I'd been struck with a whip. Two-Times instinctively rose from his seat.

Involuntary tears streamed down my face. My father ate his pot roast calmly, but I could see the vein on his temple throbbing. He was now silent. Dad hadn't slapped me in years.

I rubbed the spot where he hit me and stood. "Sit down, Two. It's okay. I was just leaving. Sorry to rain on your Hollywood parade, Dad. But if Michael De Silva thinks we're America's new family values, he's more fucked up than we are."

I wiped the tears from my face and left without looking back. I thought my father might stop me, might apologize, might even continue the fight, but he didn't. Of course, I knew why. He'd slapped me hard enough to leave a mark. When Tom saw it, no one would be safe.

I fell asleep on my bed, and as I slept I had a nightmare. I dreamed that someone was suffocating me. His hands were around my neck, but I couldn't see who it was. I fought against him, his face in the shadows, and I had the sensation of gasping for air. I startled awake and was eerily aware that someone was watching me.

As my eyes adjusted to the gray-blackness of past midnight, I saw a figure sitting in the chair in the corner of my bedroom. Watching me. Watching me as I slept.

I flicked on the lamp on my nightstand. Tom sat staring at me intensely.

"Jesus Christ, Tom, you scared the fucking daylights out of me." I pulled the covers around me, pulling them to cover my tank top, my heart pounding nearly out of my chest.

He was blasted out of his mind, and as I uneasily assumed of late, he had come in to check on me. Just as I sat on his bed to see if he was breathing, he came into my room in the night to look at me. Though I purposely had fallen asleep on a bag of frozen peas to reduce the swelling on my cheek, I had rolled over in the night.

We both sat blinking in the light, our eyes adjusting.

"What the fuck happened to you?" Tom exhaled through his nose, the way a bull might before it gored a bullfighter.

"It's nothing." I casually turned my head so he couldn't examine my face, pulling my hair forward to hide it. My heartbeat echoed in my ears. Courtesy of my father, I had traces of finger marks on my cheek, thereby eliminating the "I walked into a door" excuse.

He repeated his words slowly. "What...the...fuck...happened...Ava?"

I felt my face. It was puffy. The bag of peas was soggy on the bed next to me.

"Dad and I had a...little disagreement."

Then, calmly, icily, he spoke three words: "I'll kill him."

Tom stood up suddenly from the chair in the corner of my room, knocking it backward and against the wall. He stormed into the living room. I heard him foraging for his gun.

Leaping from my bed in my tank top and pajama bottoms, I ran to the living room and lunged at his back, trying to climb onto him, slow him down, pleading with him. "Tom, don't. Don't go over there."

"Get off me, Ava!" he barked as he put the gun in the holster he wore between his undershirt and his regular shirt.

"Don't go, Tom. I'm begging you. You want me to end up with one of you dead? One of you in jail? Is that it? Is that what I have to look forward to?" I was gasping for air for real now, not in some dream.

"I'm going over there, so get the fuck off me now." He turned to face me, his eyes flickering with rage, a rage like my father's. They never saw how alike they were in their anger.

"Give me your gun." I ran around to stand in front of him, my hands on his chest, trying to slow him down. "I'm not letting you leave unless you hand me the gun."

He stared at me, then tried to push me out of the way. I smelled the alcohol on his breath.

"Let me go, Ava. He's not doing this shit to you. No fuckin' way."

"Give me the gun, Tom." I raced to the door of our apartment and stood in front of the doorway. He stared at me, contemplated how he could knock me to the floor. We faced off, me shaking and my teeth chattering, then reluctantly he pulled the gun from his holster.

"Here."

It felt cold and heavy in my hand. But I wasn't relieved. I knew how his mind worked. My father had a set of kitchen knives, a gift from Pinky and Patricia, that could slice through metal just like on the infomercial. Pinky had even demonstrated with a beer can. Getting the gun was just half of my battle; Tom needed to go to bed, not to my father's apartment. Not to the knife set.

"Tom, don't," I pleaded. "Please don't go. It's nothing. Nothing. Just stupid shit. It's not a big deal. You know how he is. You know how we all are. We're O'Neils for Christ's sake."

"He touched you. I'm gonna kill him. Move, Ava."

His eyes were now a glacier blue. The rage had settled to a stony coldness. I accepted that all was lost. I'd never stop him. Not with a handprint on my cheek. I sank to the floor, the gun in my hand. Tom literally pulled me over to one side of the door like a soldier moving a sack of potatoes during KP duty, then he stepped over me, opened the door and flew down the stairs, his engineer boots heavily echoing in the hallway, sounding almost metallic in my ears.

I sat frozen for a minute, then stood and raced to the telephone. I dialed Two first.

"Get over there!" I shrieked. "Get over there. It's Tom!"

He hung up without even saying goodbye or asking for details.

I called Charley, having to dial three times as my shaking hands clumsily missed the correct combination of numbers on the keypad. Charlotte answered the phone groggily.

"Tell Charley Tom's gone to kill my father. Tell him to go!"

I heard her, muffled, as she covered the phone and relayed the message to him. When she spoke again, she said simply, "He's on his way."

I felt my cheek, its puffy redness. The start of another night of madness.

This was how we lived our lives. These were our family values.

17

I rocked.

Somewhere along the way, I had learned that rocking back and forth soothed me, replacing the mother long gone and, before she was gone, long crazy, and so I rocked myself back and forth, waiting for Tom to return. I believed one day he would kill my father or my father would kill Tom, or like the tragic case of Mark "Big G" Gannigan, someone would get killed stepping between them or pulling them apart. Occasionally, I believed Tom might kill me. But I pushed those feelings away as I rocked, on my knees. Back and forth.

Back and forth. Back and forth, Ava.

Then, when I felt calmer, I got up and walked, almost in a trance, to the kitchen and poured myself a cold vodka from the bottle of Smirnoff in the refrigerator. I sipped it and went into the living room to wait. I didn't dare go to my father's or even call. I'd only make a bad situation worse.

Tom didn't return until the middle of the night, close to

dawn, really, when I had drunk myself into a half sleep of exhaustion. It was like being hypnotized.

Tom had a bloody nose with some tissues stuffed up it, hanging out of his nostrils so that I would have laughed if I wasn't so worried, and a swollen jaw.

"Jesus, Tom." I shook my head. "And him?"

"Dad lost a loose molar. The one that was already loose." Like that made it okay. Free dental work.

"Uncle Two?"

"He broke the middle finger of his left hand....I think it was the left." Tom seemed a bit wobbly, his speech nasal from the tissues.

"You're lucky you're all not dead."

"Uncle Charley got the worst of it. You should've seen him. He was *wild*. He picked up a knife to try to calm us all down. Was waving it...and somehow, in the middle of the fight, he cut his own arm."

I winced.

"Really deep, too. Blood everywhere. Even on the couch."

Together, Tom told me, they had toppled a bookcase and broken a lamp. And yet, at the end of it, they had all shared a bottle of vodka. Then a second.

"All settled," Tom slurred slightly as he unbuttoned his pants, let them drop onto the floor, then half fell, half crawled into the pullout couch. "He won't never touch you again, Ava."

I gripped my sides. I had images of my very intestines and heart and stomach falling onto the floor if I didn't. That this was impossible—at least without a knife being involved—didn't matter. I felt myself, for the first time, longing to be away from Tom. Yet that very idea made my insides feel like they were slipping onto the floor faster, making it impossible to know where my insides ended and the outside of me began.

I kept holding my sides and walked over to his bed. His jaw

was turning purple. I went to the freezer and retrieved a bag of frozen vegetables. Tom didn't like his ice packs too cold, so I wrapped the bag in a dish towel.

"Here, baby." I placed it on his jaw. He was already almost passed out, his eyes glassy.

"He won't touch you no more, Ava."

"I know," I whispered.

"Don't I always protect you?" He tried to focus his eyes on me.

"Yes, you do, Tom." I stroked his forehead. "Go to sleep."

He gave in to the vodka and exhaustion. I went to my room and lay down on my bed. All of me shook. My teeth chattered so hard they made noise, and my hands trembled. Even my eyeballs seemed to vibrate, moving back and forth and making the room shake, as if a small earthquake was hitting the West Side of New York City. I sat back up and reached into my nightstand for my bottle of vodka and poured myself a glass. Vodka kept my insides where they were supposed to be; it kept the walls of my apartment from vibrating.

He won't touch you no more.

My Tom.

I knew I wouldn't sleep. I didn't want to. What came with the night but memories? So I paced and drank until morning, flipping through television channels, mindlessly watching whatever was on for just seconds before clicking to the next thing. I even saw a commercial for the knives that slice through beer cans— or human flesh. But they don't put that in the ads.

In the morning, Tom dressed in his uniform and went to work as if he'd not beaten our father. As if his jaw was fine. As if the previous night was just a regular bedtime story.

18

My father, given the right crowd, can be downright funny, bordering on charming.

Months later, Michael De Silva hosted a party for my father and the people involved with the movie. He seemed to think my father was wildly hysterical. A character. And the more my father made De Silva laugh, the more the stories regaled his Hollywood pals, the more I dreaded the entire movie ever making it to theaters. The script was finished, filming was to start in two weeks, and as De Silva was the reigning king of crime movies, a bunch of A-list stars were attached. So my father, Tom, Two-Times, Uncle Charley, Pinky, Patricia and Jack Casey all were invited to the De Silva brownstone for a private party, where, I believed, we would be studied like rats in a maze, to see what made us tick to better portray us in the film. I was dead-set against going, but my father insisted, and actually seemed hurt that I might say no, so I dressed in my best black backless dress, threw on a pair of rhinestone earrings, and prepared to spend the night in a corner.

The brownstone was magnificent, four stories tall, and the street was lined with limousines as my cab pulled up. Stepping inside, I took in the immense, two-story foyer, with a chandelier almost as big as the old one at Luchow's Restaurant, where we used to go once a year at Christmastime.

Gazing into the party, I saw tuxedoed waiters walking around with trays of champagne and finger foods. Each waiter looked like a struggling actor playing the part of a waiter. Everywhere I looked, people were beautiful in a plastic way. No matter what direction I turned, I saw someone I knew from a movie or television, or the front cover of a magazine.

Feeling totally out of place, I looked for Tom, my security blanket. I found him near a bathroom, embraced on either side by two women who were either B-list actresses or paid whores. Not that I think it matters much which. The three of them kept disappearing into one of the opulent bathrooms. I figured they were either having a three-way or doing coke. Or both.

Uncle Charley, who's handsome in a beefy way, left Charlotte at home and was also soon entertained by a young woman half his age with a set of plastic tits so firm and high he could have rested his drink on them. Two-Times planted himself near the buffet table and bar. Pinky and Patricia "mingled." Despite her Park Avenue background, she was as star-struck as a preteen with a crush on the *Tiger Beat* hunk of the month. She and Pinky made a beeline for all the movie stars and looked like they were having a wonderful time.

Dad and De Silva were joined at the hip. In fact, they had been since the start of the whole Hollywood film deal. They dined together regularly at the restaurant De Silva co-owned. They sat at "Mr. De Silva's regular table," and drank good Scotch and smoked cigars in an upstairs VIP room when they were done. They seemed to genuinely be developing a friendship, not that I really thought of my father as having friends. He didn't. He had pit bulls and bodyguards. He had blood brothers. But maybe he was making a friend for the first time. Tonight, Daddy was led from room to room, person to person, and he was entertaining all with sanitized versions of stories I'd heard before or witnessed. Instead of cutting off someone's hand, he just "scared the hell out of him." The way he told the stories, he seemed like a slightly tougher version of the dancing hoods in *West Side Story*.

Jack Casey watched it all, with an expression that was both bemused and outraged. My father had traded in his usual uniform of gray slacks and old stained T-shirts for expensive tailored pants and a black silk T-shirt. His hair was combed. He smiled constantly.

"Stop trying to make sense of it, Jack. You fucking created him," I said flatly, vodka in hand, as I approached him.

"I can't make sense of it. At all. And me. I don't get me, either. How I can find myself just as easily enjoying his stories? Even interviewing him, I would find myself laughing. What is it about me—others—that admires this crazy shit?"

"You're a writer, Jack. You should know better than anyone that there is no black and white. Only shades of gray. One man's villain is another man's hero. And now he's made you rich. You wanted truth, but truth doesn't exist. Just stories. Tell that to your old journalism professors."

"Life is strange."

"Yeah…well, every time I flip through the cable news networks and see your talking head I feel like I'm stepping down a manhole."

"A manhole?"

"Alice had a rabbit hole. Me…I fall down into the sewer system. This whole thing is fucked up. And you created it."

I walked away from Jack, always afraid that if I spent too much time talking to him, he would believe that I really did want him to rescue me. That I would go back to his apartment and make love to him, when it had never been making love that one time, but some sort of sacrificial fucking.

I wandered to the bar for a refill, watching my father from afar as he entertained yet another celebrity. I took my vodka and walked around. The brownstone had hardwood floors polished to a reflective sheen. On the walls were blown-up black-and-white stills from famous mob movies. Photos of De Silva, his arm draped around the shoulders of the famous and beautiful, hung in a hallway. I wandered down the hall, alone, moving from picture to picture, the black frames in contrast to the stark white walls, the ceilings twelve feet high, the track lighting perfectly hitting each photo to show it without a glare. De Silva's characteristic big eyebrows were expressively raised in each photo.

"He's a character, isn't he?"

I turned to the voice and found myself alone in the back hallway with Vince Quinn. Vince was signed to portray my father in the film. He was an actor who believed his own attractiveness was a detriment to being taken seriously. At least that's what I'd read. I remember once going to see one of his movies and finding myself staring at him as he moved across the screen, almost shutting out the other actors in my mind. It was as if he were the only one up there. His eyes were a clear blue, about as pale as I had ever seen, and he had dimples that settled into the crags on his face when he smiled. He was about thirty-five, hadn't yet won an Oscar, but had been nominated. He hoped, like anyone working with De Silva, that this picture would bring him the little golden man.

I stared at him a moment, unused to seeing a star in the flesh.

He repeated his question. "He's a character, De Silva. Don't you think?"

I shrugged and turned my attention back to the photo. My definition of character would not likely include De Silva, but if Quinn wanted to believe that by serving coke and whores and carousing with criminals, this made De Silva—and even Quinn himself—a character, then that was fine. I never made a habit of explaining my family to anyone.

"You're Ava, aren't you? I didn't mean to intrude on you back here. I'm sorry." There was a long pause before he said, "I'm Vince Quinn," with the tentative uncertainty of someone who hadn't had to actually introduce himself to another human being in a long, long time because of his fame. He stuck out his hand. I shook it firmly. It was strong—and without a callus.

"You're not intruding. I was just avoiding the whole crowd out there…. I didn't want to come tonight."

"Why not?" His black hair fell into a perfect haircut, as if he'd just stepped out of a shampoo commercial.

"I live this life. I don't need to see the movie."

We had, without speaking about it, walked farther down the hall, half looking at the photos. Mostly not. He laughed. "I guess I hadn't thought of that. I wanted the role. Badly. Don't tell De Silva that. My agent was cagey about it, but I wanted to play your father. They're going to age me thirty years. I thought that was a challenge. An actor may get a part like this once in his lifetime, especially with a director like De Silva. But I guess I'm just an asshole."

"What? An actor who doesn't believe his own press? I'll bite…why are you an asshole?"

"Because I kind of forgot that it's someone's life. You know, your old man is…he's a tough old guy. And I have to tell you, we had dinner together a couple of months ago when De Silva was trying to get me to sign on, and your father's an interesting guy, all right. But I didn't stop to think about you and your brother. The script is pretty heavy."

I shrugged. We had arrived at a half-open door leading into a library or study. Vince Quinn pushed the door open all the way. "Want to go in there? It'll be quiet."

More than anything, I wanted to escape. To be gone from this party, away from the silicone breasts, away from my brother who would likely become argumentative very shortly and my father's newfound mobster stand-up routine. But I liked the quiet echo of the back hall, and the empty room appealed to me.

Stepping inside, we found ourselves in a room with built-in mahogany bookshelves from floor to ceiling, as well as a small love seat and a leather chair. I sat down on the love seat, and Vince sat in the leather chair after shutting the door.

"So I take it you're not impressed with Hollywood." He smiled at me. His teeth were that bleached-white bright. As he looked at me, I thought perhaps he was studying me, and it made me uncomfortable. I found myself trying to think of answers to his questions that would reveal nothing about myself.

"Not really," I whispered. The room was still, illuminated by the green glow of a banker's lamp on a small desk. The walls of the brownstone were thick, made of plaster. You would never know there was a huge party going on in the rest of the house.

"Or me."

"I beg your pardon?"

"You're not impressed with me. You don't give a shit that I'm Vince Quinn. I'm just the asshole playing your father and helping to put your life up on the screen. And you don't want that."

"You could say that."

"Hey, look." He motioned to a side table with crystal decanters filled with, according to the engravings on the bottles, Scotch, vodka, gin and whiskey. "Want a refill on your drink? No ice, but I could go get some."

"Don't worry about it. I'll take vodka. I still have a little ice in my glass." I held it out to him.

He poured my ice into a heavy crystal glass and then added more vodka. He poured himself a Scotch.

"To the movie—" he lifted his glass in a toast "—and to your privacy." He took a long drink. "Now, if we could find a way to reconcile the two, we wouldn't be doing too badly, would we?"

Vince Quinn was as charismatic up close as he was on the screen. His eyes twinkled, as if he was always inviting you to share an inside joke. As if he knew something amusing that he was just dying to tell you. He was tall, about six feet, and his pants and shirt fit his body perfectly.

"So what's your story?" he asked me.

I didn't say anything.

"Silence," he said. "Because you won't share your story…or you don't think it's worth telling?"

"I could give you some cleaned-up fairy tale, but the silence is better. Fill in the blanks."

"And what do you think of your father's life being up there on the screen? Of all this?" He swept an arm around the room with its expensive draperies and rugs probably worth the entire contents of my apartment.

"None of it interests me very much."

"What does interest you?" he asked in a soft growl. I imagined that Vince Quinn was used to entire rooms of women responding to his flirtations, to interviewers and journalists paying homage at his feet.

"Being left alone."

"You really mean that?"

"Why is that so questionable?"

"Because I've been living in a world where people would write a press release on what they had for breakfast if they thought it would buy them more fame or better box office. I've forgotten what privacy is."

I leaned back in my chair and kicked off my high heels, letting the vodka warm me and make my insides feel a little safer. I was unused to plain small talk, to strangers wanting to know about me. Where I lived, the world knew about me before they even spoke to me. All they had to know was my last name. In our neighborhood, that said it all. O'Neil. Daughter of the Roofer. Sister of the crazy cop. Goddaughter of the bookie. Guarded by Two-Times since she was a baby.

"What do you do? Job-wise?"

I stifled a half laugh. "The guys they're making a movie about? They're my full-time job."

"Don't know if I'd want that job."

"I don't think you could handle that job." I smiled at him.

"You're pretty confident about that, are you?"

"Most definitely."

"So who takes care of *you* when that full-time job gets tiring?"

"No one." I used to think Tom took care of me. In truth, he still brought me frozen bags of peas for my hangovers and stole Percocet from apartments when he was doing busts. He bought me vodka, and he bought the groceries. But I couldn't recall, not in a long time, me telling him what I felt, inside. We both knew that what was inside the both of us was best left in the dark.

"Try me."

"Excuse me?"

"Try me. Tell me a secret. I promise not to flinch. Whatever it is. You can tell me you hijacked a bus."

"My father already did that. You read the script."

"Killed someone."

"Ditto."

"Tell me something about you that no one else knows."

Vince Quinn was flirting with me, making a game of some variation of Truth or Dare. I didn't feel like playing. Not with the truth. Not with anything important. But I liked his eyes enough to want to play with lies. Or at least truths about unimportant things.

"I like to fuck standing up."

19

I didn't stay to see what Vince Quinn would say. He had blinked twice, in surprise or amusement, and I stood and walked away from him, out of the room and down the hall into the party. It was surreal to see my family mixed in with movie stars and people from another world. Might as well have been another planet. Michael De Silva made a beeline for me and pulled me to his side.

"If it isn't the very beautiful Ava."

"Hi, Michael." I smiled weakly.

"You know who I got to play you, don't you?" he asked, his breath smelling of strong whiskey.

Actually, De Silva had told me a half dozen times who was playing me, although the daughter in the movie was named "Mary." The actress chosen was Juliette Walker, a dark-haired woman who had once been America's "It Girl" and had been nominated for the Oscar as best supporting actress five years before. After a string of flops, this was supposed to be her comeback role. Playing me on film. For a brief moment, I longed to escape into a movie myself, to hop into a pretty film, a breezy romantic comedy. A movie where people didn't cut off fingers and beat each other with crowbars.

"I know. Juliette Walker."

"Wanna meet her?"

"Not really. I'm actually going to go home. I want to thank you for inviting me."

"Don't leave so soon." He took my hand in his. His hand was firm and cool. He lifted my hand to his mouth and kissed it, his lips staying on my hand for a minute. He moved closer to me still. "You know, Ava. You could be an actress. You're just as beautiful as anyone up there on the screen." He leaned his head to mine in conspiratorial fashion, our faces almost touching. "You're better-looking than Juliette. You were tough to cast."

"Thanks."

"I could help you, you know. Get cast in a role… Very beautiful." His lips now brushed against my cheek and stayed there for a moment too long. I stepped back and pulled my black shawl around me.

"My father wants me to come to the set next week. So I'll see you then." I made my eyes go flat. I can do it without even thinking or trying. The spark dies, like blowing out a candle. Snuff. Gone. Ava isn't home.

"You do that. We'll show you all around," he said, staring at me, then releasing my hand. I wondered if Juliette would do that on-screen—with her eyes. I wondered again whether De Silva was studying me. Throw the O'Neils at a Hollywood party and see what they do. Watch Tom fuck two girls in a bathroom. Watch Ava pull into herself and disappear. Then put it in the movie.

In my peripheral vision, I saw Vince Quinn staring at me. He had come out to the party, too. I desperately wanted to leave. I didn't know what made me say what I did to Vince. Then again, I didn't know my reasons for doing half of what I did. I was an O'Neil; we operated on instinct. Instinct and alcohol.

I said good-night to De Silva, then I maneuvered toward the front door, staring up one last time at the immense crystal chandelier in the foyer. I didn't tell my father or Tom I was leaving. My father was never too concerned about where we were or what we did. We had been raised to keep our wits about us. As for Tom, our only dragon had been slayed years before. And Tom was usually too wasted to know whether I was there or not. Sometimes I would come into the living room to find him halfway into a conversation with me when I hadn't been there at all. I was in his head as he was in mine.

I stepped outside into the night. A doorman offered to hail me a cab, and I nodded, pulling my shawl still tighter around me as the wind whipped down the street.

"I'll take her home." Vince Quinn appeared at my side, smiling his megawatt smile.

"That's all right. I can take a cab. Go in and enjoy the party."

"My limo is right there." He pointed to a long black stretch limousine parked halfway down the block.

"Really, I'm fine taking a cab. Go back inside."

"Please. It's not a bother. I can come back if I feel like it. I could use a breather, anyway. That's why I was in the study with you. I needed to be alone, too." He looked at me sincerely, as if willing me to believe we were alike in some way, which I knew was impossible. Hadn't he read the script?

"Fine." Agreeing would get me home faster.

His hand on my elbow, we walked down the block to his waiting limousine. I imagined millions of young girls swooning. To be in the back of a limo with Vince Quinn.

The driver opened the door and nodded. "Mr. Quinn."

Sliding across the rich leather seats, I settled in the far corner. The bar was stocked with vodka, gin, Scotch and bourbon, also in crystal decanters as in De Silva's study, only these had little brass plaques around their necks, with tiny chains, proclaiming their contents. Little alcohol necklaces. There was a DVD player, and the stereo piped in soft jazz. The only times I had been in a limo before were for funerals. And they didn't have DVD players. And we O'Neils carried our own booze. Liquor didn't last long enough around us to need fancy necklaces. When we buried Two-Times's son, we had long black limos snaking out to a cemetery in Brooklyn. I remember grieving over Rocky. He had given me my first schoolyard kiss when we were small. I grieved for Uncle Two, whose weight seemed to grow heavier with the burden of loss. His very shoulders sagged.

"Care for a drink? A nightcap for the ride home? Vodka? I even have ice." Vince winked as he ducked his head and climbed in, and the limo pulled from the curb and into the traffic of nighttime revelers in New York City.

I nodded. "A vodka on the rocks."

"Ketel One okay?"

"Doesn't much matter." I shrugged. Tom and I would drink Boone's Farm if that was the last thing on a shelf.

Vince poured me a vodka, then poured himself a Scotch, neat. He opened the little window to the driver, and I gave the man my address.

Vince pressed a button to close the tinted window. We had complete privacy. "I'm sorry," he said. He sat at one end of the seat, me at the other. He leaned back, clearly comfortable in a stretch limo.

"For what?"

"Making you uncomfortable."

"You didn't."

"I felt like I did."

I shrugged and stared out the window, gazing at New York-ers gathered on street corners, trying to hail cabs, or walking the sidewalks with their poodles and yippy little dogs, or clustered in well-dressed groups of two and four, heading to restaurants and clubs.

"I guess I'm just curious about you. If your father did all the things he supposedly did, then…I don't know. I try to imagine it as I read the script, but I can't. I was born, believe it or not, on a farm in Iowa. Corn-fed Iowa boy." He gave a half laugh.

I looked at him. "I've never even been farther than New Jersey."

"Yeah, well…I really am from a small town. Though I forget that sometimes with the parties and the whole life. My house. My personal assistant. It's all so *fucking* weird. But my parents were good, quiet people who took us to church every Sunday and raised my brothers and sister and me to do the right thing, though sometimes I think I forget that, too." His eyes had a faraway quality.

"Doing the right thing isn't part of the O'Neil repertoire."

"I guess not." He took a sip of his Scotch.

"I hate the whole movie. I hate the attention it's bringing us. I hate Jack's book. I hate it all."

"I don't blame you." He slid a little closer to me. "There's something about you. It's not Hollywood…and it sure as hell isn't Iowa. I know this sounds like a bullshit line, but it's not. I guess when we were talking—" he took another sip of Scotch "—something about you makes me want to know your secrets."

"What makes you think I have any?"

"You're the Roofer's daughter."

"So they tell me."

"Can I take you to dinner tonight? Late supper. Anyplace you want. That's one nice thing about being famous. It's like having a magic carpet to anywhere you want to go."

"No. I really am tired. No magic tonight."

"Tomorrow, then?"

I looked at him. Vince Quinn. His face was perfect, and beneath his shirt I knew was the rock-hard abdomen that made women weak in the knees after his love scene with Susan Faraday in *Close to the Truth*.

"Yes," I heard myself say.

He looked at me intently, then he reached out and took my hand. We rode in silence to my apartment building. When the limo stopped, he climbed out of the car and helped me exit. He leaned forward and kissed my cheek. For a split second I thought I saw pity in his face.

"Good night," I said, and climbed up the steps to my building.

"I'll pick you up tomorrow at eight."

I turned and waved goodbye, then trudged up to the third floor. Opening my apartment door, I didn't turn on any lights. I locked the door behind me and walked through to my bedroom and sat in the dark. My head swirled from vodka and Vince Quinn. And in the darkness I communed with the ghost of my family's secrets. A ghost that never let me be.

20

Over dinner, Vince Quinn made me laugh. He was a wonderful mimic and did a mean version of Uncle Two. Then he launched into an imitation of Pinky. "So's I had this guy right where I wanted him, and I just choked him until he passed out, the fuckin' bastard." Everyone was a bastard to Pinky. Unless he liked you. Then, if you were male, you were "Kid." If a woman, "Sweetheart."

Vince had picked me up promptly at eight o'clock, wearing subtle cologne that reminded me of the sea, though I couldn't remember the last time I had smelled salty air. Now we sat in Nobu at a table that was the envy of all, and we laughed. He was obviously a keen observer. He had all the mannerisms down, even of my father. The way his left eye twitched when he was angry. The way Dad always shifted in his chair at dinner, any dinner, his eyes scanning across a table, looking at the cutlery in case it was needed. As a little girl, I remember hiding the steak knives in our apartment and being aware of every knife in the butcher block in the kitchen and whether any were missing. I couldn't imagine being like Vince Quinn, in a world where cutlery was something you simply kept in a drawer and took out when you ate, put through the dishwasher and put away again.

"So isn't this kind of weird, you out with the man playing your father?"

"I didn't think about that. I guess so. But you're not him...thank God." I smiled at him. I had dressed in my favorite black velvet top and a pair of black velvet pants. I wore my hair up; a few curls had sprung loose and fell against my face. "It's just odd being out with you, period. People are looking at us."

He glanced around the room. "I never notice anymore...not really. Can I ask you something?"

"Let's not go there again."

"No, I'm serious. Your brother...is he okay? I mean really okay?"

I sipped at my tiny little cup of sake—Japanese vodka as far as I was concerned. Looking around the restaurant, I noticed how people surreptitiously stared at us, then averted their eyes. Even in a city celebrities called home, in a restaurant adorned with important people, Vince Quinn was the pinnacle of the celebrity pyramid. Women wanted to be me. If they only knew.

"No...he's not okay." I bit my lip. I was unused to talking about Tom to anyone. Uncle Two and I carried him home, but we never shared a word between us about how sick Tom really was. Even just admitting that Tom was not okay to Vince Quinn, I felt a sense of betrayal. The O'Neils didn't talk about one another to people outside the family. Yet I also felt a surge of something. A desire to tell this almost-stranger everything. To have someone nod and listen to me. To have someone whisper that all was forgiven, that I was absolved of my sins. Not a priest, but a confessor. I stared into Vince's eyes.

"I don't mean to pry, honest. He seems a little…on the edge. I was just concerned."

"Tom *is* on the edge. He's——I take care of him. I make sure he doesn't…" I sighed. Doesn't what? Do what he always seemed to threaten? Take my mother's way out. He never said it, but I knew the threat was always there. It was as if she called to him like the Sirens called the sailors. *Come back to me, my children, my babies. Come back…come back.*

"I'm sorry to pry. It's hard not to care about you. You have this…quiet dignity."

"Dignity?" I shook my head.

"You do. There's something powerful about you."

I blushed and lowered my head. "I don't know about that."

"I bet you're stronger than…anyone I've ever met before."

Our waiter came to the table, and we ordered pieces of sushi and tuna rolls and didn't talk about Tom or the movie. We talked about faraway places. Vince had traveled extensively and shot films in Budapest, London, the mountains of Montana, in the desert of New Mexico. I spoke a bit about growing up in the neighborhood. He held on to my every word as if I was the one with the exotic life. I told him my second-favorite Daddy story, after the bus hijacking, the one about the time I came home from school to find four hundred cartons of cigarettes in the apartment. Tom and I had made forts and tunnels through them. Even Carol had squealed like it was Christmas. We played at soldiers for a while. Then Tom had allowed Carol and me to each pretend to be Rapunzel, and he was our prince.

"Other kids got tree houses. We got stolen cartons of Marlboros."

He laughed as I told the whole story, complete with Uncle

Two, who was a heavy smoker, periodically raiding our fort to open up packs of cigs.

"What a childhood. But you know, as funny as all that is, I'm not sure how you manage to hold it all together. It's kind of scary. Where I come from, people don't lock their doors at night. In summertime, when I was little, I would leave on my bike in the morning and come back at dusk, spend the day riding and maybe hang out in a *real* tree house. Play baseball in someone's field."

"Sounds nice."

"It was. Don't you get tired, Ava? Don't you ever want to get away from here?"

Did I ever want to get away? I wiped at the corner of my eye. Who could even think of that when each day started with cleaning up after Tom, wiping away the vomit from the sides of the sink? I paced in that apartment, the air unclean and filled with dusty memories.

I shrugged and hoped he couldn't tell I was teary. "I wouldn't know where to go."

"How about going with me? Away for a weekend. Separate rooms. No bullshit." He held his hands up like a magician showing nothing up his sleeves. "Separate rooms. Let's go play in Vegas for the weekend."

"I've never even been on a plane."

"No way."

"Really. I told you…the farthest I've ever been is the Jersey Shore. Atlantic City."

"So let's do it."

"I can't." What would Tom do without me? The thought made me feel ill. I stared again at the faces of the other diners. I didn't belong here where a plate of sushi cost forty dollars. Where women wore jewelry and watches bought legitimately—with receipts. This was a world for Vince Quinn, but it was no place for an O'Neil.

"You can." He smiled at me. The thought crossed my mind that he wanted to dissect me just like De Silva. You can. Like it was so easy.

"Can I?" I spoke to myself more than to Vince. I felt the familiar magnetic pull of the West Side. Of my apartment. My mother's voice whispered in my ear. *Come to me, my babies. Come to me.*

"What do you say? I'll have a Gulfstream waiting at Kennedy." He pulled a black American Express card out of his wallet. "We'll buy you whatever you need. We'll fly right out. Stay at MGM. Hard Rock. Someplace cool. Gamble. Relax by the pool. Doesn't it sound good to get away from here? I'll be back Monday to meet with De Silva. We're just about ready to start shooting. Tom can manage without you for the weekend, can't he? One little weekend away?"

"He actually has the nightshift this weekend." When Tom was on the nightshift, he came home and drank by the filtered gray light of the rising sun, then slept all day like a vampire.

"Say you'll go."

"All right…I'll go," I heard myself say. I felt light. I felt a sound like laughter rise up inside me, like carbonated bubbles.

"To Vegas," Vince smiled. We clinked our little sake cups together. People looked at me, wondering if I was an actress they didn't quite recognize.

"To Vegas," I said.

Vince made several calls on his cell phone, contacting his assistant to take care of all the arrangements, and three hours later I was ensconced in a jet with leather seats, a chilled bottle of Moët Chandon and a tray of desserts within my reach—little éclairs, chocolate-covered strawberries. I didn't have so much as a toothbrush, and I left a vague message for Tom, telling him

I had decided to go away with Vince Quinn for the weekend. I gazed out the window at the darkness and the clouds. I had somehow thought the clouds would seem more substantive, more like cotton, but instead as we flew through them, they were merely wisps of vapor. Staring down at the lights of New York as we turned and flew away from the city, I took a deep breath.

"You okay? Not afraid of the flight, are you?"

"No." I looked at Vince as he poured me a glass of champagne. I wasn't afraid of flying. I was afraid, a little, of Vince Quinn. I was afraid I might tell him too much. I heard a whisper in my head. *The O'Neils know how to keep secrets, don't they, Ava?*

Yes.

We did.

21

'

We landed in Las Vegas, the city a glowing mirage in the desert from the jet. As we wound our way to the MGM Grand in a limousine, I watched the people on the street and the neon lights animated like bar signs on amphetamines.

"What do you think?" Vince asked me as he leaned back and stretched his legs out.

"It's unbelievable. New York may never sleep, but Vegas sure has the glitz and neon hands down." As if on cue, a sign with a million bulbs, a cowboy, moved its hand and lassoed a million-watted cowgirl.

"Wait until you see the suite."

All my life, people have reacted to my father. And to Tom. Both of them pulse with violence. You see it on them. People, almost imperceptibly, step aside when they walk into a bar or room. It's like knowing instinctively not to pet a pit bull. But people reacted to Vince in a different way. They either stared at him outright or pretended not to notice him yet sneaked glances constantly. Some women dissolved into giggles and cries of "Oh, my God!"

When we got to the hotel, the bell captain and the man at the front desk all handled him with cool efficiency, probably used to celebrities, and ushered us up to our suite. And through it all, people looked at me, trying to decide if they should know me. This was different from being stared at as the sister of Tom, daughter to Frank O'Neil. It was different...and I wasn't sure I liked it.

I tried not to be impressed with the suite, but I had never seen such opulence in my life. The spigots were gold, and the furnishings looked antique. I laughed, thinking how Pinky and Charley would have the place stripped down to carpet tacks on the floor inside of twenty-five minutes if left to their own devices.

"What are you smiling at, beautiful?" Vince asked me.

I shook my head. "You'd never understand."

"Try me. Do you like the place?"

"What's not to like? I just can imagine my father and his friends calculating how to rip this place off."

Vince looked at me. "Sure. Wait...shit...what's the line from the script? A day without larceny is like a day without sunshine."

"Yeah." I strolled over to the windows and looked out at the night, artificially glowing with neon. "Not that we O'Neils see a lot of sunshine."

He came up behind me as I stared out at the desert stretching before us, marked by hotel after hotel after hotel. He kissed my shoulder.

"I reread the script last night after I dropped you off. I decided I didn't think it was as funny as I used to. I'm going to try to do the part justice, Ava. And now—" he grabbed my hand "—it's time to go gamble."

"I don't even have a toothbrush. Or a hairbrush. Nothing."

"Concierge, Ava love. Concierge."

He picked up the telephone and ordered toiletries, perfume, two bathrobes. Like magic, Vince Quinn had what I needed being delivered. "And can you make sure it's up here before we get back from the tables? Say 2:00 a.m., just in case my friend is tired."

He replaced the receiver. "Voilà. Now we go gamble."

We descended in a glass elevator to the casino below. I was blinded by sequins. Half the women looked like call girls. The sound was deafening, too. The metal *ching-ching-ching* of slots making their payout. People talking, roulette wheels clicking, craps table crowds erupting into screams of joy.

"Did you know you're smiling?" Vince asked me, taking my hand.

"Am I?"

"Yeah. Is a smile so unusual for you?"

I nodded. I felt lighter than I had in years, maybe ever. Someplace in my chest, perhaps my heart, laughed. I felt something I hadn't ever felt before. I breathed free, even in the noisy chaos and the buzzing lights.

We played blackjack. Vince gave me five thousand dollars in chips, and we sat side by side. He played with thirty thousand. "If you need more, you'll use some of my chips," he said, handing me the heavy chips. Every woman at the table looked at me warily, almost angrily. We were in a roped-off area, playing with high rollers, celebrities and the beautiful people. We had made our way past several muscled, intimidating men with little earpieces—security detail. If you weren't a big shot, you weren't coming to those tables. I ordered a vodka and settled in to play.

My childhood was spent learning craps, three-card monte and poker. I was *born* to play cards. I knew when to fold my hand, and I doubled down when I was supposed to. Before long I had amassed three thousand dollars more, then four thousand. Vince was down a few thousand. But every time I won, he watched me break out into a grin. Only then would he smile, as if he wasn't allowed to smile unless I did first. He paid more attention to my expression than to his cards. I think that was why he was losing. After a couple of hours, he nudged me.

"Want to go for a nightcap? We can play all day tomorrow, Diamond Lil."

"Sure. I think this whole night's going to catch up with me soon."

I collected my winnings and handed Vince back his original five thousand dollars in ten smooth five-hundred-dollar chips.

"Don't give me this. They're yours." He tried to push the chips back into my palm.

"I can't. Take them."

He reluctantly took the chips, and we headed to one of the too-many-to-count bars off of the casino.

Settled into a back table by a waitress who nearly fainted when she saw him, we ordered drinks and I felt fatigue descend on me. Every bit of me ached. Even my eyelashes were tired.

"I liked watching you gamble." He winked at me.

"Why?"

"I like seeing you smile."

I yawned and stretched. "God, I can't believe I'm here."

"I can't believe I'm here with you."

My bullshit meter rose. "Don't play with me, Vince."

"Is it so *hard* to believe that I like being with you? I like being with you because of how I feel when your face lights up. It's like giving a little girl a present. You're so different."

"What? You've never been with a woman who played with Marlboros instead of dolls?"

"No. I haven't. And I like seeing your eyes dance. So maybe it's time to trust me just a bit. It won't kill you. You might even like it."

I shrugged.

We drank in silence, the tiredness settling over both of us. Vince went to pay the bill, but the manager comped it. We walked back through the still-constant cacophony in the casino and up to our suite. It had two bedrooms and a living room in the center, as well as two baths, one of which contained a tub that I would consider a small swimming pool.

Laid out on one bed were two robes with the logo of the MGM Grand embroidered in gold thread. In the bathroom were four new toothbrushes and a variety of women's skin-care products.

"I could get used to this," I said, kicking off my heels.

"That's what I'm hoping."

I eyed him warily. In three strides he was by my side, holding my face in his hands and kissing me. The kisses seemed to swoop down into my belly, giving me a nervous rush.

"I meant what I said. Separate rooms. But if you want to lie next to me all night, I won't stop you," he smirked. "But you'll have to behave yourself."

I stood on tiptoe and kissed him again. Slowly we made our way to the bed, kissing and touching each other as we moved. He undressed me, slowly, never taking his eyes off of me. He slid my pants off by kneeling down in front of me, then kissing my belly and making his way back up my body with tiny kisses, stopping at each nipple. Then he took off his shirt and pants. He was perfect.

"I'm not sure this is a good idea," I whispered, turning out the light. I didn't mind being naked in front of him. What I minded was smiling in front of him, feeling happy in front of him. That made me feel more naked.

"Ava...I *know* making love to the daughter of the Roofer is a bad idea. If I don't keep you happy, your father will break my legs, right?" I could see his white smile in the darkness. "But I've never been known to do the safe thing, anyway. We're both taking a risk this weekend."

He reached a hand out and pulled me to him, my breasts against his chest. His breath was on my neck, and for once I didn't think about Tom or my father, or people falling from buildings. I thought about the place in my stomach that had felt a strange rush. I longed to have Vince Quinn inside of me.

He pulled me down on the bed and kissed his way down my stomach, resting his head on my belly for a moment, hugging me, then nuzzling down between my legs. When he entered me, I felt somewhere else. Somewhere far away from the West Side of New York. It was a place I liked going. A place I had never been before.

After making love, Vince lay down next to me. We faced each other on our sides, and he touched my arm, my neck, my hair, twirling one of my curls around his finger, staring at me.

"You're a mystery, Ava."

"Not really. I'm just me."

"Yeah. And for the first time in a *long* time, I feel like someone…made love with *me*. Not Vince Quinn. I know that sounds really stupid. But I think you were with me, not him. Not the guy on the screen."

I just stroked his face. Then I rolled over and pressed against his hips.

"You fit perfectly here, Ava," he whispered in the dark.

Vince yawned and curled around me, his arms rocklike and warm. When I heard his breath grow deep and even, the breath of sleep, I lifted his arm off of me and climbed out of bed.

It was the darkness, I think, that made the reality of what I'd done come hurtling toward me like a subway train. I'd left Tom alone. I'd left New York.

Walking in the blackness of the room, I pulled the curtains aside and stared down at the neon. In the place inside me that not an hour before had been filled with a strange new joy, I felt

Two hours later, after a big breakfast served on beautiful china and a silver pot of coffee, Vince and I were on the underground monorail traveling to Caesar's Palace. Vince had ordered himself a baseball cap from the MGM store, and wore sunglasses, but still people occasionally pointed and whispered and wondered if it was him or a look-alike. I had thought that I was alone in feeling like people were staring at me in the neighborhood, or that night at De Silva's party. But Vince Quinn knew that uncomfortable feeling of being looked at constantly, though for different reasons, of course. I guessed it wasn't likely his old man had killed one person, let alone five.

We got off the monorail at the Palace. Stores lined the shopping area, everything from Versace to Fendi. Shopping with Vince was surreal. He never looked at a price tag. He also didn't head for any sales racks. Like in a fairy tale, I picked out jeans and tops, a dress and shoes. A sweater in case the restaurant was chilly. Underwear and a beautiful silk pajama set. A black bikini and cover-up for the pool. Each purchase was wrapped in tissue paper and placed in a glossy shopping bag. Every time they ran Vince's credit card through the machine, the women at the cash registers quivered with excitement, and yet in each store, Vince made certain it was me who had fun. He bought himself outfits, but he didn't look too carefully at them, didn't try them on. Instead he wanted me to take six dresses into the dressing room and come out in each one to twirl around for him.

Bags in hand, we ate at Spago because Vince said he ate at the one in L.A., and it would be like a bit of home. Then we headed back to the MGM Grand and changed into our swimsuits. Within an hour we were sunning ourselves in a cabana complete with misting machines so we wouldn't get too hot in the desert sun.

"They think of everything here, don't they?"

"Yeah, and if they haven't thought of it first, and you think of it, you just call someone and they'll make sure it's done."

The sun itself felt foreign to me. First of all, the whole "but it's dry heat" thing is bullshit. Las Vegas was hot. Hotter than New York City in the dog days of August. And in New York, the sun always plays games, peeking through the buildings and skyscrapers, through the smog that hovers, through the dirtiness and grit. It is as if we never see sunlight in her full glory. Not like in Las Vegas. And in my apartment, sun never poked through to my world with Tom. We kept the shades drawn, the better to face a morning hangover.

In the brilliance of the desert day, I sipped a cold vodka and tonic and felt the sun hitting my face and my arms, warming me. I liked the sunshine. I had convinced myself that I didn't. But I did. I wanted to stand up and spin around like a little girl catching snowflakes on her tongue, only I wanted to catch sunbeams.

"Don't get sunburned, beautiful," Vince warned me.

"I won't." I pulled my lounge chair back into the cabana, into the shade.

"You having a good time?"

"I'm having a fabulous time."

"Tell me…"

"What?"

"Would your Dad and Two-Times really take everything that wasn't nailed down?"

"Vince, they'd take the stuff that was nailed down, too. The TV set. Every towel. The robes. They'd take the bath mat. They'd take stuff they didn't need and would never use, like the plastic shower cap."

He laughed. "Then how did you turn out so normal?"

"God, Vince, I'm not normal. Not by a long shot."

"You're not crazy though, or a thief."

"How do you know?" I raised an eyebrow at him. "Have you checked your wallet lately?"

"No. And you know I don't recall seeing my watch this morning, either," he teased.

"See. You thought we should trust each other. They make 'em naive in Iowa, don't they?"

"Yup. I'm just a dumb ol' farmhand."

"With a black American Express card."

"So I'm not your typical farmboy."

"And I'm not your typical New York City girl, either."

"That I never doubted." He sipped a cold beer.

"You know...the movie, it shows that sort of American mob story glamour. The easy money, the loyalty, the lifelong friendships, the 'fuck you' to authority. Everyone wonders what it would be like to walk into a room... Well, let's put it this way, if you're a guy, you wonder what it would be like to walk into a room and have every man fear you. And every woman looks at them up there on the screen—in De Silva's movies—and wonders what it would be like to fuck a man who can take everyone in the room."

He smirked. "When the movie's done, they'll just want to know what it's like to fuck me." I flicked an ice cube at him. He flicked one back at me.

"But the truth is, the life with my family is crazy. No one watching that movie is going to get that. Not really. De Silva won't show my life. Tom's. Not how it really was when we were kids. Not how it is now. They just can't show that—no one would pay to see that. But as much as I resent De Silva for immortalizing that life in such a way that people think it's 'gangland cool,' there is a side to it that is...I don't know."

"Yes, you do. What?" He sat up on his lounge chair, his chest glistening with sweat, his sunglasses reflecting me in their dark glass.

"They're pit bulls on the end of a short chain. My father, Tom, Uncle Two. If someone truly harmed me—truly harmed me—there would be nowhere that person would be safe. It's not the kind of love most people experience. My father probably wouldn't be able to tell you what color my eyes are, or what music I like, or whether I like to eat Italian food, or what year I graduated high school, or even my birthday. He wouldn't be able to tell you very much about me. But I know if I need him, there would be no questions asked."

"Do you ever ask him about…killing people, or about what he does?"

"No."

"Not even curious?"

"No. Not really… Plus a lot of it we lived through with him."

"Ever make you sad?"

"Not really. Are you sad that you're from Iowa?"

"No."

"Well, then I'm not sad I come from where I do." I rolled over on my stomach to tan the backs of my legs, which were still in the sun, though my face was shaded by the cabana. People floated by in the distance on a lazy river of a pool.

"Do you love your father?"

I leaned up on my elbows and cupped my chin. "I suppose I do."

"Are you afraid of him?"

"No. I'm afraid that one day he or Tom will kill each other. But I'm not afraid of him. This is the guy who dragged me to Central Park the night of the first snowfall of every year. First big snowfall. And we'd go find some open spot and lie down and make snow angels. There is nothing like being in the snow in Manhattan at night. The stars are usually out. You can catch sight of a few of them, but what you sense the most is the silence. Fewer cars and cabs in a big snow. The whole place slows down and the snow muffles the sounds. And we'd just spend an hour or two in the snow, dancing in it. Me and him and Tom and Carol. Then we'd go to John's afterward for a glass of rum. Mine was in a little shot glass."

"When was the last time you did that?"

"It's been a couple of years, but I know we even went after I moved out of his apartment. It's a standing date. Sacred. He'll call me when Al Roker predicts a big snow to tell me to get ready."

"Doesn't sound like the same guy who throws people from the rooftops."

"But it is. And so I suppose that's why when they show him throwing someone from a roof in the movie, I'm not in denial about it, but he's still my father and there are some parts De Silva will never know. Some parts Jack Casey never found out about. Those are the parts that belong to me."

Vince Quinn climbed from his lounge chair and knelt in front of mine and kissed my forehead, then each cheek.

"What was that for?" I asked.

"Nothing. No…something. This weekend belongs to me. To us."

"I won't ever forget it."

"Wait until tonight."

"What?" I asked.

"A surprise."

Vince moved his lounge chair over to mine and rested his hand on the small of my back. I liked being near him, and I couldn't understand why I didn't feel claustrophobic. I was usually so cautious and concerned with having my own space, my own air to breathe.

"Vince?"

"Hmm?"

"I told you a little bit about me, now can I ask you something?"

"Shoot."

"Did you really have a half-alien baby with Margot Summers?" I asked, referring to a tabloid headline of the week before.

His laughter filled the cabana. Rich and deep, he howled.

"Well, did you?"

"Yes. He had horns and a slimy lizard tail. We named him Damian."

"I knew you were too good to be true."

He leaned over to kiss me, and as he got close to my face he started laughing again. I kissed his cheek.

"Thank you," I whispered.

"For what?" he asked. But I couldn't articulate it. For what? Freedom? Sunshine? Laughter?

I decided it was for resting his hand on my back and knowing his hand wasn't covered in blood, real or metaphorical.

23

That night I dressed in the simple black cocktail dress Vince and I had picked out together. He wore a black T-shirt and gray slacks, with eight-hundred-dollar loafers. I know. *He* may not have looked at price tags, but I did.

A limousine was waiting at the front of the hotel and drove us to the Mandalay Bay Resort. Without a hat to shield his face, we were again stared at as we made our way to the vodka vault. In the Mandalay Bay was a restaurant whose claim to fame was housing a literal vault of vodka—rare bottles of clear liquid imported from Russia, Poland—all over the world—and housed in safety deposit boxes in a subzero vault. Vince's surprise for me was an evening of tastings of the world's best vodka, with proofs so high I breathed fire, followed by ringside seats for a title boxing match at the MGM.

The vodkas were perfectly chilled and each one went down my throat cold only to turn to an inferno in the pit of my belly. With each shot, I felt New York slip farther and farther away. Each time a thought came—a thought of my room or of Tom, or of a picture in my mind, frozen, like the time my mother forgot to turn off the stove and nearly set the apartment on fire—I pushed it away. I would live, if only for the weekend.

In the vodka vault, the man who catered to us put a mink around my shoulders to keep me warm. I rubbed the fur against my face. From the desert to Siberia in minutes. Only in Vegas.

After several vodkas, some caviar with a price tag I had to blink at several times, and dinner, we took the limousine back to the MGM.

"You're a fight fan, right?"

"How'd you know?" I looked at Vince as we took our seats ringside.

"Read it in the *Chronicle*."

"*I* didn't tell Jack Casey that. My father and him must have got on the subject of boxing. I don't know that I'm a fan, it's just my father taught me how to score the matches when I was a kid. Ten-point must, can't be saved by the bell, standing eight counts and all that."

"So who do you pick tonight?"

"Terry Jones. He has the best cornerman in boxing, and he hasn't been cutting rap records and fucking an MTV veejay in his free time like Jimenez. Distractions are bad for boxing."

"Care to make it interesting?"

"Sure."

"Okay. You take Terry Jones. I'll take the other guy. If you win, we have dinner at your choice of a restaurant on Friday night back in New York after shooting. If I win, it's my choice, *and* you have to come with me to Atlantic City the next time I have a two-day break."

I shot him a look. "Seems like I win either way."

"Depends on how you look at it. Maybe I win either way."

I smiled and listened as the ring announcer addressed the

crowd. Part of me assumed when we went back to New York, this weekend would be just a dream of sunshine and palm trees and nothing more. He was, after all, one of *People* magazine's fifty most beautiful people. And I was me. But Vince wanted to see me again. I let myself believe that was possible.

The fight began, and it was bloody. Close up, a boxing match is nothing like what you see on TV. Live, you hear the men's grunts and the sound of the air being forced from their lungs with body shots. You hear the sickening crunch of cartilage in the nose being smashed, and you see blood spraying across the canvas. It isn't video. It isn't the TV screen. It's living-color blood and snot flying through the air. No wonder my father loves the sport.

Terry Jones lost after a strong uppercut by his opponent sent his eyes rolling to the back of his head and his body falling to the canvas.

"Looks like you'll be packing your bag for the Taj Mahal, darlin'," Vince grinned. "And I have a two-day break next week."

I stared at him, seeing sincerity in his eyes.

"Don't look so disappointed."

"I'm not."

"And you know, if you hate Atlantic City, we can fly anywhere you want."

"Atlantic City is fine."

He leaned in close to me and licked my neck, seductively, looking to the crowd as if he was simply nuzzling me.

"Let's go upstairs," he whispered.

I nodded, and we stood and made our way through the crowd. Three photographers cornered us as we tried to exit. Vince smiled for them, draping his arm around my shoulder for one shot, drawing me to him at the waist for another. His motions were practiced, while I felt overwhelmed by the flashing lights and turned my face to the side. Safe in the elevator later, I asked him if the attention bothered him.

"No. When they stop paying attention, then I'll worry."

"But what about when they print the pictures, and it says underneath them that you were in Vegas with the Roofer's daughter?"

"I don't care."

"Why do you want to be famous?"

The elevator opened on our penthouse floor.

"I suppose it's because I'm not good at anything else. Your father and Two-Times are good at the things they're good at. I'm good at acting. I'm good at smiling for the camera. I can't do anything else, and if they want to pay me an obscene amount of money, then fine. But this movie, Ava…this one is my chance for a bit of respect. I don't want to be the pretty boy anymore. I'll take the money, but if I could have people see I really am good at what I do…that would be…it would be something I would have for the rest of my life."

He slid the key card into the slot and the door clicked open. Fresh fruit baskets and flowers filled the suite. Our bed had been turned down and two Godiva chocolates were placed on each pillow. Vince didn't turn on the light. Instead he went to the curtains and opened them, letting in the neon lights from the strip. The room was mostly in shadows, but the light from the strip cast a glow over us.

"Ava….when I saw you at the party, I admit I was curious about you. I was swept up in the movie and wanting to know everything I could soak up about the O'Neils. But this weekend has been no bullshit. This was our weekend. Not De Silva's, not your family's."

He pulled his shirt over his head and came over to me, sliding the spaghetti straps of my dress down and letting the black fabric fall to the floor. My whole life making love had been a force of nature, fury, a pounding to make me forget, force me to forget. Vince Quinn wasn't about fury.

"Kiss me," he whispered. "There's a part of you that is so gentle…and you share that with me." He pulled me to him, and I felt a need to make him part of me. Tomorrow we would return to New York City. I wanted to make sure neither of us forgot Las Vegas. I kissed him and slid my hands down his stomach, stroking his belly with featherlike touches.

"Ava…if I don't fuck you, I'm going to go out of my mind."

He pulled me over to the bed and took off his pants. I slid my panties down my legs and then watched him approach in the neon half light.

"Make my ghosts go away, Vince," I whispered as he entered me. He didn't ask what ghosts they were, he didn't stop fucking me, he didn't stop pulling me to him. In the wee hours of the Vegas night, I found a haven for the first time in my life. I found a place that was safe, for a night. A place without rooftops.

As the jet descended on New York City, I felt my spirits deflate.

"Come with me to my apartment." Vince held my hand.

"Aren't you staying in a hotel?"

"No…the shoot is too long. De Silva got me a furnished apartment. Comes with a housekeeper. Stocked fridge. Stocked bar. What do you say?"

"I can't go with you."

"Why not?"

"Because this is my real life now. You have your real life. I have mine. Though yours is a lot better as far as real life goes. My apartment doesn't come with a housekeeper. I *am* the housekeeper."

Vince grinned, but his eyes were very flat.

"What's wrong?"

"I found myself pretending while we were away that it was just about me and you and no one else. Promise me you won't let that neighborhood and your family pull you away from me?"

I shrugged. "What about Hollywood? What about all the beautiful people and the fact that you'll be making out with some gorgeous female on camera."

"Trust me. Kissing a stranger in a room full of cameramen is overrated. Promise me you'll at least try to remember last night."

I squeezed his hand. "Promise."

Within two hours, our limousine had pulled up in front of my apartment building. I kissed Vince goodbye, and we arranged to meet for drinks in two nights, when Vince's rehearsal schedule would be a short day because of how the scenes were arranged.

I took my suitcase—which we'd had to buy to bring home my new clothes and things—and climbed out of the limo, waving goodbye.

"Thank you." I smiled, running back to hug him as he stood by the open limo door. As a bunch of neighborhood kids walked by, they stared at the car.

He pulled me to him and whispered, "The weekend was ours."

I made my way to my apartment. Fighting tears as I unlocked the door, I took a deep breath. I didn't want to go back into a world without neon and brightness and sunshine and laughter.

"Tom?" I called out, setting my suitcase down as I shut the door behind me. He didn't answer, but I sensed him. I flicked on the lights and gasped. The apartment was wrecked from one end to the other. Chairs were overturned. Dishes were broken. The bookshelves had been emptied, knickknacks smashed on the floor and books thrown in a pile.

He came charging out of the spare bedroom, his eyes wild. I searched for sanity in them, but could find none.

"Where the fuck have you been?" he shouted at me, his footsteps pounding across the floor.

I startled and shrunk back from him. "Vegas," I said meekly.

"With that pretty-boy fuck?"

I nodded, and tried to move past him to my bedroom.

"I won't have you acting like a whore, Ava. I won't have it."

Afraid as I was, the word "whore" made me angry. I whirled around. "Look at this place," I hissed. "Look at it. You've destroyed it! This is my home, too. Leave me alone, Tom. Leave me the fuck alone."

I went into my bedroom, but he followed me and pushed me down on the bed, his hands pinning down each of my shoulders.

"I mean it, Ava. You can't leave me just because you feel like running off for a weekend."

I turned my face to the side, wouldn't look him in the eyes.

"Look at me."

"No! I hate you!"

"Look at me."

Finally, I stared up at him. Then I spat at him. "I hate you. I hate who we are."

He took his hands from my shoulders and pressed his hands into my wrists and held me down. "I'll let you have this one...whatever. This guy. But this is just about the movie. Nothing more."

He suddenly let me go after roughly pushing my hands down one last time, then he left my room, kicking a chair on the way out to his bed.

My breath was ragged. I looked at my wrists where he had grabbed them. They were mottled red.

I don't know how long I lay there, rubbing my wrists. Tears flowed out of my eyes and down the sides of my face. The weekend was ruined. Tom had ruined it. After a while, he came back to the doorway. "I was just worried," he said, his voice softer.

He looked at me, then turned and shut the door. I sat up and surveyed my room. He had smashed photos in frames. Had slept in my bed. I could smell his alcoholic scent on my sheets. I shut my eyes and tried to remember making love with Vince Quinn, but already the memories we had created were fading.

24

I refused to believe in fairy tales. I believed, I suppose, in ogres, evil kings and monsters underneath the bed. So I expected, with my whole heart, that my weekend with Vince in Las Vegas would be something I remembered, but would never be repeated.

But Vince Quinn surprised me. Though I respected what Tom said—that it could go on as long as the movie did, but that it was about the movie, nothing more—I suddenly found my life revolving around someone else other than my brother. Vince called me every break in shooting he had. We spent hours on the phone talking about everything and nothing. I told him how my mother died, not as it was written in the script, but how it really was. I told him about the Creature Feature. About the time my father broke Tom's nose. About the dinner that had gotten so insane that *I* was the one to grab a knife and wave it, telling everyone to calm down. I also told him about peaceful times, the birthday I had gotten a Barbie house. The way my father made happy faces out of pancakes, using raisins for the eyes and nose and mouth when I was little. And Vince told me about leaving Iowa and this burning desire to create and leave a legacy. He told me about his mother's slow death from cancer. About how, since he could remember, he was afraid of dying anonymously.

We went away every time shooting stopped for more than a day, whether it was because of the weather, or a scheduled break, or scenes were being filmed featuring only Uncle Two or Jack Casey (both played by actors bearing an uncanny physical resemblance to the real thing). Most of the time, we slipped away to Connecticut or up the coast as far as Rhode Island, staying in small bed-and-breakfasts. Most of the innkeepers, even if they recognized him, were discreet, and we slept in, had breakfast in our room, then would take off on long walks. I had never breathed in so much fresh air in my life. We always returned to our room, my cheeks almost ruby-red from the cold, and made love, curling around each other and sleeping away the late afternoons.

Our time together became something sacred to me, to us both. We shut out the world. He turned down invitations to openings, premieres and parties. We tried to keep our relationship as quiet as possible. But of course, it wasn't long before I saw my name in a tabloid. I actually hadn't spotted it. Charlotte did because she bought the gossip rags every week.

HOLLYWOOD HUNK IN LOVE WITH MOB MURDERER'S DAUGHTER. And there we were, a snapshot taken in Atlantic City. Blurry, out of focus, but definitely me.

"What's the matter, baby?" Vince asked when I showed it to him at his apartment that night, over a bottle of white wine and a dinner of delivered Thai food.

I was shaking. "This…"

"It's a good picture of you."

"But this…I…Tom and I have always lived our lives quietly."

"Quietly? What about last weekend?" His voice was challenging.

The previous weekend, when Vince had arrived to take me to his apartment for the night, Tom was throwing up in the sink, and I was changing the sheets on his bed and crying, begging Tom to knock off the vodka for a day or so. Tom, in between puking, was yelling at me to shut up. He had refused to acknowledge Vince even was there.

"I don't ask you to understand, Vince. I owe it to Tom to care for him, and what we do is private. I just hate the idea of people reading about me. Judging me. I like being invisible."

"I would make myself invisible for you if I could. As it is we stay away from parties and nightlife. You're beautiful. People are curious about you. About the movie. But after a while, it won't be such a hot story. You'll see."

I shook my head. "By then the movie will be over."

"So?"

I bit my lower lip and shrugged.

"What? What are you saying to me? That when the movie is over, we'll be over, too?"

"I don't know."

"You do know. You always know, Ava. That's something I love about you. You're always precisely sure of how you feel about things, even if you don't come out and say it right away."

"Vince…after the movie you'll be shooting another movie. Far away."

He put his ivory chopsticks down and came over and knelt by my chair. I tried not to look into his eyes, which had a way of making me feel an ache in my stomach.

"You know, baby, I used to spend my money on clothes, furniture, art, houses. But now all I can think about is how to spend it on you. Wherever I am, you're flying to visit me or you're coming with me. This isn't ending. I don't care what you say. What Tom says. I won't let it…. I love you."

I said nothing, just looked at him. I was a murderer's daughter. I didn't get to have happy endings. I just couldn't make Vince Quinn believe that. His life was geared toward making people believe in fairy tales, at least on-screen.

Five weeks into the filming, Vince had three scheduled days off. He told me to pack my bags, that we were flying someplace secret. Bring warm-weather clothes. No other hints.

We flew by private jet. He was exhausted by the previous week's filming schedule, in which he'd worked fourteen- and fifteen-hour days. He was sleeping almost as soon as we taxied down the runway for takeoff. I watched him sleep, amazed at how chiseled his features were; how, even with his eyes shut, there was something about his face that literally compelled you to look at him.

I took his hand in mine and turned his palm over, memorizing the lines, bringing his fingers to my lips and kissing them. I leaned my seat back, and holding his hand, I fell asleep.

Five hours later, we landed at LAX airport. He woke, instinctively, when we landed, and I woke because he did.

"Welcome to L.A., baby doll, city of dreams."

"L.A.?" I peered out at the runway, lit only by small lights down on the ground, the air traffic control tower in the distance.

"Yup. I wanted you to see my house. I wanted to show you where I live."

A driver was waiting for us and took us by a Mercedes limousine to Vince's house in the Hollywood Hills. When we passed through the gates and up the driveway, I couldn't help but exhale loudly.

"What?"

"It's enormous! And beautiful. I can picture you here." And in truth, I could, though I couldn't say the same for myself.

The front door was opened by his housekeeper, Rosa, a chubby woman who spoke Spanish to him. He answered in broken Spanish. He introduced me to her, and she smiled warmly and told me she would have a light supper ready for us in about a half hour.

Stepping inside, I felt as if I had walked into a magazine on home design or architecture. I couldn't have described it precisely. Vince later did, telling me that much of the furniture was French Country, or if not that, then antiques he had picked out himself. Vince had not gone to college, but he had educated himself…read books on things that interested him, including antiques and design. Art. He had two paintings by Marc Chagall, and other artists' work hung on the walls, less well-known painters but coveted by collectors.

The overwhelming feeling I got, however, was one of tranquility. He had a fountain flowing into a koi pond in the entranceway. Candles were lit. I felt almost as if I had walked into a church. The ceilings were high and vaulted.

"Come on," he said, taking my hand. "This is what I've been waiting to show you."

He led me through the house to sliding doors that opened onto a pool area and gardens. We stepped outside, and I could see stars twinkling in the sky. I smelled jasmine.

"Just a little farther," he whispered. We stepped to the edge of the garden and there was a teak deck with a table set for supper. And from there, L.A. was lit up in the night sky like a jewel below us, the wind from the Pacific blowing my hair around my face wildly.

"It's—I can't even put it into words."

"I realize it's not Hell's Kitchen," he breathed in my ear, "but could you be happy here?"

I nodded. "I wish it were as simple as that, Vince."

"It can be."

I shook my head.

"It can. Don't be fatalistic."

"I can't help it."

"Just look at how pretty it is. Just be here, with me, in this moment. Okay?"

I nodded. But part of me realized my life with Vince was about moments. As long as we stayed in the present time, with no past and no future, it was perfect. But the minute we left the moment, reality had a way of crashing down upon us like the waves of the Pacific. I was defying my brother each extra moment I was with Vince, and the end of filming was fast approaching.

25

My mother strode across the living room and lit a cigarette. Not my mother, actually, but a woman who looked remarkably like her.

"Come, my babies. Stay up with me."

The actress gathered up the two children playing Tom and me. Carol had been excised from the script in the very way she had cut us from her life, and we, in turn, had chopped her out of ours. When she'd given birth to my one and only niece, we had all shown up for the baptism because my father felt it was the right thing to do, but now Carol's daughter had started kindergarten and we hadn't seen her since she was in diapers.

The child actor playing Tom had pale blue eyes rimmed with thick black lashes, and he had a smattering of freckles across his nose. Prior to winning the role in the movie, he had made a commercial for a hamburger chain. He was adorable, and I looked at the bright lights above the set in an attempt to force the tears in my eyes back into their ducts and to fight the dizzying way my world spun around when I visited Vince on the set. I clenched my fists, digging my nails into the fleshy part of my palm as the little boy, this little Tom clone, allowed the actress playing my mother to engulf him in an embrace. She smelled his hair, just as my mother had sometimes done. The actress had an uncanny way of duplicating my mother's mannerisms.

The girl playing me was named Lulu, and she was an absolute spitfire. Each day Lulu greeted me with a hug, her arms wrapped around my waist. I watched my mother pull her to her side. The little girl looked up at my mother, full of hope. Had I ever looked like that?

"Daddy is going to be away for a little while, children. It will be just us...just us, my darlings."

I couldn't bear it anymore, and I turned on my heel and retreated to Vince's trailer. He had been on the set watching the scene, too, but he followed me.

Shutting the door behind him, he was at my side, stroking my hair. "It's okay, Ava. This is just a movie. It's not exactly what happened. That woman isn't your mother, and that little girl isn't you. It's Lulu."

I pulled away from him. "Let's look at what this scene is, at what's coming up, Vince. My mother out there is going to slit her wrists—Hollywood dramatic license." I paced the trailer, fighting my anxiety. "She's going to cut open her wrists so they can get a little more blood into a film that's already a bloodbath."

"Baby, you know what? I don't think you should stay on the set this week. This is too hard. It's too hard for *me,* so I can't even fathom what this is like for you. Loving you has made every bit of this movie very hard for me. I never cared before. Not about a movie script. Not like this. Some days, I just leave here exhausted."

Despite Tom's rages, Vince and I had continued our affair after L.A. My father was pleased, thinking I might at last settle down—with someone legitimately rich, not pony and shylock and bookmaking rich. I was actually with someone who thought the word *laundering* meant taking your shirts to the dry cleaners, not combining dirty money with legitimate receipts from a saloon, or elsewhere.

"I know. I won't stay here. I just can't. This is just too hard for me, Vince." I reached out a hand to touch a stray strand of hair that fell across his forehead. In the months since our first weekend together, I had marveled at the way a simple gesture, a strand of hair, a hand resting on mine casually during an evening in front of the television set, transported me somewhere else, a place real people lived. A place where, according to Vince, parents kissed their children good-night and read them a book, and the final line before they shut out the light was "Good night…don't let the bed bugs bite," not "If you get hungry in the middle of the night, whatever you do, don't look in the freezer."

Vince engulfed me in a hug and whispered in my ear, always seducing me to the real world. "Let's get away, Ava. Let's go away Friday night. Not out of the city, just over to the Plaza to get away. Room service. Quiet. A walk through Central Park."

"Vince, what you don't ever seem to grasp is I can't run away from what my life is forever. And what's more, I don't know if I'd want to. If you really love me like you say you do, then you would learn to love the ugly parts, too."

"There's nothing ugly about you."

"Bullshit, Vince. What if I told you I killed someone, just like my father? What would you say about me then?"

"But you *haven't* killed anyone."

I turned my back on him.

"What if the sins of the father fell to the daughter, Vince?"

He came behind me and ran his tongue along my neck to my

ear. "I know you, Ava. You're not responsible for the sins of the father. Have you thought about coming with me to those meetings?"

Vince was convinced that half my problems could be solved
by a little twelve-step bullshit. We would go to Al-Anon he said
and tough-love Tom into sobriety. Of course, I suspected Al-
Anon was really a twelve-step cult for the real world and real
people, and they wouldn't let me join and still drink my way from
morning vodka to late-night sleep chaser. Though, with Vince,
even that had slowed down. He kept luring me into the light.

I turned to face him. "I've thought about it. We'll see. Okay?
I just can't even picture Tom accepting help of any kind."

"Okay. No pressure. It's just because I love you, and I see the
way you suffer over him. You know, we both could use some
TLC. Can we go to the Plaza?"

"Sure."

"Tell me you love me."

"Why? You get sacks of fan mail a week. Everyone loves you.
The female population of America and most of the gay men, too."

"You say it. You're the only one who counts."

I pressed my breasts against him and immediately felt his
cock growing hard against my crotch. I kissed him viciously on
the mouth, and he returned my kisses with equal intensity. Then
he pulled away, breathing hard.

"Say it, Ava."

"Say what?" I leaned forward and tried to kiss him again, putting my hand on his cock, and then trying to unbutton his pants.

"Ava…" His hands shook. "God, you drive me fucking crazy.
I've never had sex with anyone like this before—I can't get
enough of you. Ever. But I want you to say you love me. I want
to know you're fucking me."

"Why is this such a big deal?"

"Say it!" He grabbed my face roughly in his hands. "Say it, be-cause I know you feel it."

I struggled free. "I'll see you at the Plaza on Friday night."

"I love you, Ava."

I turned to the door of his trailer. "Me, too," I whispered, and quickly exited, not turning around toward the set to see the ghost of my mother hugging the ghost of me. *Come, my babies. Stay with me.* I heard her. I heard her in the night. Calling me. Calling Tom.

26

Thursday night, my father and Uncle Two appeared on a television talk show, along with De Silva, to continue building the buzz that already swirled around my father and his life, now that the movie would shine its klieg lights over the West Side of New York. Jack Casey was also sitting in a big green armchair as the female host asked him how he felt about being just a few feet away from the men who may very well have flung his uncle off a roof to splatter on the grimy sidewalks of West Fifty-second Street below.

America. We call this entertainment.

Uncle Two wheezed his way through the interview and insisted on lighting a cigar. When the attractive female interviewer told him there was no smoking in the studio, he just looked at her and lit the cigar, anyway. My family. Our reaction to anything like that is to say, "What the fuck? You gonna throw me in jail?" In the first place, because most of them had seen the inside, it was hardly as if jail was the most frightening thing you could hurl at them. A buzz saw, perhaps. A crowbar aimed at their teeth (Black Tom has all caps and major bridgework), and now we may be talking, but what the fuck, as Uncle Two was surely thinking. *What the fuck, exactly?* the hostess must have been thinking. Ah, but this is entertainment, so he lit up. Rules like no smoking and no parking zones are for pussies, my father used to say.

Uncle Two's cigar smoke swirled and curled around his face in the studio. I could practically smell it through the TV screen. De Silva and Daddy sat side by side, the new best friends, and talked about how the streets have a code, and we must admire the men who live it. A code. I could see Jack Casey clench his jaw.

The interviewer, with her apple pie dimples, said to De Silva, "But in the heavily guarded screenplay, word has leaked out about dismemberments, people thrown from roofs, men tossed in front of buses, people killed for gambling debts as little as fifteen hundred dollars. Children raised in the arms of killers. Is this really a 'code,' or is it part of the celebrity we make of death and violence in our society?"

De Silva just smiled. "We're telling a story. I'm not saying we should admire, per se, a man who might toss someone from a rooftop, but then again, I don't think we should sit in judgment, either."

The moral cop-out. It's all okay. Judge it within the context of the neighborhood. That was what we all did. And now America would do the same. My father, in the lexicon of the media, was really just an overgrown teddy bear. In interview after interview, he was characterized as "charming," "gregarious," "sly," "funny" and "an overgrown pit bull puppy." Yeah. And my mother was just a "little" crazy.

Tom sat next to me on his bed, watching the show. We passed a vodka bottle between us.

"You believe this shit?" he asked. "Do you fuckin' believe it?"

I nodded. "Actually, I do."

"Man...fuckin' Casey must be pissed out of his mind. Poor fuckin' bastard."

"Yeah. But he's rich now. So...he sold out, too. He sold the options. He took the book deal. He saw where this was all going when the article came out—maybe even before. He saw it all, but he wants fame as much as the rest of them. And money. He's now TV's talking head on all things mob and gangster. He was on Court TV the other night, commenting on a case."

"So where does that leave us?"

"It leaves us exactly where we were before."

I poured some vodka into my glass and clinked with him.

"What's going on with you and the pretty boy?"

"Pretty boy? Oh...would that be my *boyfriend*, Vince?"

"When this movie's over, Ava, you guys are finished. You know it. I know it." He stared at me, his eyes like sheer blue cliffs of ice in Antarctica. "I think Vince even knows it. Come on...you're from here, baby. This is where you belong. He gonna move down here to Hell's Kitchen? Gonna come and hang with us in this dump?"

"No."

"You gonna go to Hollywood with all the plastic people? All the silicone sluts who're always gonna be hanging on him? You gonna leave me, Ava?"

I looked at my Tom. "No, Tom. No...I wouldn't do that. I wouldn't leave you."

He leaned over, his eyes glassy, and kissed my neck. "Good girl, Ava. Good girl. Just play it out for the movie, baby, and have some fun, but in the end, it's you and me. We've got each other. We can trust each other."

After our fight when I returned from Vegas to an apartment in shambles, we never spoke of Vince again—until now. He said nothing when I left for weekends or the night, but I lived more cautiously when I was home, always sensing that he was closer than ever to harming me. Then I would force the thought from my mind. He would never hurt me, I told myself. I was his Ava, and he was my Tom, as we had been from the first time I curled my tiny infant fingers around his little-boy pinky and we stared into each other's eyes, my father said, the day I was brought home from the hospital in a pink bunting.

Later that night, long after Tom passed out, I couldn't sleep. We had taped the interview, and I went to the living room, took the tape as Tom lay sleeping, and brought it back to my room and popped it into the VCR. After the in-studio interview, there was a montage of images, old photographs, and a narrator's voice-over. The faces of people I loved flashed on the screen. Uncle Two and Dad had given the TV program photos. There we all were. Two-Times and Rocky. Tom in a Halloween costume, when he had dressed up as a cowboy. My father as a young man, handsome and gangly, yet with a charisma that made him stand out in a photo of five guys mugging for the camera in an old bar called the Twilight, a place where it wasn't safe to enter unless you were known by the regulars. My mother on her wedding day. My father's father. My aunt Brenda, long dead from ovarian cancer. They floated past on the TV screen.

I laughed at a picture from a long-ago Christmas. It had ended in a poker match of epic proportions that lasted all night. The grown-ups were so concerned about who was drawing an inside straight that Tom and Carol and I, and little Rocky, and Uncle Charley's daughter by his girlfriend at the time, all stayed up playing with our Christmas gifts until we literally passed out from exhaustion on the floor or on our beds. Tom and I slept in one bed, I remember, and Rocky slept in another. Carol slept in her room. And Charley's daughter Lisa fell asleep under the

Christmas tree. Some time in the night, someone put a coat over her to keep her warm. We had eaten Christmas cookies until I was certain I would never want another green-leaf cookie with chocolate icing in the center again. And all the while, as we had played Operation and Battleship and dolls and cowboys and Indians, Tom with his new toy gun, we were comforted by the sounds, not of Christmas carols, but of the shouted "fucks" and "assholes" from the other room as the men grew louder and laughed harder. They were happy. They were closer than brothers, the best of friends. No one was in jail. They had bought us everything we wanted, and their wives and girlfriends were decked out in new jewelry. The picture of that Christmas remained frozen on the screen as the show went to commercial.

After the commercials, which I sped through on fast-forward, came the pictures from Riker's Island, the mug shots, the photo of Rocky so far gone on heroin he looked like a walking cadaver. The shot of my mother's headstone. The photos and remnants of the other side of that life. Why couldn't it all be about Christmas?

But I knew.

Shortly after that Christmas, King Conway was busted for the only thing they had on him—income tax evasion. So my father and Uncle Two-Times and Pinky took over his shylock business, a little shy, a lot of book, collecting even though the King was locked away. And that meant more people pushed in front of buses, more people thrown from rooftops. Because in order to collect from the citizens of the West Side, from the neighborhood people who were inclined to borrow from a man like King Conway, you needed respect.

So I had grown up, not hating the way my father earned his living, but hating the cops and the feds who put King Conway

away, and then later put my father away. Left alone, the neighborhood had a system that worked just fine. But when the real
world came knocking, it wasn't Christmas anymore.

27

I never had dreams of real life. When I was a little girl, I didn't dream of being a ballerina. I don't recall ever wanting to be anything when I grew up. I didn't, like other girls in New York City, long to have tea at the Plaza and skate around the ice at Rockefeller Center.

As time went on with Vince, I had to stop myself from dreaming of that elusive "real life." Tom was right. When the movie was over, where could we go? Where could we exist? Vince had flown his widowed father to New York to meet me. Mr. Brown—Quinn was a stage name—was a dairy farmer, a sweet man, lonely, anxious for Vince to settle down with a woman not from the Hollywood establishment, and create a real life, make babies. Of course, the Roofer's daughter wasn't what he had in mind. He had twisted his linen napkin around his large fingers, thick with arthritis, at the lunch we had, nervous around me, nervous in the city. His eyes were pale like Vince's, but Mr. Brown's were rheumatic and yellowish. Vince sent him enough money that he never had to work his farm another day, but still, Vince said, he rose and tended the farm because it was how he was. He awoke before dawn and went to bed shortly after sundown.

Vince had a sister named Carla, and a niece and nephew by her and her husband. He had bought them a house in the same Iowa community he'd grown up in, and he'd set up trust funds for his niece and nephew, so that even if they chose to go to Harvard, they would never have a single student loan, book or bill to pay for. Vince did all these things, but he found himself increasingly separated from his family by this gulf of experience they could never understand. They couldn't know what it was like to have lies written about you in the magazines—to have your every word and move dissected, to order a Perrier instead of a beer and have it interpreted that you were struggling to quit drinking, to go out for the paper without shaving and have your photo taken and plastered in the supermarket tabloid revealing that you were a drug addict. They couldn't understand, no matter what he bought them, how wealth really does change everything. Why he needed a housekeeper and a gardener when he knew perfectly well how to keep any kind of plant and how to do his own laundry. Vince was isolated from the very people he loved, and maybe that was why he clung to me and loved me, even as I understood what Tom said to me.

I arrived at the Plaza, not with dreams, but with a sense of resignation. We would enjoy what we had, enjoy it here in this city with the dreams of a million others—but not mine.

I spotted him across the lobby and noticed how my heartbeat quickened. No one else would notice it. I didn't flush. Didn't smile. But my heart beat faster in anticipation of the moment we were alone. I never tired of his body, of his touch, even if it was just as simple as his hand wrapped around mine as we strolled Central Park.

Our room was, like the other rooms where we had stayed, filled with flowers and opulent. We ordered room service and made love, slowly, him licking his way down my belly and making me squirm, waiting for the feel of his tongue on me between my legs, dying for him to enter me, to pull him into me. His cock was made for me, I thought. It was as if I had waited my whole life to find him.

After we made love, we decided to take a bath, candles lit around us. We soaked in silence, a peace settling over us. Vince's shoulders, tense from a week of filming, were softening. I felt a stillness. The world became this room. I tried to force dreams of something more from my mind. Tom's voice echoed and reverberated off the marble walls and floor of the bathroom. *But in the end, it's you and me.*

We climbed out of the tub, still afraid, I think, to break this pure stillness, this complete symbiosis. Vince toweled me dry and helped me into my robe, and then, holding my hand, we went to the couch and turned on the television. We lay there, his back against the arm of the sofa, me between his legs, his chest my pillow, and watched television until we both were so sleepy our lids were heavy.

"I love you, Ava." He stroked my hair. The way my mother used to. Soothing. Gentle.

"I know."

"I could stay here forever."

"Me, too. I wish I could. Really. Stay here forever."

"Ready for bed?"

I nodded, and we made our way to the king-size bed, shutting off the television in the sitting room and turning on the one in the bedroom.

Curling around me, he said again, "I love you."

Now that we were in the dark and I faced the TV and not him, I nodded. "I love you, too. I love you from a space that was never touched before."

"Me, too," he whispered, though I didn't think he could really know what I meant. Soon he was sound asleep. So was I—I thought.

Maybe it was the stillness. In the middle of the night, I awoke with a start. I lifted his arm from around me and tiptoed into the bathroom. From lying on the pillow, I had sheet marks creasing my cheek. I looked into the mirror at myself and knew. In the end, all I would ever have was Tom.

Part Three

Daddy's Wake: Night Three

In revenge and in love woman is more barbarous than man.

—*Friedrich Nietzsche*

28

The third night of the wake was so crowded that people milled on the sidewalk waiting to pay their respects. Besides the neighborhood faces, journalists snapped pictures, TV crews were double-parked, and most of the movie cast and crew were there, from the grips and drivers to De Silva. All but Vince.

Uncle Two-Times pulled me aside, toward a large floral arrangement of a horseshoe done up in red carnations, sent by Boxcar Flynn. Uncle Two bent his head to me, speaking in a loud whisper, his forehead practically touching mine.

"Why isn't Vince here?"

"Uncle Two, we've been broken up for a while now. He doesn't have to be here. Besides, I hear he's off filming in Toronto or something."

"If Quinn was a stand-up guy, he'd be here."

"Yeah, well...you don't know what happened. If I were him, I wouldn't be here, either." I pulled back and grinned at Uncle

Two, trying to mask how I absolutely ached that Vince wasn't there, yet dreaded the idea of seeing him in this crowd of people, anyway.

"You okay with that? Really okay with it?"

I nodded. Ever since Rocky died, Uncle Two and I had become co-conspirators over Tom's alcohol and drug use, tried to shield my father from it. Two had a daughter about six years younger than Rocky who had moved to California. He had a grandson by her whom he had never seen. His daughter had discovered, through therapy, that her family was dysfunctional. Big news flash. She also didn't want to speak with her father ever again, which broke Uncle Two's heart a second time, their break coming six months after Rocky died. Uncle Two told me his daughter had died in a way, but he hadn't even had a casket to weep over or a gravestone to visit. All he had was the knowledge that she was out in "Flake Land," as he called California, with a Jewish husband and a kid who didn't know he had a grandpa who would have gone to prison two times over for a chance to take him for an ice cream.

"Yes. I'm okay with that, Uncle Two."

"I don't think it's right you guys breakin' up."

"I know. But…we tried, Uncle Two. We just had too much to overcome."

"Sounds like therapy talk to me," he said, suspicious of anyone with a sheepskin on the wall and a couch.

I stood on tiptoes and kissed him on the cheek. "I love you, Uncle Two."

He just clasped me to him. My arms were barely able to encircle him in return.

Out of the corner of my eye, I spotted De Silva walking toward me.

"Ava, love…so sorry about your father."

"Thanks." I released Uncle Two and stood with my hands clasped in front of me.

"He was one of a kind." De Silva hugged me, though I didn't hug him back. He shook Two's hand and clapped him on the back. Then Uncle Two waved to Trigger Smith and excused himself, leaving me alone with De Silva.

"Vince here?"

"No."

He shook his head. "I would have thought he'd show...I'm surprised."

I shrugged. "Don't judge him."

"If you were mine, Ava, I'd be here."

"I'm not yours...and I'm not Vince's anymore."

"Wouldn't matter."

De Silva had a girlfriend. She was an actress mostly known for being De Silva's girlfriend. With a quirky smile and a nose that looked like the botched result of a plastic surgeon on a bender, she was also known as a bitch, but I'd heard my father say she could suck the chrome off of a Cadillac, so she obviously had a certain charm with De Silva. Now he moved closer to me.

"You need anything, you call me."

"Thanks."

"I mean it. Even if it's the middle of the night...you need someone to talk to...you call me, I'll send my car."

I thanked him, but couldn't avoid his kiss on my cheek that lingered, as always, too long. Then I weaved through the crowd to the ladies' room. I always felt like I had to wash my hands two or three times after I touched De Silva.

Coming out of the ladies' room, I spotted Tom and a cop friend of his heading toward the men's room with conspiratorial looks on their faces. I shook my head and knew we were starting a very long night.

* * *

John's was definitely in violation of the fire code. With people packed five deep at the bar, I couldn't even squeeze past and would have to wait for someone to go to the men's room or toward the back for me to move a few feet.

Tom was lining up shots with his cop friend, a guy named Jimmy O'Toole, at a booth in the back. His pupils were pinpoints, and he was clenching his jaw.

"Ava, baby, you know Jimmy, right?"

I nodded, glancing around John's for Uncle Two. I knew he was my only hope for hauling Tom back home when the sum total of the evening toppled him.

Jimmy pulled me to him. I hated him. Hated the smell of Polo cologne, thick on him. Hated the medallion of St. Christopher he wore. Hated everything about him, because I knew that he wanted to fuck me, and I also knew that he had a never-ending supply of cocaine, courtesy of a dealer he turned a blind eye to.

"When are you going to let me buy you dinner, Ava?"

"You know, Jimmy, I'm burying my father tomorrow. How about a little respect?" I loved how we all tossed that word around. No honor among thieves.

"Ava!" Tom snapped at me. "Jimmy's a good guy. How about cuttin' him some slack?"

I smiled and said, "Let me have one of those shots, boys."

Downing the vodka, I eyed my brother and prayed for Two to get to John's. I didn't breathe easy until he showed up a half hour later. We exchanged looks from across the room. I worked my way through the crowd, preferring the heat and bodies packed tight near the bar over Jimmy's wandering hands. Uncle Two, Uncle Charley, Black Tom, Mick and Benny C-note and I stood nursing our drinks and laughing over old stories. Sure, I'd heard about the time they'd hidden a body in the back of Benny C-note's sister's car and then she'd decided to take a surprise trip to Atlantic City, not realizing the contents of her trunk, but the story was still funny the tenth time around, particularly when Benny C. acted out the phone call he got. Not just from his sister in Atlantic City, but from his ninety-year-old mother, who'd smacked him for being so stupid. Not for killing—for being so stupid.

And then the men turned nostalgic, telling tales of my father, and even my mother. There was a progression; first told were stories of my dad's boyhood. He had once descended into the basement of the tenement he and his parents lived in, turned on the light and surprised a rat the size of a small cat gnawing on the body of another rat. My father, then ten years old, found an ax, hanging on the wall with some old tools, covered in dust and dull-edged, and whacked at the rat, not killing it until the third or fourth whack. Blood splattered everywhere—and rats can squeal surprisingly loud. I got the heebies just listening to them laughing over it. My father had emerged from the basement the toughest boy in the neighborhood. You can whack a rat *that* size to pieces, you can do a lot of things at ten years old.

As they reminisced, Uncle Charley told the one about when my father first laid eyes on my mother. "Mary was the prettiest girl in the dance hall. And every guy wanted to dance with her, but she just shook her head no to each guy who asked. She was holding hands with her best girlfriend—what was her name, Two?"

"Anita."

"Yeah. She wasn't moving from this Anita's side. So your father sees all these guys just shot down, boom, boom, boom. No, she ain't dancin' with any of 'em. So your father knows this guy, Ugly Bobby Fitzgerald, who ain't ugly at all, but the best-lookin' Mick on the whole West Side. He figures he can't lose if he can get Ugly Bobby to ask Anita to dance because she'll say yes and then your mother will say yes to your dad."

"It must have worked," I said, laughing at my father's scheme. "I'm standing here."

"Bingo," said Uncle Charley. "It worked, all right."

Next, they told me the story of the drill sergeant, which of course I'd heard before. Then his prison stints. My mother's death, and how broken up my father was. They went from stories of boyhood bravery and young love to the spiral of the Westies and loan-sharking, the book, the vig, the points, the beatings. Yet still we all laughed. We filled our glasses, and I realized, as we stood in a small circle, sweating in the crowded bar, that this was my family. These men and Tom were all I had left.

At the thought of Tom, I looked to the back of the bar. I could see he was no longer able to stand but was slumped in a booth, his head back against the filthy wall of the bar, Jimmy slapping his face trying to rouse him.

"Uncle Two?" I caught his eye. Without a word, we left the men to continue their tribute to my father and pushed our way to the back booths. Uncle Two cut through the crowd, and I put my hand into his belt loop and sort of rode to the back in his wake. It reminded me of days spent riding atop his shoulders or my father's, or dances on my father's feet, my little stockinged feet on his shoes, as we played old records in the living room. For the first time, I felt a surge of grief stab my heart, a physical pain that reminded me my father was gone forever.

Two and I reached the table, and he pulled Tom up on his feet. It was of little use. I glared at Jimmy, though he likely thought that was a look of love, he was so obliterated himself. Two, Tom and I went out the back door, Two maneuvering Tom on one side, me on the other. Tom's feet literally dragged on the floor, sweeping through old beer, streams of piss and, in the alley, trash and half-eaten food. I stifled a gag.

We dragged him to our apartment, then lugged him up the stairs. Two helped me push him on the pullout sofa.

"Don't let his shoes touch the sheets," I begged, staring at the filth we'd tracked home.

Uncle Two nodded, pulling them off Tom's feet. I fought the urge to vomit, but Uncle Two didn't even flinch. He was stone-faced. I couldn't help but think of Rocky. He had been so good-looking with his curly brown hair and big eyes with lashes that curled like a little boy's, and he'd been the funniest kid I knew before he fell in love with heroin. I know my father urged Uncle Two to toss Rocky out, to stop giving him money, to "knock some sense into him." But Two resolutely refused.

Tom began to gag. We rolled him on his side.

"Do you think we should take him to a hospital?" I asked Two.

"Tomorrow's the funeral. We do that, and he maybe misses his own father's funeral. Now, that's not right. We'll sit here with him all night. We'll sit here. You sleep for two hours. Then me. And we watch him."

"I can't sleep. You go lie on my bed. I'll come get you when I start feeling sleepy. I'll watch him."

"Ava...your father's funeral..."

"Two. Go."

Reluctantly, he rose. He paused, as if he wanted to say something to me. He even inhaled, as if gathering his thoughts. But then he thought better of it and just kissed the top of my head and went into my bedroom to sleep for first shift.

I sat down in a chair next to the pull-out bed and watched Tom sleep. His face was beautiful in the half light of the small table lamp in the corner of our living room. His hair fell across his forehead, boyishly. He had circles beneath his eyes, but other than that, he showed no signs, when sleeping, of the way insanity had come to roost on his shoulder. My Tom.

He wasn't always like this. He wasn't always sick.

29

The person Tom admired most growing up was my uncle George. He was a cop. He had a badge and a gun. He was one of the good guys.

I remember when we were very little, before my mother killed herself, we would sit, rapt, around Uncle George as he told us stories that weren't all that different from Pinky's. We learned to see the world as a gray land of neither black nor white. You were simply on the side that didn't get caught. We switched alliances often and maintained a neutrality that would shame Switzerland, though Tom seemed partial to Uncle George's escapades, memorizing them and then making me act them out later.

Pinky told stories of detectives on the take, of an FBI agent who took book over on Fifty-first in his bar, and cops who saw crimes happening right in their own neighborhoods but were too stupid to really figure out what was going on. He told us stories of men who held guns to the temples of their enemies, or who pistol-whipped former friends and colleagues in dingy basements of bars known for keeping actual testicles in jars behind the bartender, alongside the bottles of cheap vodka and gin. And Uncle George told us stories about the "bad guys," men who used guns and knives to commit crimes that seemed *remarkably* similar to the crimes our father and Two-Times committed.

After my mother's suicide, my father went, in the words of his friends, "off the rails," for a time. I didn't understand this, as the words seemed to have something to do more with trains than Daddy, who, I knew, never took a train to work. But off the rails he was. He spent long hours in John's, drinking until he punished and drove out whatever it was inside that made him moan when he tried to sleep in the bed that had been theirs. He usually slept on the couch, or he came into my room and slept on my bed, curled around me, in a fetal position, snoring.

We never saw him actually drink in John's. He usually deposited me, Carol, Tom and Rocky outside on the stoop of John's, with a small bag of marbles. Then he held up, with some ceremony, a crisp five dollar bill, and said, "I will give you kids this five dollar bill here—and that's a lot of candy—if you can stack these marbles in a pyramid. It can be done. You just have to figure out the secret."

It never occurred to us that there *was* no secret. Every bar trick in John's we had ever witnessed had a stunt behind it. There was, indeed, a way to pull a dollar bill out from beneath a shot glass full of liquor without toppling the glass or spilling a drop. There was even a way, using a bar towel, to steady the hand of someone with the d.t.'s so he could literally pull a drink up to his mouth without splashing the booze all over the bar. So when Daddy told us to stack the marbles into a pyramid, we never questioned that we were being played for baby fools. Instead, the four of us sat outside trying desperately to win five dollars. We would manipulate our tiny little hands around the cat's eyes and agates and try to stack them—to no avail. While we did this outside, scheming and plotting and thinking of every trick we could, my father drank vodka until he emerged hours later, drunk and subdued, sometimes angry, with Uncle Two by his side.

Our refuge was Uncle George. He was similar to my father in coloring, with the O'Neil family dimple in the chin, but he was made spectacularly beautiful, elegant even, by his dress blues, and by his physique, which was honed by weight lifting and jogging five miles a day. In the neighborhood, he wasn't like anyone we knew. He even went to college—St. John's. Our greatest treat was being invited to go to St. John's basketball games.

My father and his brother had an uneasy truce between them. Uncle George wasn't a totally straight-and-narrow cop. He gambled and he drank, and though they fought the way my father fought with many people in his life, we never doubted that they loved each other. Though of course, back then, we knew men in my father's crew didn't *love* each other. Hugs were for pussies— at best they gave a drunken back-clap at Christmastime. Handshakes ruled the street. But we knew they were brothers, and that meant something. Uncle George was a good guy, but he was also smart, and wickedly funny, and he attracted all the best-looking women in any bar he visited, so even the neighborhood bad guys didn't mind him too much. They gladly took his leftovers.

A year or so after my mother died, I guess I was eight or nine, my father had to spend eleven months at Riker's for a possession-of-stolen-property charge, along with having beaten up a cop at the time of his arrest. My father sustained four broken ribs, though the cop had to have his jaw wired shut. Still, the cop hadn't followed perfect procedures, which opened the door to a plea bargain, perhaps helped along by Uncle George's many connections. My father accepted the deal. Uncle George and his new wife, Aunt Charlene, became our surrogate parents.

Though Tom missed my father, and he cried surreptitiously when we had to say our goodbyes, he thought Uncle George was a superhero. Getting to stay with him was something that Tom had dreamed of, something he later told me he felt guilty about, as if he had willed my father to prison—as if my father could be willed to do anything.

"Bang-bang, Ava." Tom aimed his finger like a toy gun at me at bedtime, the first night after Uncle George and Aunt Charlene tucked us in. They had sublet their apartment and moved in with us, because we had a three-bedroom and there was room for us all, even if Carol's bedroom really wasn't much bigger than a closet.

"What are you doing?" I whispered into the darkness.

"I'm shooting you. You're the bad guy."

"Am not."

"Yes," he said firmly. "You are a moll."

"A what?" I asked, missing my father, aching for my mother. Aunt Charlene smelled of beer in the same way Uncle Two did, and I found this very un-Mommylike. She had long black hair and she frosted the pieces up front and wore blue eyeshadow.

"A moll. Uncle George and I watched *Bonnie and Clyde* today. Bonnie was a moll. A lady bad guy. And I'm a G-man. I'm a *good* guy. You be a bad girl."

"I don't want to be a bad girl," I whispered into the night. "*You* be a bad guy, you big jerk. I'll be a G-man."

Tom climbed out of bed. He was wearing Spider-Man underwear with a matching T-shirt. "I can't be a bad guy. And you can't be a G-man. You can't be a policeman, Ava, because you're a *girl*. You are *so* dumb, Ava. A big stinkin' dummy. I'm Spider-Man. That makes me a good guy."

"Then how come you have a gun? Spider-Man doesn't have a gun."

"Now I'm not Spider-Man. I'm Uncle George. He's a police-man. And he's a good guy."

"I'm not being a moll."

"Fine. We'll make *Carol* the moll." He crossed his arms and stared at me expectantly.

"Okay."

This agreed with me just fine.

My father didn't believe in us visiting him when he was in pris-on. He said there were "bad elements" in prison that he didn't want us exposed to. So we wrote to him. Whether my aunt Charlene actually mailed these letters, full of giant *X*'s and *O*'s and kisses—"S.W.A.K."—I have no idea. Aunt Charlene made us lunches for school, and she helped us with our homework, but when we looked into her eyes, they were flat, like two dirty brown buttons. She had married Uncle George, in love with his good looks, and he had married, my father said, the neighborhood beauty queen—with a real fine "rack." But whether she counted on being instant mom-my to three kids whose mother had just died, I doubt it. She wouldn't even wash me in the tub. She said she didn't know how. So Tom washed my hair, and he got water up my nose most of the time. I missed my mother every day until the feeling that I would throw up missing her faded to a pain like a perpetual stone in my belly.

My father sent us letters once every week or so, one for each of us.

Dear Ava,
    Hope you are being a good girl for Uncle George and that you are listening to him and Aunt Charlene. I'm okay.

My roommate is a guy I know from the neighborhood a long time ago. So it's not so bad. I can't wait to come home. I want pizza. With pepperoni.

I miss you, baby doll. When I come home we'll watch us the Creature Feature.

Love you,
Your Daddy

Roommate. Like Dad was off at summer camp.

As we spent our time with Uncle George, he taught Tom about his gun—how to clean it, how to load it. He told Tom, in "men talk" I was forbidden to listen in on but did, anyway, about different arrests he'd made, and about women who sold their bodies, about good versus evil, about men who thought they could pull one over on Uncle George. It never occurred to me, then, how very much like my father Uncle George was. My father was the center of all the action, but so was Uncle George. In the way he told it, there wasn't a single bust in the city that didn't "go down" without him being in the know about at least part of it. He cultivated "rats"—guys who turned on their buddies. In general, Uncle George was just someone you didn't want to mess with.

So the first time Uncle George came into my bed while Tom was sleeping, and slid his hand down my underwear, and touched me, then left without a word, I never thought that what he did was wrong. Uncle George was one of the good guys. He had a gun. He was a G-man. I thought that meant a good man.

30

I can't remember what kind of toothpaste I used as a little girl. I can't remember what I had for dinner on October 2, 1978. Or any specific day for that matter. I can't remember whether I wore my hair in a ponytail on the first day of second grade. The details are lost. They are a part of the vague recollections of childhood where huge gaps blend together. A single instant might jump out when a person recalls second grade or third grade. A single present—a bicycle, maybe—or a special occasion may come to the fore, but the rest, the day-in, day-out, is lost forever. It's just a blur, like zipping by a forest at high speed in a car. Can you recall a specific leaf on a tree? Childhood—life—blends together unless something calls a detail to mind.

So it was with Uncle George.

I cannot remember what days he touched me, how his hand stroked me down in my underwear, how he forced my hand to touch him as his monstrous thing grew hard then soft, then hard again, how he forced me to look at it or to lick it. I can't remember when he did it or how he got me alone. I cannot recall, because for me, touching Uncle George was as routine as brushing my teeth. I could no sooner remember brushing my teeth on any specific morning than I could recall touching him. I only knew that after brushing my teeth, I didn't kneel at my bed and beg my mother to come from heaven and rescue me. If she couldn't rescue me, then I hoped she could kill me. In this way, life with Uncle George was different from watching toothpaste spit swirl down the sink.

I grew withdrawn. Even Uncle Two noticed.

"Come on, kid," he had coaxed me with a small bag of jelly beans. "Your uncle George and aunt Charlene ain't so bad. And your dad will be home soon enough. So you don't be sad, Ava."

He patted my head and brushed his thumb against my cheek, worry in his eyes.

I tried to make him not worry. I tried to behave. When Uncle George used to show me his gun, and tell me that bad things happen to girls who don't keep secrets…and to their brothers, and to the people they love, I tried to take myself far away. I would look at a spot on the wall, illuminated by our night-light, a little gray spot where the paint and spackle failed to fully cover an old nail hole. I would stare at it until I was away, free, in heaven with my mother, soaring and flying with Mommy. Her hugs in heaven were like a breeze, not solid arms, that swept me away over the city to someplace far away with green grass and tall trees, and butterflies and flowers. She smiled a lot, my mother did. Heaven agreed with her. When she called me darling, it wasn't with the desperation of earth, but the peaceful love of the angels. After traveling through the sky with her, I would come back into my body. Then I would become a rock. Cold, hard. And oblivious of Uncle George, his hot breath in my ear. He was far away. Like an echo from across a field in heaven.

Still, though I traveled to heaven with my mother and visited her often, I lived life in a daze. My teachers gave up on me, assuming my mother's death and my father's unfortunate incarceration meant I was disturbed. I couldn't be expected to read Dr. Seuss with all that was going on in my life. Uncle George told my third-grade teacher that he and his wife were doing the best they could "under the circumstances," and Mrs. O'Leary clucked her tongue and agreed. He was a great man, my uncle, taking in three kids on a cop's salary.

So his nightly visits continued, at least nights he wasn't on duty. He would wake me up after Tom and I fell asleep. I have no idea what Aunt Charlene thought. She divorced him years later, anyway. All I knew was each time I landed back into my body with a thud, he was there. He was always there.

He convinced me he loved me. Not love like an uncle loves a niece, a dad loves a daughter, a brother loves a sister. He said ours was a love that surpassed the ages, a love like Romeo and Juliet's. A love that no one would understand. That's why it had to be a secret. And because I was an O'Neil, I was used to keeping secrets. Uncle George said he would protect me, marry me, love me for all times. I was his Ava. He made me stand before him, my hair in a little bun he arranged himself, tendrils falling about my face like the *Playboy* models of the day, naked, and smile at him. He loved me. And in my world, love was in short supply. So when he told me that when I grew up and turned fourteen he would take me to Maryland and marry me, where it was legal to marry a fourteen-year-old girl, I believed him. He had convinced me, brainwashed me. "We" were victims of a society that couldn't understand that what we shared was beyond the love of ordinary people. What we had was something other people would envy. They would be jealous. So we would have to keep it between us, this sacred pact.

I remember we had this ritual. He would make me use hand cream. Jergens hand cream. He would pour some in my palm and make me rub my hands together until they were slippery and creamy and moist. Then I could touch him. Only then. It made moving my hand up and down him easier, though still my arm cramped.

And afterward, before I went to sleep. He made me recite, "And now I lay me down to sleep, I pray the Lord my soul to keep. If I should die before I wake, I pray the Lord my soul to take."

My life was lived in two psychotic halves. There was Day Ava, the girl who dressed in knee socks and the plaid jumper of the Catholic school we attended and played at being street cop and damsel in distress with Tom, and there was Night Ava, who flew to heaven with her mother while pleading for the Lord to take her soul.

Uncle George singled me out, lavishing attention on me and ignoring Carol, further driving a wedge between us. And Tom was too full of hero worship to suspect anything.

When my father was released from prison, I was literally quivering with excitement. Not only had I missed him, I understood that with my father home, Night Ava could go away. Uncle George seemed to understand it, too. The night before my father came home, he finally tried to penetrate me for the first time, angry, bitter, urging me not to forget that I was his. I remember only a very sharp pain, and then my mother descending from heaven to take me away. My darling, she whispered, and I looked down on my own body, on the bed, the humping figure of Uncle George on top of me, the way an oversexed dog humps someone's leg, and then Mommy and I left the apartment through the window and out over the city, sparkling with lights and traffic.

The next day, my father came home and looked, for the first time I could remember, rough and scary. He was unshaven, and he seemed to have grown wrinkles while he was away, but at the sight of me and Tom and Carol, his face crinkled into a smile that took away the tiredness. Uncle Two-Times, who'd seemed so worried about me, pushed me toward my father, pushed me toward my salvation. Daddy was home. I clasped my hands around his neck, breathing him in. My eyes felt hot, and my throat burned. I would no longer need to visit my mother in heaven. I could be Day Ava again.

I believed this.

I also believed in Santa Claus and the Tooth Fairy.

Day Ava was happy for a time. Tom and I invented elaborate games of cops and robbers, and Tom told me how he was going to be like Uncle George.

"He was in the newspaper, Ava."

Tom could read. I was behind in school. I could read words with three or four letters, and it helped if they rhymed. Like *Cat in the Hat*. Crook in a book.

"He caught a drug dealer, Ava. The mayor's going to give him a medal."

I shrugged. Was Uncle George the evil man my mother told me he was in whispered dreams, or was he my future husband, as he told me? I was never sure.

Tom stood on his bed, jumping up and down as if it was a trampoline, in his underwear. "I am king of New York. I am Super Cop! And you are under arrest."

I shrugged. "Am not."

"Are, too!"

"Am not!"

"Are, too!"

My father poked his head into our room. "Tom…how many times do I have to tell you not to jump on your bed? 'Cause if you fall and crack your head open, I'll make Pinky put the stitches in."

Tom stopped jumping immediately. Though we both liked Pinky, we had seen even Uncle Two and Black Tom wince at kitchen-table stitches.

"And what are you still doing in your underwear?" Daddy asked.

Tom didn't answer.

"And what are you wearing, Ava?" He looked at me, puzzled. Instead of my usual pink nightgown, I was wearing a cast-off pair of Superman underwear from Tom and a Superman T-shirt. I wanted to look like a boy. I wanted to *be* a boy. If I was a boy, then Uncle George wouldn't want to marry me.

"I want to be like Tom."

Daddy rolled his eyes. "Jesus Christ, we need a woman around this place. Well——" he crossed his arms and smiled, eyes now twinkling as only an O'Neil's can when teasing "——I guess you two kids don't want to go to the candy store and then to John's if you're still in your underwear at lunchtime. But that's okay, I guess. I mean, I could go by myself…I can ask Uncle Two to come with me and leave you with Grandma O'Neil."

The Russian knuckle-slapper!

"Ah!" I shrieked. Tom and I ran around our little bedroom. With our two twin beds in there, we had just a two-foot-wide pathway down the middle of the room to walk. We raced from one end of the room to the other, knocking each other over like in a bad Keystone Kops film, and tried to dress ourselves as quickly as possible, all the while screaming and squealing.

We were fully ready in three minutes; all the while my father laughed. I remember slipping my hand in his to go down to John's. I leaned my head against his waist and nuzzled into his belly.

"Hey there, baby," he said, lifting me up. "You miss your old man while he was gone?"

I was unable to speak. I started crying, the sobs rising up from my gut in great gasps. Dad clutched me to him. "Hey, baby, it's okay," he shushed me. "Daddy's home now."

Tom came running over. "Don't cry, Ava." He rubbed my back and took my hand and squeezed it. And as suddenly as I had started crying, I stopped. I let Tom and Daddy love me and protect me, and I believed my world was returning to normal. It would be okay. Tom looked up at me in Daddy's arms and winked at me. I smiled wanly. Daddy put me down.

"Ready?"

I nodded.

He mussed my hair. "That's my girl." We knocked on Carol's bedroom door. No, she didn't want to come. She was old enough to stay home alone. So off we went to the candy store to peruse the Necco wafers and Life Savers. Then to John's for Cokes and maraschino cherries. Maybe because I had cried, Dad didn't ask us to stack marbles in a pyramid. Instead Tom and I shared a bar stool and practiced bar tricks and played at sword fights with the little cocktail straws. Tom let me win…because he loved me.

That night, I slept peacefully, and my mother didn't visit me. I knew all was well. And it would have remained so.

If my father hadn't violated his parole.

31

Justice moves quickly or slowly, depending on whose side you're on.

My father was picked up for RICO-related charges for running book in the neighborhood. RICO, as even I knew as a third-grader, was, in the words of Pinky, "The way they get you when they got nothin' to get you on."

By the time my father left for prison again when I was ten, it was an open secret that Aunt Charlene was hiding bottles of gin underneath her bed and small fifths in the pockets of Uncle George's winter coat in the hall closet. The day I had to say good-bye to my father, I resolved to die. Inside I turned to a statue. I traveled far away to a place I cannot describe, a world for little girls who need to die but don't know how many pills to take or how, exactly, to rig a hangman's noose.

My father served nearly two years. I served two years in Uncle George's prison. I don't remember most of that time. All I remember is Tom.

He dressed me. He held my hand. He whispered to me in the night as dreams twisted and turned and grew dark as a moon-less night.

"Mommy came to visit me," I finally confessed to him one night when I saw her hovering near the ceiling.

"She's an angel, Ava." He sat next to me, holding my hand, his lip quivering.

"Why are you crying?" I asked him.

"Because you're scaring me."

"Why?"

"'Cause you can't *really* see Mommy."

"I can."

And then he broke down. He cried, shoulders shaking and his trembling hand wiping his little-boy brow. He stifled the noise, biting his hand, not wanting Aunt Charlene to hear him.

I touched his cheek. "Don't cry, Tom."

He couldn't even speak.

"I won't talk about Mommy anymore. I promise. Just don't cry."

I remember he slumped down to the floor. I climbed out of bed and sat next to him, more terrified than ever. I knew I was bound to my secrets, but I wanted to tell him. I wanted to tell him why I was confused. Why I could not sleep.

But I didn't.

When my father was released from prison this time, he was nearly a stranger to us. We had grown and changed in the way of children who overnight go from freckle-faced, almost-babies in long-john pj's and bare feet, to sulking adolescents, baby teeth long gone to the Tooth Fairy.

I tried to be the Ava he remembered. We watched the Crea-ture Feature. We went to John's. We ordered pizza and played blackjack for Apple Jacks and pennies. I watched the fights with him, and we listened to Bobby Darin sing "Mack the Knife" over and over and over again. But he was different, darker, and more angry at the police than ever. This led to a falling-out with Uncle George, who, a short time later, disappeared, just disappeared from his apartment and his life; I both missed him and was relieved. But try as I might, I wasn't the Ava who believed everything my father told me anymore. When he left us alone at night, I no longer believed his activities were innocent or legal. Every time I heard him in the kitchen getting ready to go out, I watched him, stared him down. I tried to say with my eyes what I could not say aloud, tried to will him not to get into any more trouble, to stay home, but he never understood my eyes. As I approached junior high school, as Tom became a teenager, Daddy stopped understanding us at all.

Our apartment became a battleground. Carol left as soon as she turned eighteen. All those years alone in her bedroom had turned her into a superbrain, and she got a scholarship to Villanova, where she was a science major, of all things. An O'Neil who was not only smart but studying fucking botany. As my dad said, if that didn't beat all. While there she met her future husband, and she never came home again, not for more than a couple of days.

Tom and my father fought through Tom's teen years with a fierceness that scared even the fearless Uncle Two. Then again, Uncle Two had his own battleground, with Rocky showing up at home after two-day benders out on the street, and clearly coming down off a high, shaking, with tired, bloodshot eyes. My father and Tom fought over something far vaguer than a needle in the arm; they fought over attitude. Tom didn't accord my father the respect Daddy felt he deserved. It wasn't ever what he said, but how he said it, the way he held his body, as if his entire face and neck and shoulders were curling into a sneer. They snarled at each other, Tom defiant that he would never, ever end up like my father. He would never drink himself to sleep, would never spend his nights in John's. He would have a family and be a good father who was home every night.

Tom's dreams were all about going far away from our father—but Tom swore he would never leave me. He would take me with him, and we would buy land in upstate New York somewhere. He would be the town sheriff, and I would have a horse. We created a world where we would need no one but each other, a world populated by people we imagined from television shows or occasional books. We couldn't yet name what was different about us, but we knew we were unique. Some Saturdays, we'd crisscross New York City on a single token, taking subways uptown, often to Lincoln Center. We people-watched, laughing and sharing Cokes and pretzels and watching lovers and families of tourists. We knew what we wanted. We could almost taste the normalcy. Could smell it around us, so close and yet unreachable. It seduced us, like the faint call of my mother across the fields of heaven. We wanted it in a way I have never ached for a lover since then, a longing almost orgasmic and primal. We wanted what *they* had, those people whose fathers weren't ex-cons.

My times with Tom as I entered high school, too, were the most blessed of my life. My time in purgatory with Uncle George faded. I decided those earlier years were like my own prison sentence. I had served my time, and now I was free. It's as if I was able to pull the velvet curtain on a performance at Lincoln Center. The stage was darkened, and it was all a grand performance. Nothing real.

I felt myself hoping. What a strange emotion, this bubbling up from within me, this crazy, reckless exhilaration, like getting caught in a rainstorm, at first ducking your head beneath your arm, sheltering yourself, then deciding, fuck it, and dancing in the rain with total abandonment, catching raindrops on your tongue. Hope surged through me the way heroin raced through Rocky, giving me my own high. The darkness wouldn't win.

What a fool I was. Tom, too. I crashed to earth like a jumper from the Empire State Building, like a roofed victim, bloodied and shattered. The summer after my fourteenth birthday, Uncle George returned, wifeless, to the neighborhood. And my father embraced him as the prodigal brother.

32

What is it about the scent of pussy that weakens men? Uncle George didn't wait a week before he was cornering me for stolen kisses, forcing his tongue down my throat and feeling my recently bra-encased breasts.

"Miss me, Ava?" he asked me, breathless as I tried to push him away.

"No." I tried to look fierce. I wasn't my father's daughter for nothing.

He slipped his hand to my crotch. "I bet you did."

Hell is too overused a word for what my life became. Uncle George said he had quit the force, left his wife, spent a couple years drunk in Vegas, and was now looking to join my father and his friends. He was with us all the time. And though Tom seemed disappointed he was no longer a cop, he would sometimes ask him questions about his days as one of New York's finest.

The faces of my father's crew had aged slightly, but they were still the same old guys, with the addition of George. As men were sent to prison or died, they were replaced by young punks, skinny Irishmen, sometimes with a brogue. I remember Curly, who'd shaved his hair off and was a musclehead, Tom said. The steroids he took made him volatile, but carefully controlled; he was valuable to my father. And though I'm not sure whether it was the freewheeling eighties, the economy or the young turks of the stock market, suddenly we had a lot more money than ever before. The bookmaking business traditionally does well when the market is strong, as the turks blow off steam and bet on their alma maters. When the market dives, there's always the shylock business, loaning people money for a hefty bit of interest. Recession-proof. But with George's arrival, my father seemed to be making a killing. Maybe literally.

I managed, because of school, my weekend rovings with Tom and sheer cleverness, to avoid Uncle George. My life was an elaborate ruse of escape routes and excuses. When he did get me alone, often by dropping by unannounced on a night Tom had other plans, I found my mother's waiting arms.

One night, after I had flown in my dreams to the upstate farm my mother picked out for Tom and me, a place so perfect I wondered if it really could exist or if it was only her invention, I landed back in my body to hear him tell me to get dressed.

"Why?"

"You're going to meet a friend of mine."

"I don't want to."

"Yeah, well, I don't want to do a lot of things, but I do 'em, anyway. Get the fuck up and get dressed."

His friend was a bartender in a bar I had never been in before, yet it was like all the rest of the bars of our lives: dark and dirty, with a sticky floor and tough guys lining the stools and the occasional whacked-out lady alcoholic flirting pathetically with men too gross to even consider letting touch your sheets.

"Sammy, this is Ava," my uncle said. "Give her a blackberry brandy."

"I don't want one," I whispered.

"Drink it, anyway." He stared straight ahead, virtually ignoring me.

Sammy was olive-skinned, dark-haired, with a double piercing in his left ear, two little gold hoops dangling. His tattoos, on his rather impressive biceps, weren't jailhouse, but well done, including a bald eagle, wings fully outstretched on his right arm. If I was fourteen, he was probably thirty.

"Here you go, gorgeous," he said, pouring my blackberry brandy. I took a sip. It tasted like fire and smelled like jam mixed with Scotch.

"And for you, George?"

"Vodka. On ice."

Sammy poured my uncle his drink and then he leaned over the bar.

"George here tells me you're a high school girl."

I nodded.

"Ever go out clubbing?"

"No."

"You'll have to let me take you sometime."

I glanced at my uncle, feeling as if the world had gone even crazier than ever before. My uncle looked at me and nodded. Then he looked at Sammy. "She'll go."

I was confused, and I told him so on the way home. "But I don't want to go on a date with that guy."

"You'll go."

"No, I won't."

He grabbed my arm like a vise and wheeled me around. As he stared into my eyes, I realized this was the first time we had been face-to-face, eye-to-eye, in a long time, when I was actually present, actually *there*. For a moment, he faltered. He blinked, and I had a sense of my own power, a sense that if I defied him, I would win.

"Look, you little ungrateful bitch, you owe everything to me."

"I owe you nothing." I spat in his face.

His slap was quick and hard. "Shut the fuck up."

My uncle then explained to me, in a hushed voice, angrily, that all along he had been on a mission. He was with the Drug Enforcement Agency. He was DEA and Sammy was a friend of his who liked high school girls. I would do this for my uncle for his case. I would do it because the DEA was going to bring down the scourge that had settled into our neighborhood. I would do it because he told me to do it.

My head reeled from the brandy, from the simple math I did in my mind. He was looking to take down King Conway. That had to be the reason he'd returned to the neighborhood. But like with many secrets, he simply looked at me and told me the price for telling anyone was my life.

"I'll kill you without even thinking if you tell anyone. I'll kill you and deposit your body like fucking trash in the East River. It won't even wash up on shore."

"I don't care anymore." I stuck my chin up into the air. I had spotted his weakness. His weakness was in having to face me, with the reality of what he had stolen from me traced on my face like crease marks from the sheets of my bed. Some days, he used to fuck me with my face pressed on his unloaded gun. I would carry the mark of the handle on my cheek, and he would tell me I couldn't leave the apartment until the mark faded. So I learned to stare at my reflection in the mirror. To memorize my face. But my face was now *my* weapon. "I don't care what you do to me anymore."

"You stupid whore. It's your life. And your father's. He'll go away forever. Gone. Dead in prison. You think I give a fuck?"

I wanted to say again, I don't care. The words were there—right there—on my mouth where they had been just a minute before. I wanted to say the words, to will myself to say them. But they didn't come out. They couldn't.

"Yeah…that's it. I thought you'd see things my way. So you'll go out with Sammy there, and you'll fuck him the way I've taught you. You'll do it to save your father."

That night, my mother stopped visiting me. Maybe I sensed that my salvation didn't lie in heaven. Inside me, I felt the first tiny root of anger, a quivering nerve like a throbbing toothache. After that, when I had to do anything for him or to him, I simply went inside to a place that was dead and cold. Then traveled still deeper somewhere hot, like the earth's core. And there, I imagined all the various ways I would kill him if I ever got the chance.

33

Eventually, Tom decided to become a cop for real. He abandoned his Spider-Man underwear for weight lifting, and his adolescent aspiring swagger for real confidence and a presence. People noticed Tom, and when he flashed his smile, it seemed like no one, from waitresses to his teachers to his fellow cops, could resist his charm. His ultimate dream was to be a detective. And though we no longer talked of moving upstate and getting a horse, we did assume on some level that we'd always be together.

He graduated from the police academy, a striking figure in uniform, full of pride. We had gotten out of the habit, after my mother died, of taking pictures, but this was one occasion I wanted preserved forever. I snapped away, cautious to make sure Uncle George wasn't in a single picture.

Dad, ostensibly, was upset Tom decided to become a "dumb cop." Corruption woes plagued the NYPD at the time, and wearing a blue uniform wasn't about being a hero. But Tom believed in what he was doing in a way that bordered on religious fervor.

Each day he came home to tell me about arrests he'd made or about his partner, Derek, a guy who'd grown up in the projects but who had decided, like my brother, to turn his back on the way his family was—his father also had a rap sheet, his mother was a drug addict—and instead focus on doing right.

With Tom gone for long shifts on the street, Daddy was left to focus on one person: me. If I went on a date, which was rare, he called me a whore. If I stayed home, he called me a freak. When I cooked for him, he criticized what I made. I overcooked the chicken and undercooked his roast beef. When I did his laundry, I didn't get the whites white enough. When I made his bed, it wasn't military-style with tight corners the way he liked them.

Uncle Two-Times and I were left alone one night watching the World Series when my father left abruptly after a phone call from Jimmy Tomatoes, named for his perpetually ruddy complexion.

Two patted my knee. "You and your father really gotta learn to get along, Ava. I hates seein' you fight like the way you do."

"Please…give me a break, Uncle Two. *Nothing* I do makes him happy."

"Not true. He's always braggin' on youse down there at John's. On Tom being a cop and on you…"

"Me what?"

"You bein' very pretty and very smart."

"Uh-huh. He doesn't think I'm smart. He doesn't think I do anything right."

I stood and took the old plates from our earlier dinner into the kitchen and starting washing them. Uncle Two followed me in there, and without saying anything, picked up a dish towel and dried.

"He loves you," Two offered, putting a dry plate away.

"You'd never know it," I said, no trace of emotion in my voice. "I hate him."

* * *

Tom now stayed in our bedroom, and I had moved into Carol's old room. On a Saturday, we had painted it sky blue. The color of heaven. But with my father's rages increasing in intensity, and Uncle George hovering around me like a bee around a spring flower, my room, our apartment, was no sanctuary. I grew desperate and knocked on Tom's door one afternoon.

"Yeah?"

"Hey." I walked in and sat down on his bed. He was lying underneath his comforter, a monstrosity of plaid that had me convinced he was at least partially color-blind.

"What's up, Ava?"

"Tom..." I lay down next to him and snuggled, curled in the crook of his arm, my sole remaining safe place on earth. I adored him. He was, truly, one of the good guys. The only good guy I knew.

"Yeah?"

"What if we got our own apartment?"

"Me and you?"

"Yeah."

"How would we pay for it? You ever looked at a rookie cop's paycheck? It sucks."

"I'll waitress. I'll temp. I'll do whatever. I'm just so tried of fighting with Daddy.... I'm so unhappy here, Tom. Really unhappy. I just want it to be me and you."

Tom sighed, I'm sure mentally calculating what rent would cost us. I had graduated high school but felt aimless. I picked up waitressing shifts at the Shamrock, saving every penny to escape.

"I don't know, Ava."

"Please," I pleaded. "You won't have to do *anything*. I'll cook and clean and I'll even make your bed every day. Please, Tom? Please? Please?"

He mussed my hair. "All right, you little brat. I'll see what I can find. I'll ask around."

I kissed his cheek, knowing I had just manipulated him, but my years with Uncle George had taught me lessons.

When Tom brought up the idea of our moving out to my father, he reacted with his typical fury. He called us ungrateful, and he hissed at me over his vodka. But in the end, he let us move into the co-op he owned, and we paid him a small rent that we could afford. When we packed, it had been with a feeling of elation on my part. Again, that bubbling hope had sprung from deep inside, like an old water pump long thought dry, but if you primed it over and over again, your arm growing tired, it might surprise you with a small gush of cool water.

We took our mother's things. They'd long been boxed but without labels—no Clothes, Old Photos, Books. After she had died, her things pained my father. When he opened the hall closet, we would hear him sometimes choke off a sound at the sight of her off-season winter coat, dark blue to match her eyes, hanging there next to his old jackets and our little snowsuits. Eventually, Uncle Two had come with boxes from the grocery store and had shoved her things into them, taped them shut and put them on the top shelf in our closet and Dad's closet, and one or two small ones underneath my Dad's bed. Now that we were leaving for our own place, Dad suddenly wanted us to take them with us.

Thinking about it, I imagined his feeling of heaviness, of knowing a dead woman's things rested on the floor just beneath where he slept. We gladly took them. I imagined putting her books and old perfume bottles on shelves Tom would build me.

The day of our move, my father recruited some of his pals to help us. Uncle Two may have had the build of an ox, but he winded easily. Uncle Charley gathered up some union pals, kids who owed their union cards to him, and we set a keg up in the bath-tub of our new place and turned the event into a party. That was the O'Neil way…everything was cause for hoisting a beer. Thanksgiving we played poker; Christmas we shot craps.

Our moving crew drank all night, finishing a keg between them. Tom's friends, cops, not the ones he later fell in with—alcoholics to a man—were bright young guys going to Fordham at night and dreaming of detective status. They drank with us and helped me put boxes away and then down in the basement for the trash collectors.

"Hungry?" I asked them all as they sat laughing, on boxes and folding chairs around the card table that was our temporary dining room.

"Starvin'," my father said. "Order us some pizza, okay, Ava?" He slipped an arm around my waist as I stood there. All seemed to be forgotten, the arguments about us moving. He once again was placid—if only, like all his serene moments, for just that, a moment. Maybe he decided that he liked having our old apartment to himself, after all.

"Sure, Dad." I stood on tiptoe and kissed him. I placed a call to the local parlor, then slipped out of the apartment to get some paper plates and napkins at the grocery store two blocks away.

The night was brisk so I walked quickly. I turned a corner, tucking my face into the collar of my jacket, walking against the wind. And then I ran right into Uncle George.

"In a hurry?" he leered. "Going someplace? Or no…maybe settling in. Like your new place?" he asked, eyes taunting me.

"Yeah."

He could have no idea just how much I liked it. I was break-ing free, tentatively grasping at a real life.

"I'll have to come up to see it, Ava."

"Don't bother." I brushed past him, fear making my stomach

churn, nauseating me. I glanced up and down the block for someone to respond to a cry of help should he grab me. Around Uncle George, my mind always maneuvered like the high-speed chess players in the park, the ones who lifted and slid their pawns to timers, slamming their hands down with lightning speed on the stop button on the clock as they completed each move. Their hands moved like the three-card-monte kings, in a blur. My mind, too, plotted three moves ahead of him, trying to outwit him at every turn, playing for my life. For my body.

"Don't walk away from me, Ava." He spoke sternly, like my father. "I'll make you regret it."

I kept walking, hearing him call after me. "I love you. No one will love you like I do, little girl."

That night, I made Tom's friend Joseph put three locks on the door. Tom mocked me for being paranoid, but my father, who wouldn't trust a stranger with a nickel, let alone his life, nodded approvingly. "You never know," he muttered. "A lot of nuts out there."

It wasn't the nuts out there, of course, but the nut within our circle of family that I feared most. The locks, which I faithfully dead-bolted each night, gave me a sense of safety. I retreated to our apartment and rarely left, creating the kind of world Tom and I had once daydreamed of. I cooked meals for him and his partner. I lit candles and hung pictures on the walls, even buying a horse painting at a flea market Tom and I went to in Greenwich Village. We called the horse "Midnight," and talked of one day buying a horse, even though neither of us had ever ridden, except for a pony ride at a fair we went to once out in Jersey. In my dreams, I rode Midnight through fields far away. She was a good horse, in my dreams, tireless and able to carry me away from Uncle George and the city.

Tom encouraged me to date, to leave the apartment for the

evening, but I was afraid to go out. Every time I did, Uncle George showed up at the bar where I was. Inside I screamed. Could Tom not see how Uncle George latched onto me? Tom knew me better than anyone. How could he miss the way I grew nauseated or asked to leave the minute I saw my uncle? It was as if my uncle George was some sort of evil comic book villain, with just a thin mask between his real identity and his treacherous alter ego.

In chess, there is a move to "castle." I ensconced myself in our apartment, my defenses high. I "castled" myself. But Uncle George had decided he had waited long enough. One night shift, with Tom gone until dawn, he showed up and banged on the door, waking our neighbors, who threatened to call the cops.

"Call the fuckin' cops!" he had yelled down the hall, knowing full well that as a DEA agent he could swagger out of any trouble he might be in.

He continued banging on my door. Banging, banging. Louder. His fists pounding the door, as I sat, shaking, my back to the door on the other side. The door was actually vibrating and I kept staring up at the locks, hoping they would hold, knowing deep down they would, but investing Uncle George with superpowers.

After he had banged on the door until, I imagined, his palms bled, he started crying.

"Ava…Ava…baby…I need to see you. I won't do nothin', just open the door. Open the door. Open the door. Open the door. I won't do nothin'. I'll be good." He sobbed and pleaded like a cast-off lover.

Eventually, sometime in the night, he left. I had fallen asleep on the floor, my eyes swollen shut from crying, and I had even been too afraid to go to my bedroom. I had Tom's revolver, a spare one, on the floor next to me. Tom came home at dawn after the night shift. He called my name through the dead-bolted door, and I let him in, then sank to the floor again.

"What the fuck's going on?" Stepping inside, he saw me in my nightgown, lying in a fetal position. He looked at my face. He looked at the gun.

I glanced at the painting of Midnight on our wall. The only way I would ever be free would be to tell my brother the truth. I shook and threw up on the floor, retching with dry heaves.

Tom knelt down next to me, tears in his eyes. "Whatever it is, Ava, if you're afraid of someone, you have to tell me. Are you in some kind of trouble?"

I nodded.

"Someone bothering you?"

I nodded.

"One of your old boyfriends?"

I shook my head.

"Okay," he soothed. I could see why he was a good cop. He stroked my hair and put his hand to my cheek. "Just tell me, Ava. Just tell Tom. Who is bothering you?"

And so I squeaked out, throat desperately dry, "Uncle... George."

And then, in a torrent, I told him everything.

For some, the truth sets them free. For me, it created a whole new prison.

34

Tom had put me to bed, carrying me as a father might carry an infant, watching over me as I slept the sleep of a person who has had a cathartic episode. I don't remember if I dreamed, or even how long I slept, exactly. When I awoke, Tom was no longer sitting in the chair in my bedroom, and I started shaking again. I had spared Tom nothing, not the way I was pimped out to Uncle George's friends, not anything. Well…one thing. That he was DEA. I would have to think about it before I told Tom that. I had to be careful. For my family's sake. The DEA were the rogue agents of the criminal justice world. Like high-flying, coked-up cowboys. And I didn't see the sense in telling Tom that. Not yet. I had hurt him enough. After I told him my whole story, he had gone into the bathroom and retched. Then he'd held on to me fiercely, tighter than I'd ever been held in my life.

The next day, pulling my robe around me, I opened my door cautiously, feeling queasy. Tom was shirtless and sweating in the living room, building the bookshelves I had been begging for since we moved in.

"Hey…" I looked at him and started to cry. I had ruined Tom's life. I had done it by not keeping my secret. Now he would carry the same rock in his belly that I did.

"Shh…don't cry, baby." He put down his hammer and came over to me. Wood was stacked everywhere. I hadn't even heard him go buy the stuff. It was long past midday and heading into winter dusk.

"I'm…so…sorry," I babbled through tears. "So sorry. I shouldn't have told you. God…what have I done?"

"Shh. Baby…I'm the one who's sorry. I'm sorry I didn't put up these shelves when you asked me. I'm sorry that it's not the exact wood you wanted. I'm so sorry…I never——" He choked on the words and left it unsaid.

I hugged him, clung to him like a drowning person hangs on to a life preserver tossed into the ocean. I swam to Tom, and he held me.

"Look, Ava…" He showed me the shelves. "You can put all the books you want here. You can read about horses or anything you want. You can put Mommy's things on the shelves."

"They're beautiful." I nodded, rubbing my bathrobe sleeve against my runny nose. "You didn't have to do this. Not today."

"Gave me something to do." He had tools scattered about the floor, sawdust had settled into a film over the area he was working in.

"Where'd you get all these tools?"

"Where does anyone get this stuff in the O'Neil family?"

"The convenient truck it fell off of?"

He winked. "Exactly."

"I'm going to take a shower."

"You know, honey, I have to tell you something."

"What?"

"Uncle George is going to come over here around ten o'clock tonight."

"What? You can't, Tom. No. Not here. This is my one safe place. My only safe place. With you."

"Listen——" he put his hands on my shoulders "——I just want to talk to him. I'm going to tell him to stay away from you…and all of us. Just to get lost. He's done it once before when he fell off the map and went to Vegas. If he's a man, any sort of man, he'll go now that I know. You won't ever have to worry about him again. I won't let you."

"I don't want to be here when he comes."

"You have to. If I need you to say something to him, you're going to have to do it. It'll unnerve him. You're an O'Neil, Ava." His eyes stared at me, determined, willing his strength into me. "You can do this. I'll be here. We'll deal with this together. You and me. Like we've always been. Now, go take a shower."

Waiting for Uncle George to come was like waiting for the executioner. The shelves were finished. Tom had worked in a fury, like a machine, his demeanor changing over the course of the afternoon. He was now pacing, edgy, his face like granite.

Uncle George knocked on the door. My palms were sweating, and my breath came in ragged gasps. I sat on the couch, not trusting my knees.

"Uncle George!" Tom was a great actor. He opened the door and clasped him in a bear hug and patted his back, then showed him to a chair, quietly locking our three dead bolts behind him.

"Ava…" George smiled at me. "Nice place, kids. I'm just insulted you haven't invited me up for a drink until now." He laughed.

"We'll make up for that," Tom answered. His eyes were flat. "Can I get you a vodka?"

"Sure."

Tom went into the kitchen, and Uncle George made his usual small talk. My hair looked pretty. My eyes were pretty. He liked my makeup. I could see Tom out of the corner of my eyes, stiffening. He was playing connect the dots and realizing he had missed all the clues.

"Here, Uncle George." He handed him the vodka. "Can I ask you something?" He stood to the side of Uncle George, his facial muscles twitching.

"Sure."

"Why have you been fucking my sister since she was a little girl? You sick motherfucking bastard!"

"What?" Uncle George's eyes shot to me in a panic. "She's a whore and a liar."

But the look on his face told Tom everything, no matter what denials fell from his mouth. And in an instant, Tom had pulled out his gun and swung with all his might and pistol-whipped Uncle George on the side of his head, knocking him to the floor in a violent crash, a trickle of blood coming from a spot on his temple. I jumped, shocked, too shocked to even speak.

Uncle George groaned, putting his hands up defensively. Then Tom picked up a claw hammer and swung it into Uncle George's skull, smashing the side in with a sticky thud, followed by blood, more than I had ever seen, gushing from Uncle George's skull. I shrieked and Tom turned to me. "Quiet, Ava!"

"Tom, don't. Stop!" I went to him, my feet sliding in my uncle's blood, and tried to stop him as the hammer came down again. Tom shook me off with one swift movement of his arm. He swung again, this time caving in Uncle George's eyes, by striking the bridge of his nose. I saw brains spattered on Tom's jeans. We were both covered with flecks of blood, looking like medics in a MASH unit.

"Oh, my God..." I grabbed my chest and stepped back, hyperventilating, surveying the mess. "Tom...Tom...I thought you said you were just going to make him go away."

"I did.... Permanently."

I looked at Tom, looked at the wall, the ceiling. Looked everywhere but at the dead person lying on the floor of my living room. Uncle George didn't even look like a person anymore. He looked like a pool of blood with some skin and muscle and bone mixed in. His skull was more a soup bowl that a human skull. I wanted to throw up, but I think, after the exhaustion of the previous night, that I was too numb. Or my stomach was too empty.

I stood there, absorbing what had just happened, that my brother had killed a man, our uncle, in cold blood. Tom was already on the move, dragging the body onto a large, clear-plastic sheet that I thought had been placed on the floor to collect the sawdust that fell as Tom built the shelves. I realized in an instant that he had planned it all. This hadn't been an act of spontaneous madness.

"Oh, my God, Tom. What now?" I shivered, pacing.

He grasped my shoulders, his fingers leaving bloody prints on my shirt. "We grew up with the Westies, Ava. It's perfect. What are the Westies known for?"

I shook my head in horror, pleading with him with my eyes.

"Don't look like that, Ava. Listen to me...we won't get caught. We won't. Neighbors saw me hauling wood, tools. When people lie, when they don't back up their stories with witnesses, they run into problems. You just have to think like the cops. But if anyone comes snooping—which they won't—if the neighbors hear the saw going, we can point to these shelves."

I stared at the shelves he had built me, giving him the perfect excuse for power tools. I put my hand to my chest, gasping at air. He turned his attention to the dead body on our floor.

"I've thought it all out, Ava. It was the only way."

The moment felt surreal. I was having this conversation as he was dragging the body to the bathroom. Tom was sweating from the exertion. The Westies, like King Conway, ran bookmaking and shylock operations. But they also were known to have a few psychopaths mixed into their lineage. Even the Italians, if they had a messy hit they wanted done, would turn to the Westies. Because the psychopaths among the Westies would not balk at dismemberment. In fact, they were known for it.

"No…" My teeth chattered. "You're not going to cut him up."

"In the bathtub." Tom grunted as he dragged the body along. "I'll cut him up and put the pieces in Hefty bags. We'll pack 'em in suitcases and borrow Two's car to take a trip upstate. Day trip. We'll bury him in the Catskills somewhere, come home. They'll never find him. We'll stick his head in one place, a leg somewhere else."

"Tom, this is sickening." I tried to avoid looking at the plastic sheeting.

He dropped Uncle George with a small thud. "No…what he did to you was sickening. This is the way we do things around here. In this neighborhood."

"You've never talked this way before."

"I thought about it," he said, the dead body between us. "I thought about it while you slept. If we handled it the right way, nothin' would ever happen to him. He'd get away with it. And we couldn't just let him be. He wouldn't have been scared off. I don't think so, anyway. If I had asked him to get out of town tonight, he would have just said you were a liar. So we handled it the Westie way. It's the life we were born to, we just didn't need it till now."

"Tom…I left out something. Oh, God, what have I done?" I

put my hand to my mouth, saw there was blood on my hand and then wiped it on my pants.

"What, baby?" His eyes softened. He looked at me like I was a child. Treated me so gently. He naturally reached out to touch my cheek. There was blood on his hands.

"He's DEA."

"What?" Tom stepped back, then looked down at the body. "Fuck. How do you know?"

"He told me two years ago. Maybe more. Maybe three years. It was how he kept me quiet. Said he'd get Daddy put away forever. King Conway. Uncle Two. He pimped me out, Tom. That bartender I told you about? I think the place is a front for the DEA, anyway."

"Fuck."

"They'll look for him."

He took a breath, then exhaled slowly, thoughtfully. "Maybe not. He was under deep cover, Ava. This may be good." Suddenly he seemed gleeful. "This could be *great*. They'll just assume he crossed someone."

"And what if someone finds his body?" I shuddered. "Or a piece of it?"

"No one will come looking for us. No one. If he's an agent…they'll look at King or they'll even take a look at Dad. Or some dealer. But they won't look at his niece and nephew, the kids he raised for three years or whatever the hell it was. The fucker. Motherfucker." He bit his lip. "And the DNA won't match King's. Or any known dealers. And as it is, we'll bury him so far down, so scattered, that won't be an issue."

"I'm scared."

"Don't be. Now…you go clean up the living room. I've got industrial cleaner in the kitchen under the sink. And bleach. Scrub it all. Every bit of it. There're rags. And then double-bag a Hefty. Put it all in there—the rags. Your clothes. Even your underwear. Any mess. We'll put it in a suitcase, too, and take it to the Catskills. Burn it."

I looked at my brother. He didn't seem bothered by what he had done at all.

"Go on. I'll be in the bathroom."

I walked out to the living room and began to clean up the blood. I scrubbed until my hands were chapped red from the chemicals. I scrubbed and shut my eyes, wishing I could shut my ears to the sounds of an electric saw. I kept retching. It was the sound of my brother taking apart my uncle, bit by bit, in our bathtub.

35

I scrubbed all night. Our apartment smelled like bleach, but it was spotless. As if nothing had ever happened.

But it had.

Eventually, I fell asleep on the floor, my head resting on my arms. Tom shook me gently the next day.

"Ava...wake up. Go look at the bathroom."

I rose, stiffly, and went into the white-and-black-tiled bathroom. It was spotless. Even the tub.

"How'd you do it?"

"Lots of Drano. Lots of bleach." He looked proud of himself, but at the same time, his eyes were troubled.

"Tom...I wish I never told you."

He grabbed me and shook me, staring into my eyes. "No. Don't you ever fucking regret telling me. Think how I feel that it went on in front of me all these years and I didn't pick up on anything, like some stupid fuck. No...you don't ever regret it. He got what was coming to him, Ava. He's in hell now."

In a flash, like a strike of lightning, my mind traveled to the bartender, Sammy. He used me like a paid prostitute, never having any conscience that I could see. Never treating me like I was a human being. After he fucked me, as if ashamed of what he'd done, he always closed his hands around my throat, choking me, only to release me and sob "I'm sorry," unable to look me in the eye. The fact that my eyes were dead to him as he climbed on top of me infuriated him. And always, after I had gone to Sammy's apartment, my uncle waited in the stairwell to the building, and when I came out, he made me tell him what happened in detail. Uncle George did get what he deserved.

I nodded. "Are you okay?"

"Fine. Come on... Two's car is out in front of the building. Anybody asks, we're just taking a trip to the Catskills. Getting away. I'll carry all the suitcases down. You go get changed." I saw he was wearing casual clothes, a flannel shirt, for all intents and purposes, a guy ready to take a hike in the country.

Four suitcases stood in the hallway. I imagined body parts sloshing around inside. Tom hefted two of them and left the apartment and went downstairs. I walked into my bedroom and then into my bathroom. I took a shower, then dried off and dressed in jeans and a heavy black sweater. By the time I was done, Tom had made a second trip and was waiting for me.

"Come on, baby. No time to blow-dry your hair. Let's just beat it."

I followed him out the door, then turned and locked our three dead bolts, reasoning it was the last time I'd ever need them.

We drove out of the city in Two's big boat of a car, then headed across the Hudson and up the New York State Thruway.

"We'll go to the four corners of New York, baby," Tom said. We had been riding, not talking. The Rolling Stones were on the radio.

"What if they come looking for him? What if someone saw him in our building?"

"No one did."

"But what if——"

"No one did, Ava. If he was DEA, that son of a bitch——" his hands gripped the wheel "——there'll be so many suspects they won't know where to fuckin' start lookin'. We'll be last on the list. Don't worry. I wouldn't let anything more happen to you." His voice caught, and he looked out his driver's side window.

I folded my arms and stared out at the scenery. I had a headache.

"Didn't it bother you," I asked, "doing it?"

"Didn't bother me killin' him. Can't say I liked carving him up. But no. I just kept picturing you....being used." The words caught in his throat.

I reached over my hand and touched Tom's leg. He patted my hand. "We'll be fine. Me and you. Just fine."

We drove into foggy weather as we got farther upstate. He took an exit and drove until he saw a turnoff into the woods. We parked the car and then got out.

"I have two shovels. We dig a hole. We dump the contents of each Hefty bag, along with some acid. We bury it. We drive away. We go to the next spot," he said, opening the trunk.

I stared at the four battered suitcases in the trunk. It was hard to imagine that the contents of the four suitcases had once been a whole walking, talking person, no matter how evil he had been.

We trudged through the woods with one suitcase and our shovels. The ground was hard, and we struggled to break through the earth and dig a deep-enough hole. When Tom was satisfied, we poured the contents of one Hefty bag in the hole, an arm tumbling out and almost making me sick. Tom added acid he had bought in gallon jugs, I think some kind of pool cleaner, and then covered up the hole and put leaves on top of it.

"Nature will take her course," he said, turning away from the first grave.

We stopped for gas past Orange County and drove toward Port Jervis, and then turned down a side road to another patch of woods. We did the same thing. I found myself working mechanically. The only time I got sick was when the head tumbled out into the ground, the brains visible through the hole in the skull.

Darkness set in early. Still we drove and found abandoned roads and turnoffs. By ten o'clock we had four empty suitcases.

"Now what?"

"We fill 'em with rocks and dump 'em in the Hudson. The Hefty bags, too."

We drove through the night and found a cliffside overlook. The Hudson ran dark beneath us. Edging himself onto a ledge, Tom hurled a suitcase as far as he could out into the water. We heard a splash. Then it was back to the car for more driving.

"You tired?" I asked him, my eyes feeling heavy.

"Not really. Kind of wired. Like I can't shut off my mind."

We drove even farther upstate, toward Potsdam, and found a lake, where we hurled another suitcase after walking to the end of a dock in the pitch darkness. Then it was back to the car. Tom favored classic rock, and we listened to the radio, as if this was an ordinary road trip.

"What if a suitcase gets found by a swimmer in the summer?"

"Just look like a battered old suitcase."

We drove until dawn, scattering our sin to all parts of New York. We didn't arrive home until almost one in the afternoon. We entered our apartment, and without speaking, each of us went to bed, utterly exhausted. But I couldn't stop thinking.

What if we got caught? What if Tom was arrested for murder? What if our secret was found out? What if the DEA came to our doorstep?

About three hours later, I padded out to the kitchen, quietly. Tom was sound asleep. I opened the refrigerator, found the cold vodka bottle and poured myself a huge juice glass full. On my way back to my room, I stopped to look at Tom as he slept, the shadows of dreams crossing his face. He and I would never sleep in peace again.

36

My father and Uncle Two thought, at first, that Uncle George had disappeared to get laid. After that, they assumed he had either turned traitor, gotten killed while doing some sort of dealing on the side, or had gone back to Vegas. As Tom predicted, no one came looking for him. No police. No DEA. No one. We were never questioned. Months went by, and then a year, then two.

We were free.

Until the hunter.

He was a deer hunter, aiming at a six-point buck. Had his dog with him. The dog's name was Digger, because, the hunter told the cops, that's what he did, morning, noon and night. Digger had made the man's yard look like the pockmarked landscape of Vietnam during the war, as if a hundred land mines had blown up. And Digger was the one who found my uncle. Or at least a part of him.

At first the hunter thought it was just a cow skull, or maybe the jawbone of a deer. Only when Digger brought the bone to his master's feet did the hunter realize it was part of a human skull. He called the cops, the cops looked at the burial spot, and eventually they figured out it was the murdered body of Uncle George. The first person the cops talked to was my father.

"Cocksucker," my father had told me. "Fucking cocksucker."

"What, Dad?"

"You think someone finds a head…a fucking head… what…from natural causes?"

"No," I said quietly, breathing deeply, trying to slow down my heartbeat. I felt it pounding in my ears and wondered if my father heard it, too.

"So he was a rat. A rat…or into shit he hid from the family. The fucker. I never trusted him. Not really. Like his time in Vegas. What was he really doing out there?"

Of course, it had been what he did within the family's embrace that was worse. The detectives interviewed Tom and me, only because we were family. I let Tom do the talking.

"No," Tom had said solemnly. "I can't really recall the last time we saw him. Can you, Ava?"

I shook my head.

"So what did you think when he disappeared?" the older detective asked, his appearance rumpled and tired-looking.

Tom shrugged. "Look…I'm a cop, but I also grew up around here. You learn not to ask too many questions. I think Ava and I both figured he got into some sort of trouble. Gambling…maybe something even worse. And I guess we weren't wrong."

I marveled at how steady his voice was, how casually he leaned back, his arm draped across the sofa back—we had made up the couch for a change, waiting for the detectives to visit.

"And how do you feel now?"

Tom tried to look appropriately troubled. "It's a damn shame."

He shook his head. "He raised us for a while…he wasn't a saint, but he didn't deserve whatever happened to him."

"I hear you," the detective said. "I've got a kid brother into all kinds of shit. I've washed my hands of him, but I still worry…know what I mean?"

"Absolutely." Tom nodded. "And it gets to me that I don't think we'll ever know what really happened to him."

The two detectives had then stood, handed us their cards with the clichéd "Call us if you think of something that might be useful" line. And they were gone.

We weren't caught.

After they left, I remembered when I had scrubbed Uncle George's brains from the floor, I remember thinking I would never get over the sight of him, his head smashed in like a bad melon in the grocery store. But I did. Surprisingly quickly. While my memories of what he did to me continued to play through my mind and wake me from a dead sleep, the sight of his dead body, or the memory of Tom lugging suitcases down the stairs of our apartment and flinging them into the trunk of Uncle Two's car, brought me a sense of relief. I had seen his dead body. He would never return to touch me, to force his tongue into my mouth or to give me to the highest bidder.

But Tom was gone. My Tom. Replaced by a nervous cop who drank his way from the end of his shift to oblivion. He couldn't sleep without alcohol and sleeping pills, and he couldn't wake up without a hit of something, a jolt of uppers, or at the very least a pot of strong coffee.

Tom grew edgy. He didn't like to shower in our bathtub and took to showering at work whenever he could.

"You need to forgive yourself," I whispered to him one night as I helped him into bed.

"I can't. It's not cutting him up—though, God, Ava, that was bad...I wake up screaming at it. You ever cut anyone up, cut through bone like it's a fuckin' side of beef? No. You haven't. No. But no matter. That ain't what bothers me. It's that I didn't protect you, Ava. And you didn't tell me. And he was going down on you when I was sleeping in the bed next to you...in my pj's for Christ's sake. I think about it, and I get sick. And then maybe, a little of it's the cutting him up. A little."

He rambled incoherently sometimes. Other nights, he cried.

I have wondered all my life where God was in all this. We went to church; we took Holy Communion. We took the sacraments. I once said the rosary, in my head, without the beads, as my uncle touched me, hoping God would deliver me from evil. But the response from God was silence. And later, still darker nights and danker bars.

All I wanted was to breathe free. I used to have a box of treasures when I was a little girl. I stored it underneath my bed, in an old shoe box from my father's size-twelve dress wing tips. In it, I collected the sacred things of childhood—a robin's feather I found on the sidewalk, a smooth rock I had uncovered in Central Park, movie stubs from the time my father took me to my first scary movie at the theater, a pink parasol from a virgin piña colada I had when we went to a beach club out on Long Island once, a handmade get-well card drawn in crayon Tom made me when I had the croup, a wheat penny, a silver dollar, a pinecone. The box was crammed with these trinkets and discovered bits of fantasy. I colored the top of the shoe box with a rainbow. But when Uncle George came to live with us, he found it one night and mocked its contents, holding each one up for derision, sneering. Snapping the parasol in half. After that, I stopped finding treasures. They were still there—the pennies on the sidewalk, the parasols in drinks—but I stopped noticing.

Once Uncle George was gone, I noticed again. My world had

been in shades of gray, and suddenly it burst forth in Technicolor. I had my freedom, and I gulped it in. I believed in treasures, and I believed in a God that resided in the pool of crimson blood on my living room floor. God was in my uncle's death. I believed it.

But then I realized God was a master deceiver. For though I had my freedom, and though I saw the world in crimsons and azure blues and amethysts and mossy greens, the price had been too high. It seemed as if I was always being bought and paid for. This time, the price had been the soul of my brother.

Part Four

Daddy's Funeral

All, everything that I understand, I understand only because I love.

—Leo Tolstoy

37

The night before the funeral, after spending the hours thinking of how Tom had both saved my life and damned it, I saw that he was breathing regularly and that I could go rouse Uncle Two, send him home, then take a nap before the funeral.

"Why didn't you wake me up, Ava? You were up all night?" Uncle Two was groggy.

I nodded.

"Ava...you got the funeral today. This ain't good for you." Uncle Two wore his pants and a white undershirt. His dress shirt from the wake the night before hung over the chair in my room. We trotted our good clothes out for weddings and funerals.

"I'll be okay. Just a little tired... I'm not sure I could have slept, anyway. Today's the big day."

Two nodded. "Is Tom all right?"

"Yeah. His head'll be killing him today, but he's all right."

Uncle Two dressed slowly. He seemed to be thinking about something. He opened his mouth, let out a breath, then shut it.

"What?"

"Nothing."

"Say it. What?"

"I just...I just think Tom's no good for you, Ava. Your father used to get very upset every time he thought about how you always take care of Tom."

"Daddy was just mad that I had less time to take care of him."

"That's not true."

I patted his back. "I'm sorry. I'm just tired."

I showed Uncle Two out of our apartment and watched Tom sleep. His eyes were moving beneath his eyelids. He was dreaming. I wondered of what.

When I got back to my bedroom, the phone rang. I picked it up on the first ring. "Hello?"

"Ava?"

"Yes?"

"It's Carol."

I said nothing for a moment, too shocked to speak.

"Hello? Hello? How are you?"

"Fine."

"How's Tom?"

"Fine." I figured I should ask about her child—my niece. "How's little Mary?"

"Good. She doesn't really understand death."

"Yeah, well neither do I."

"Listen...I...I..." She stammered and I heard her stifle a cry. "I want you to know that I am really sad about Dad. You all may think I didn't love him, but I was just...I just wanted to survive, Ava. Can you understand that?"

"Yes," I whispered.

"I have a normal life. I...my...my daughter doesn't have to worry she's going to come home from school one day and find someone like Pinky pulling black sewing thread and a needle through someone's hand. Or see her mother talking to the furniture. Or her father too drunk to climb into bed so he's passed out on the floor."

Carol was speaking faster, and her voice was rising, not getting louder, just more high-pitched.

"She's never been to a bar. She's in kindergarten, and she's never been to a bar. Imagine that. Imagine it! And most especially she has never been to one with testicles in jars." I could hear Carol crying. Then she started speaking again. "She's never seen someone on heroin. She's never watched her father beat someone up in front of her, taking a man's face and smashing it into a wall. And you know what? You know what?" Her voice was trembling.

"What?"

"That's *normal*. That's normal, Ava. And I wanted that."

"Good for you," I said flatly.

"Don't you want that? Don't you?"

"It's…it's not a question of what I want. This is my life. This neighborhood. Tom. I can't just leave Tom. I owe him my life, Carol."

"Why? How?"

I didn't answer.

"That's fine. You don't want to answer me, I understand. But no matter what it is, you don't owe him anything, Ava."

"It's all stuff from after you left. You went off to your fancy college and never looked back."

"Bullshit!" she screamed.

"It's not bullshit."

"It is. I looked back. I talked to Dad a lot about you. I worried about you home alone with him and Tom, and all those guys—Two and Pinky—no mother. I worried about you. But he, Dad, he had a way of letting me know I should just get lost. And after a while I got tired of trying and tired of screaming into the phone from my college dorm. And I gave up."

"I'm fine, Carol. I don't hate you if that's what you want to know." I remembered my sister from the previous night of the wake. She wore a black suit, very expensive-looking, a set of pearls around her neck. She had black hair, too, and wore it in a ballerina's topknot. She looked scary to me, like the women in Hollywood who seemed to see through me when they wanted to get to Vince.

"You can hate me. You can hate me all you want. I just…I just want you to get away from the neighborhood. Daddy's gone now. Do you think he and Mom really want to see you taking care of Tom for the rest of your life?"

"You…you—"

"I what? I wouldn't understand? I don't know what it's like to look at people I love and want out at the same time I want to stay? Don't do it, Ava. If you stay with Tom, if you stay now that Dad's gone, you'll be committing suicide. Just like Mom."

"Leave me alone, Carol, you don't even know me."

She was silent a long moment. "Fine. But if you decide to leave, you can come to Connecticut. You'll always be my sister, even if you won't let me in."

"I won't come to Connecticut."

"Look, I told myself I would say my peace, Ava. What you choose to do is up to you."

She hung up. I went into the shower and scrubbed a night of memories from my skin. I wasn't a suicide case. No one knew why I stayed. Not even Vince.

* * *

I knew what people thought. That Tom had broken up Vince and me. Or that Vince had decided to go back to Hollywood to fuck a few starlets. But the truth wasn't anything like that....

The movie premiere was insane. I had never seen such a crush of people in my life. Camera bulbs flashed, and I had to lower my gaze to avoid being blinded by popping bulbs and bursts of bright light.

My father and De Silva worked the red carpet, my dad signing autographs. Entertainment television shows wanting sound bites allowed Uncle Two and Charley and the neighborhood guys who were invited to pontificate about what it all meant. I imagined all the "bleeps" on tape as they edited out the curse words, the native speak of the neighborhood.

Vince smiled and signed autographs, gravitating to young kids behind the barrier gates, letting them snap photos of him. I held back, fighting the urge to go running down the long carpet and back to the safety of our limousine and then to the safety of my apartment, far from this other world.

Finally, we all went in to watch the film.

De Silva, for all the ways he made me uncomfortable, was a genius. He somehow made the actors up on the screen *become* us. Vince *was* my father, the mannerisms, the way he had that underlying seething energy.

Jack Casey sat just a few seats away from me. I watched him during the first roofing scene. In the flickering light of the movie screen, I saw him look down at his lap. He had made us all naked up there on the screen. His article, his book, all of this attention, had brought us into a glare that none of us was quite prepared for.

After the premiere, Vince was scheduled to go to the West Coast to plug the movie on the late-night talk shows. The mov-

ie was instant Oscar talk. He wanted me to travel to L.A. with
him and then go on to San Francisco for a short vacation. And
for some reason, he insisted on coming to my apartment before
we left. For the past several months, we had lived our lives out
of suitcases and hotels, and he just wanted to have a night in my
home.

I reluctantly agreed, arranging the night when Tom would be
working. I cooked Vince the one dish I make halfway decently—
linguine in white clam sauce, from a recipe Uncle Two's mother gave me one time when I wanted to cook something special
for my father's sixtieth birthday.

We ate by candlelight. I had actually made up the couch, but
Vince, like all good actors and journalists, was an observer. He
looked all around the room. Nothing escaped his gaze.

"Is that Tom's room?" He nodded at the door of the spare
bedroom.

"No. We use it for storage."

"Where does he sleep, then?"

"On the couch."

"Every night?"

I nodded, and poured him some more red wine. I could tell
the evening was a mistake.

"How does Tom feel about me?"

I shrugged. "I don't think he's given it much thought."

"I know your father likes me."

My Dad, in fact, thought Vince was a great guy, particularly
since he picked up thousand-dollar bar tabs when we all went
out after a day of shooting, or because his celebrity got us into
good restaurants without a wait.

But as we were discussing this, Tom came flying through the
door, unlocking it clumsily and staggering in, still in uniform.

"What are you doing home?"

"Called out sick."

"Hi, Tom." Vince rose from his chair.

Tom ignored his hand and went over to the couch and started pulling it out, tossing the cushions on the floor, undressing to his boxers and T-shirt in front of us.

"Don't mind me." He sneered at us.

"Tom…" I started to say, standing up.

"*You* shut up." He glared at me. "You have company and think you can just pretend like I don't exist. This is *my* bed—this, in fact, is *my* room. And if your boyfriend doesn't like it, he can go fuck himself." He clicked on the television and went straight to the porn channel.

I shook my head. "Vince…let's just go."

"No," he said firmly, coming to my side. "You made this nice dinner, and this isn't right, Ava." Under his breath, he added, "Stand up to him. Don't take this."

But Vince had a legion of people to stand up for him. From publicists to business managers to agents.

"Let's just leave," I said, pulling Vince by the hand.

He shook my hand off and put on his jacket and went over to Tom, looking down at him just lying there, eyes glazed over. "You get off doing things like this to your sister? You like making her miserable? She takes care of you, and this is how you repay her?"

Tom glared up at him. "You don't know what the fuck you're talking about."

"I think I do."

"You don't. So butt out where you're not wanted, pretty boy." Tom rolled over, putting his back to Vince and me. Then he muttered, "Homo."

Vince stiffened. He looked at me. "This is fucking bullshit. Pack your bags. You're not staying here anymore."

"I can't."

"You can." He grabbed my arm. Tom, as if blessed with a sixth sense about me, whipped around, leapt off the bed and rushed Vince, tackling him in the gut, like an offensive lineman and knocking the wind out of him. They crashed into a wall; Vince grunted.

The two of them started fighting, more like wrestling, hugging each other in a vicious death grip as they rammed into things. A vase fell off a shelf and shattered on the floor. I started smacking Tom on the back. "Get off of him!" I screamed in a high-pitched voice. "Get off of him! Get off or I will leave with him and never come back."

He heard that, visibly turning his face to me, then angrily disengaging himself from Vince, who then leaned over and gasped a few times, catching his breath.

"You're nothing," Tom said to Vince, spitting in his direction, then coldly turning and making his way to the kitchen, where we could hear him pouring a drink. I took Vince's hand, and we went into my bedroom. He faced me.

"You have to leave or your brother will kill you. Don't tell me about code and honor and that this is the neighborhood. You have to leave.... I bought you this." He reached into his pocket and pulled out a small box, holding it out to me. "I want you to come to L.A. with me when this movie shoot is over. I want you to marry me."

I didn't make a move toward the box. He tossed it on the bed and came close to me, putting his palms to my cheeks.

"I have to ask you something, Ava. I have to ask, and whatever you tell me...I swear to you I will move past it. But I have to know. The not knowing is killing me."

"What?" I asked, my voice dull.

"Is there—not *is* there..." His breath was ragged. "*Was* there something going on between you and Tom? There's something not right, more than just that he's on drugs half the time. Something else. I can feel it."

I exhaled slowly. I could never tell him the truth. Not just that we cut up Uncle George into pieces and scattered him to the four corners of the state of New York, but that I'd been touched in that way, been a *thing* for my uncle for almost as long as my memory took me back. I didn't want to be pitied, and I never wanted to look across the bed at the man I loved and see it there, between us, the misty ghosts of that bar, of Sammy, of so many things.

"Vince…" My voice caught and I stepped back. "Please go."

He moved toward me and tried to hug me. But I was too practiced in the ways of shutting down.

"Forget I said anything." He looked desperate.

"Just go."

"No. I won't."

"Vince…I can't do this anymore. Can't be torn in two, your world versus my world. I can't."

"Fine. You don't have to choose. Ava, I just want you to be happy. And safe. I love you. I'll call you tomorrow."

He hugged me, but I kept my arms to my side.

"Please, Ava…"

"I can't."

"Ava, you deserve a real life. Not this."

I refused to look at him.

"Fine, Ava. I'll go. But I'll call you tomorrow. We're not through with this. I'm not through. I love you. I love you so much I can't breathe right unless you're with me."

Still I refused to look at him. I was afraid I'd weaken.

I heard him leave, shutting the apartment door. I heard Tom watching the TV. And then I sat on the bed and cried, the velvet box sitting in the middle of the mattress.

Vince did call. He called twenty times a day for over a week. He sent flowers. He had my father talk to me. He came by. But I never answered the door. And I never saw Vince Quinn again.

After showering, I dressed in a pair of black pants and a long black sweater coat, with a white silk blouse. Before I buried my father, I had things I needed to tell him. I put on my makeup and went out to the living room and woke up Tom, sitting down on the pullout couch and gently touching his shoulder.

"Jesus Christ..." He clutched his head.

"Percocet in the medicine cabinet."

"Get me some."

"Can't. I'm going over to the funeral parlor."

"What time is it?"

"Eleven."

"Funeral's not until two o'clock."

"I know. But I want to say goodbye to the old man. Myself. I'll meet you there."

Tom looked puzzled but leaned up and kissed me on the cheek. "All right. See you later."

I stood and grabbed my purse and made my way out of the apartment and downstairs. I wanted to be alone with my daddy. I wasn't sure what I was going to say to my father. I only know we hadn't said all that needed saying while he was alive. Few people ever do.

38

The room where my father lay was empty, rows of chairs like silent sentinels keeping him company. The place was half dark, only the light from the hall trailing in, casting the room in a sort of murky gray. I told Mr. Constantino, the funeral home director, to keep the lights off. My father and I had always spoken better in the dark, when we couldn't see each other's faces, when he had a vodka bottle in his hand.

"Hey, Daddy," I whispered, staring down at him. "Funeral's today. . . . I think wherever you are, you must be cracking up at the fuss, the reporters and the TV cameras. I didn't see him because I had left with Jack Casey, but Mike Collins, one of the producers for the segment of *20/20*, was here. For you, Dad. A guy from the neighborhood.

"I know you killed people, Daddy. I sometimes wake up at night, and it eats away at me. Why do the O'Neils settle everything with blood? But I know you just did what you did to survive. Maybe if Mommy had lived, if she wasn't sick, we would have been like the Martins. Remember they lived upstairs? And they moved out to Rockland County. The kids went to good schools. One of them is a doctor now."

I was afraid to touch him, to feel him stiff. So instead I touched his hair, held in place by hairspray, but still his hair, his real hair, even at his age not thinned much at all.

"If you're someplace, Dad, someplace where you see and hear everything, then you know.... You were either greeted by Mom in heaven or Uncle George in hell. Either way, you know now...." I felt it rise in me, this primal scream that I suppressed but came out, instead, in a moan. I fell to my knees and cried, my face on the railing.

"I should have told you, Daddy. I should have told you he was touching me, but I thought you would kill him or he would...put you away forever. Or kill you. And I should have told you what Tom and I did. I should have. Then you wouldn't have spent all those years angry at Tom for going the way of Rocky and all the sons of your friends who ended as fuck-ups. You would have forgiven him, and we would have forgiven you."

The tears streamed steadily, and my nose was running. I rummaged through my purse for tissues.

"See...Daddy...I was braver than you thought. I remember him touching me and telling me if I didn't go along, we would end up in foster care, separated. Tom would go one place, I would go another, Carol a third. No one wants three kids, Daddy. Not in foster care. Not in the city. He told me that. And I knew he was right, that son of a bitch. I did it for us all. I did it for the family. I was a loyal O'Neil. I did it for...us. Can't you see now, Daddy?" I shuddered. "I had to do whatever he made me do. And I am so, so sorry."

I looked at his body and then up at the ceiling. "Where are you, Daddy? With her or with him? And where will Tom and I go when we die? Will God let us all be at peace together? Finally?"

Sobs came from deep in my stomach. I lay my head on the rail again. I could only feel one emotion. "I miss you. I miss my daddy."

And there it was. I missed the daddy who curled me in his arm and watched Godzilla with me. That he had struck me, or called me a whore, or done a thousand barely forgivable things didn't matter. He had killed people. And I had hidden a drive to the Catskills from him. But I believed he was somewhere, someplace, where time stretched out in front of him, backward, and he could see all that had happened. In the end, in that gray room, he was my father, the only one I ever had. We loved each other. I felt it. I loved him so much it overwhelmed me, and I felt like I was slowly suffocating among the flowers. And I knew, if he could, he would say, *I'm sorry, Ava. For it all. I love you. Don't ever forget it. The Roofer loved you. Now, quit your crying and get ready for the funeral. I hope you ordered enough kegs of beer for the party.*

39

Tom came to the funeral with a fifth in his pocket. He wore his best suit and the white shirt I'd picked up from the dry cleaners for him. Even hungover, he was so striking that people who didn't know better assumed he was one of the actors from the movie.

After we said a prayer at the funeral home, we all climbed into limos. The funeral cortege seemed to stretch for ten city blocks. We had a police escort, and I'm sure people on the sidewalks thought a head of state had died, or maybe a politician. We went to St. John's Catholic Church. Because of my father's reputation, we were not permitted to have a mass, but the priest was an old friend of King Conway's so we did get to have a service. Just no communion. Like my father would have cared.

Uncle Two-Times delivered the eulogy. He cleared his throat several times in the church vestibule. Then he slowly made his way to the pulpit, his lumbering gait getting a little arthritic in his old age, his emphysema causing him to wheeze a bit into the microphone before he spoke.

"Frank O'Neil was like a brother to me. He ran things around our neighborhood. I suppose everyone kind of knows that now since he's…you know…kind of famous. But that wouldn't be everything about him. There was a lot more.

"He was tough. The toughest SOB—excuse me, Father—that you ever met. Scared of no one or nothin'. Except maybe that something might happen to one of his kids."

Uncle Two cleared his throat. I looked at Tom in the pew next to me. He squeezed my hand. I glanced at the end of the pew at Carol. She caught my gaze and gave me a conciliatory smile. I smiled weakly back.

"I remember when my son Rocky died, Frank was with me. He got me through it. And I got him through it when his beloved Mary died. That was loyalty and friendship. It wasn't just the bad times, either." He chuckled a little. "I could tell you *stories*. Such stories. We used to take the ferry out to Staten Island. We were kids. And we'd go girl-watching. Summers at Rockaway, eating raw clams. I was with him when he met Mary." He looked down from the pulpit at Tom and me. Then he looked over at Carol. "It was love at first sight. No kidding."

Uncle Two looked out over the packed church. Pinky and Patricia, Mick the Prick, Black Tom…the young guys just coming up through the neighborhood. Old guys from John's. Slick Jimmy. Uncle Charley sitting with Charlotte. "The neighborhood has changed. Was a time when we ruled the streets. Now you got condos going in. In our neighborhood! I can't believe it. And Frank O'Neil is gone. It's the end of an era. He represents a time when a man's handshake was worth something. Loyalty."

Uncle Two looked at my father's casket. It gleamed in a stream of sunlight coming through the stained-glass window. "He was a real man. A man's man. He was a father, brother and friend. We'll miss you, Frank."

Uncle Two stepped down and took the two steps down from the altar area slowly. He walked over to the front pew and gave me a kiss on my forehead. Then he took his seat in the second row.

Father McCann concluded the service, and we stood and made our way to the back of the church. I spotted De Silva. He nodded at me. The movie set had been the first time I had been part of a group that wasn't my immediate family. I saw makeup artists and the actress who played me sitting in the pews. Everyone but Vince.

Stepping out into the cold air, I walked down the marble steps to the limousine and climbed in the back with Tom. He immediately put his head in my lap.

"We're orphans now, Ava. Did you think of that? We're orphans now." He shut his eyes and was dozing before we hit the Long Island Expressway.

I stroked his hair. "Yeah, baby. We're orphans."

40

My father, years ago, didn't have the foresight to buy the plot next to my mother so they could be buried side by side. She was out in a cemetery in Queens. We visited her once a year, Tom and I, on Mother's Day, with all the other motherless children. We clean the stray weeds from the grave and put fresh flowers there, sometimes a potted plant. The last time we visited, we brought mums.

Unable to place my father next to her in the already overcrowded cemetery, we turned to Pinky. He got Dad a plot in a rolling-hilled cemetery on Long Island. He had insisted on paying for the plot.

"Patricia and I have a plot right in the same area. I kinda like the fact that your Dad and me will be neighbors again," he had said. Pinky had also helped pay for the casket and had been on the phone with me every day since we got the word my father had died in his sleep. After all the violence, that had been it. Died in his sleep. His heart.

The day was beautiful. When you live in New York City, you forget about trees and sunshine. Blue sky. Sands Point, Long Island, overlooks the Long Island Sound. Sailboats dot the sea, even in fall and winter.

Soon, the cortege wound its way through the wrought-iron gates of the grassy hills and tree-lined lanes of the cemetery that was to be Frank O'Neil's final resting place. His plot was waiting for us, and flowers were unloaded from the hearse and the coffin set up. A row of chairs waited for the immediate family. I sat between Carol and Tom. I held his hand. She put her hand on my thigh and squeezed it once, then placed her hands in her lap. She wore sunglasses so I couldn't see her face, but a single tear traced its way down her cheek. I reached over and squeezed her hands.

The priest, a ruddy-faced Irishman with a brogue, greeted us all. King Conway was there. King was looking very old of late; he had a palsy shake to his left hand. But he still had those ebony eyes that would scare the shit out of all of us when we were kids. His son, T.C., Tommy Conway, to distinguish himself from my Tom, was as powerfully built, but a lot less wise. He flew off the handle often, and he ran his crew with fear, not mingled with the kind of semifatherly fucked-up love King had for us all. Times really had changed. King had never dealt drugs, at least nothing too hard, but that wasn't the word on T.C.

They were my life, these men. They had seen me through my mother's death, had raised me in that apartment. I drifted in time, coming back to the gravesite when the priest began talking about ashes to ashes and dust to dust. I stared at the coffin. Inside it was my father. He was going into the ground. We were going to leave him there. Two had put a bottle of vodka in the casket. As if that would make the cold ground warmer.

People filed past the casket, taking roses and tossing them on top of the coffin. Some of the women—and even the men—

kissed them first. Finally, it was our turn. Carol and her husband went first. Yesterday, I might have thought she was bullshitting us all, but when she started crying, I believed she meant it. She was an orphan, too. Her husband pulled her to his side. I went next. I picked up a single red rose and held it to my lips. I smelled it, and the petals were soft against my skin.

"Goodbye," I whispered, and placed the flower on the casket. "Good...bye."

Tom stepped up next. He didn't take a rose. He didn't say anything. He simply patted the top of the casket like a man might pat the top of a child's head.

The priest had announced we would have a luncheon at the Sands Point Country Club. Pinky and Patricia had taken care of that, too. We snaked our way in the cortege to the stone mansion, passing by horses grazing in a field and a golf course.

The luncheon was classy. It was much nicer than any funeral luncheon I had been to before. Open bar. A beautiful buffet with filet mignon. I was drained and walked through the room greeting people, exhausted. This was it. When the luncheon was over, Tom and the rest of us would head back to the city. Uncle Two and I and Uncle Charley and Tom, we would try to stay the family we were. We would eat Sunday dinner at Tom's and my apartment. And then one by one, the old gangsters would die off. We had no relationship with T.C. After all the old guys were gone, it would just be about drugs and money. Cold things.

Tom nuzzled one of the actresses from the movie. She played the girlfriend of the young Charley. A bit part. The women always were. I saw De Silva making a beeline toward me, and I quickly ducked out to use the ladies' room. Standing in the lobby, I heard a voice say, "Ava."

I turned...and stood face-to-face with Vince Quinn.

41

He enveloped me, putting both arms around me and whispering in my ear, "I'm so sorry."

I was furious with myself, because I couldn't speak. Every time I tried, a choked-off sob came out.

"I'm sorry for not coming sooner. I've been in Toronto. I basically shut the damn set down to get here." He rubbed the small of my back and kept kissing my cheek, my ear, my hair. "I'm so sorry." Now it was his turn to stifle a cry.

"I'm okay," I managed to whisper.

"Not just for your father. I'm sorry for…everything. Me, you. God, I'm just so damn sorry. I've missed you. I wanted to call but I was afraid you'd just hang up on me."

"I've missed you, too."

He stepped back and stroked my face. "Baby, let's take a walk."

I nodded. We walked out onto the grounds of the country club. The autumn sun was already setting, and the air smelled like a first snow.

"Ava——" He held my hand, and we strolled, as if this was a lovers' walk "——I don't care about you and Tom. I don't care about any of it. I was wrong to ask you about it. I don't care what your father did or what your uncle Two did. I don't. None of it."

"Vince, let's walk farther over here." I didn't want there to be any chance someone could approach us, or overhear what I felt I had to tell him. Being near him made me dizzy. I had missed him so very much it was physical.

What was I thinking? I fought with myself. Tell him? I couldn't. Then I heard my father. I heard him in my head, saying this was my chance. *Take it! Seize it!* The truth never held much weight in my family. But I would be buried along with Frank O'Neil if I didn't say it now.

"I've never been with Tom. Not like you think."

"I never thought——"

"Stop!" I held my hand to his lips. "I have to say it all or I'll chicken out."

"Whatever it is won't matter." He leaned in and kissed me hard on the mouth. I kissed him back, the rush through my body making me weak. Then I stepped back and moved toward a large oak tree, leaning against its trunk for strength.

I looked down at the ground. "Let me just say this…let me get it out. I'm so tired of carrying all my secrets…. I was raped."

It was the first time I had ever said the words aloud to anyone besides Tom. I felt like I was going to throw up, and my teeth chattered. "My father's brother started fucking me when I was eight years old. And he never stopped." I looked up at Vince and saw him staring at me intently. "It never stopped. Relentless."

He moved to hug me again, but I put my hands up and kept him at arm's length. "It was everything that must be running through your mind and more. Uncle George was a DEA agent. That was part of Jack Casey's book, but Jack never knew what happened to him. Well…deep cover has a funny way of messing with agents' minds. In my uncle's case, he thought he was going to marry me. That I would have a baby with him. That he could pimp me out to his undercover friends. I don't know who was DEA and who was his prey. I was with them all. I hate the fucking DEA. I hate the feds. I hate the police. Except for Tom. And lately, I sometimes hate him, too."

I looked over at Vince in the fading light. He was clenching his jaw, and he started to pace, shaking his head.

"I'll understand if you can't handle it, Vince. There's no shame in saying this is too much for you."

"I'm just so fucking mad I wasn't there. That somehow we had met back then when I could have protected you from that bastard." His face was wet, and he wiped at his eyes. "I'm just so fucking mad, Ava. God, haven't you been through enough?"

I let him talk, his voice rising and falling with anger and sadness, his pacing quickening as he struggled to accept what I told him.

"Ava, however you lived doesn't matter to me. It can't change what I feel about you."

"There's more, Vince. My uncle…is dead. Pieces of him scattered to the wind. I won't say how…you can guess who. But know—know this—I helped cover it up. And I wasn't sorry. So whatever you think of Tom, know that he did whatever he's done for me. And I'm responsible for it, too."

Vince squatted down and held his head in his hands, rocking gently forward and back in a rhythm. "How did you ever survive?"

"I'm an O'Neil."

"If I could have, I would have killed him myself."

"You say so, but it was sickening. It was over before I could even scream. And you say you would have, but look at Tom. He wasn't always like this. He was such a good boy. He was…so good."

"He loves you, Ava. And I do, too."

"How can you? How can you after I've told you this?"

"I don't care, Ava." Vince was near me in an instant in the growing darkness, kissing my neck and my hair.

"You think you don't. But if we ever had a baby some-day...would you wonder if I would really make a good mother? I was on that drive with Tom. I buried my uncle and told no one."

He shook his head. "I would kill someone who hurt you. Don't judge yourself."

I turned my back to him. "You say you would kill. All men say they would. But it's more than just talk. It's a life, Vince. A human life." I clutched my stomach.

"Men who abuse little children give up the right to life."

I crumpled to the ground. Speaking the truth, first to my father's body, and now to Vince, was like large sections of my soul were re-arranging themselves. I didn't know what I believed anymore.

Vince sat down on the dried autumn grass next to me. "We can get through this, Ava. But you have to know that, even though he did this for you, even though he loves you very much, Tom is dangerous. And you're not responsible for that. He has to want to get help on his own. But you'll die if you stay with him."

I nodded.

"Do you still love me?"

I nodded again. Vince leaned his back against the tree, drew his knees up and then slid me between them, my back against his chest.

"Ava, after the luncheon, we're going to go back to your apartment and pack your bags."

I nodded.

"We'll offer Tom all the help we can. We'll get him help. Get him into rehab. But you cannot stay there with him anymore. He *will* kill you. He won't mean to, but I've seen that look in his eye."

"I don't know if I can leave him. Vince, I wouldn't exist if it wasn't for Tom. I would be dead. Do you hear me? Dead."

"But that doesn't mean you owe him your life."

I took a breath. "I love you."

"Say it again."

"I love you, Vince."

"Let's go now."

"But the luncheon—"

"In the words of Frank O'Neil, fuck it. We have to leave now."

I stood and brushed the dried grass and leaves off my ass. I held out my hand to him. When he took it, strangely, I felt like I was taking my first breath of life.

42

"The place hasn't changed much."

I looked around my apartment. Tom's bed stood unmade. We never had gotten a real dining room table. A card table stood beneath a cheap chandelier.

I nodded. "You're right.... I guess it hasn't," I said nervously, making my way to my bedroom. Vince followed me. I pulled out a suitcase—the very suitcase Vince had bought me in Vegas.

"Memories, huh?" He smiled at me, looking down at the suitcase.

"Everyone will wonder where I am."

"We'll call your uncle Two. Everyone will understand. You have to know that."

I opened drawers, shoving sweaters and pants and jeans into the suitcase.

"It's pretty cold in Toronto."

"My winter coat is in the hall closet."

Vince went to retrieve my coat. I picked up framed photographs. Me and Tom. Me and Daddy and Tom. A family picture from a Christmas when my mother was still alive. We stood in front of the Christmas tree with our mother, all in our pj's and bathrobes. I wrapped each frame in a sweater and put them in the suitcase.

Vince returned with my coat. "Please hurry, Ava. We need to be gone before Tom realizes anything."

"I know." My hands shook.

I packed all my winter clothes, and eventually the suitcase was full, so I found a duffel bag and started filling that, too. How do you place a life into a little bag? A carry-on? A box?

At that thought, I raced from my room and went to the spare bedroom. I wanted something of my mother's to take. Something. I opened boxes, most of which were unmarked and dusty. The smell of mothballs overwhelmed me. I pulled things out, teacups and saucers, sweaters and trinkets. The third box I opened contained books, including a baby book. I opened it. My baby book.

In my mother's neat Catholic schoolgirl handwriting, she had filled in my birth weight (seven pounds, one ounce) and length (nineteen inches). And there, on a page that read "My Dreams for My Child" she had written that she hoped I grew up to be "happy…just happy."

I grabbed it and some photos, a framed picture of my parents' wedding, and ran back to my room. Vince was emptying my closet. We worked frantically. I ran to the bathroom for my toothbrush. I opened the medicine cabinet. Rows of pills stared back at me. I slammed the cabinet. I didn't need them anymore, I told myself.

Vince was on his cell phone making arrangements. His limousine was waiting for us downstairs. A plane would take us to Toronto. He called his assistant and made arrangements for a limo in Canada. He came over to me and grabbed my face and kissed me hard. "We will make this work, Ava. You're not alone. We'll face it together."

His teeth were chattering. "Are you okay?" I felt his forehead.

"It's nerves. What you told me…it's hard. I picture you, my love, going through all that alone. Someday, you'll tell me everything, and then you won't ever have secrets. Not with me."

I took one last look around my room. I grabbed a picture of Uncle Two, and one of Rocky and Two. "I'll miss Uncle Two-Times."

"He'll visit. You'll see him again. I promise you. Now come *on*."

But it was too late. I heard the apartment door slam open. Vince and I exchanged a look of terror.

"Tom?" I called out.

"Get out here," he shouted, his voice deep and harsh.

Vince and I emerged from my room, the duffel bag and suitcase in Vince's hands. He set them down on the floor. I noticed him loosen his stance, as if expecting a fistfight.

"You going somewhere, Ava?"

"Yes. She's coming with me," Vince said calmly and very slowly.

"No, she's not."

"Yes, she is."

Tom sneered. "Pretty boy, you think you know her just because you've fucked her? You think you can just waltz in here and take my sister away from me when we just lost our father? She just lost her daddy, asshole. She's not thinking right."

Tom's eyes were past any sense of sanity. I couldn't even see my Tom in them. He was gone.

"Tom…" I took a deep breath and exhaled. "I am leaving."

"No, you're not. Did you tell him? Did you tell him the truth about you? Did you tell your pretty boyfriend how George passed you around this neighborhood like a bottle of cheap whiskey between bums?"

"Don't, Tom…" I felt like he was swinging the hammer into me, splattering me around the apartment. "Don't say that."

"She's a whore. She's a whore, Vince. And when you get out to Hollywood, you think he's going to keep you, Ava? Think so? Guess again. He's a fucking Hollywood pretty boy. You're not anything to him. The only one—the only one—who has ever loved you totally and completely is me. I've been the one to save you, to protect you. Me, Ava. If you leave, don't ever come back. Not ever."

"Tom…you can't mean—"

"I can, too, mean it. You betray me like this, you're dead to me. I buried you the day I buried my father."

I felt a physical pain in my heart. I started to cry. And then I heard my mother. I hadn't heard her in years. She had stopped visiting me years before. But I heard her. Calling me. Telling me to just walk through that doorway. *Go, my baby. It's time for you to go.*

"Fine, Tom. I'm dead, then." I picked up the duffel bag and Vince took the suitcase. Tom stared at the bags. I started walking through the apartment, toward the door, each step feeling as though my legs were sinking into quicksand, heavy, clumsy.

"Ava?" Tom looked at me tearfully, as if he didn't recognize me. He outstretched his arms to me. "Ava, don't leave me," he wailed, then collapsed on the floor. He wasn't crying, just that sort of silent sob like when a child is crying so hard that only air comes out of his mouth.

Trembling, I dropped my bag and sat down on the floor next to him. I touched his hair, pushing it back from his forehead. "Don't, baby," I soothed him.

Vince took a step back, as if affording us some privacy. His eyes were tearful, and he didn't rush me.

"I didn't know where you were." Tom stared past me, crying, pulling at his face, his cheeks. "I didn't know. One minute you were there...and then you were gone. And then someone told me they saw Vince, and I knew he would steal you, Ava."

"Tom...it's not like that. I have to go now. I still have to go."

"You can't do that, Ava."

"I have to."

"You can't leave Tom. You can't do that to Tom." He wrung his hands together over and over, nervously, his fingertips shaking.

I pulled him to me, and he rested his head beneath my chin. "I have to, Tom."

"Ava can't leave Tom. Ava can't."

"She has to. Come on. Let her put you to bed. You'll get some rest. You need some rest. You've needed to rest for a long, long time."

He let me pull him up from the floor. I led him over to the bed to put him to sleep one last time.

"Ava loves Tom," I soothed. "Ava loves him very much." Vince watched me, his hand over his mouth, tears falling silently, letting me play out this scene, as I always had.

Tom slid onto his bed, onto the pullout couch. I unbuttoned his dress shirt and helped him slide his arms out of it. I unbuckled his belt, and he wriggled free of his pants. I went to the kitchen for a bag of frozen peas, which I wrapped in a towel, then returned to the bed. He was drunk, of course; he had probably drank all the way back to the city in his limousine. I put a blanket on him and rolled him onto his side in case he vomited in the night. I rested the ice pack beneath his head at the temple.

"Go to sleep, Tom."

"And Ava won't go away?"

"Just go to sleep, Tom. In here." I touched his bare chest, near his heart. "Ava will always be with Tom. Forever."

"Tom loves Ava. Tom saved Ava."

"Yes, Tom did. Tom saved his Ava."

I could see him fighting against sleep, against blacking out. He clenched and unclenched his jaw. I kept stroking his face. I massaged his jaw, trying to get him to relax. He was so lovely, my brother, had been such a good soul, a boy who would have been a sheriff. What had the West Side done to us? I stroked his skin, a touch of five o'clock shadow coming in. I massaged his shoulder.

"Ava loves Tom. Ava loves Tom...." I repeated the words over and over like a mantra. "Ava loves her Tom. Forever."

After five minutes, he was breathing heavily. I touched his shoulder and leaned down to kiss his cheek. I let my lips remain there, and I rubbed my face against his. Instinctively, I reached for his hand and wrapped my fingers around his pinky. It was how we first met; it was how I would say goodbye.

I stood. It was time.

Without speaking, Vince carried my bags to the door. I unlocked the dead bolts and sent him down the stairs. I turned around to look at my brother sleeping one last time.

"Ava loves Tom," I called out to him. I felt my mother's presence, and my father's. They would protect their boy now. Their dear sweet boy.

I went downstairs where Vince waited in the limousine. Opening the door, I climbed in.

"I love you," he whispered.

"I love you, too."

"I never understood....I do now."

I nodded.

The chauffeur pulled away from the curb, and I watched the apartment disappear from out the rear window. I left Hell's Kitchen. I left New York. I left Tom. I left the rooftops. I left the ghosts of my parents, and John Corrigan, the people we killed

and the people who died because that was our way. It was a ce-
ment graveyard.

Ava loves Tom. She always will.

I wondered, without Tom, where I would get my strength
from. Without Uncle Two and Pinky and Uncle Charley. Then I
heard my father.

You're a brave kid, Ava, now go live your life. If you don't...I'll have
to break your legs.

Yeah. Dad was sentimental like that.